Francesca felt very peculiar.

Sebastian Thorne was a man who could give her unlimited pleasure, and he fascinated her and frightened her at the same time. Or perhaps she was more frightened of herself.

How did it feel to kiss a man like this? In her life she had been kissed, of course she had, but usually by bumbling boys who slobbered on her cheek before she pushed them away. She'd never let herself imagine how it must feel to kiss a real man, an attractive man, and one she was attracted to. She had been too afraid.

But now here he was, the man of her dreams, and suddenly desire outweighed fear. Impulsively, she threw her arms about his neck and stretched up to place her lips on his.

Surprise gave way to passion. He grasped her roughly in his arms, and he was strong. She felt caught up in something she mightn't be able to stop and she was afraid, but just for a moment, before his mouth plundered hers . . .

Other AVON ROMANCES

DESIRE NEVER DIES by Jenna Petersen
GOOD GROOM HUNTING by Shana Galen
NIGHT OF THE HUNTRESS by Kathryn Smith
THRILL OF THE KNIGHT by Julia Latham
TOO WICKED TO TAME by Sophie Jordan
WHEN SEDUCING A SPY by Sari Robins
WILD AND WICKED IN SCOTLAND
by Melody Thomas

Coming Soon

THE DEVIL'S TEMPTATION by Kimberly Logan
WILD SWEET LOVE by Beverly Jenkins

And Don't Miss These
ROMANTIC TREASURES
from Avon BOOKS

AND THEN HE KISSED HER by Laura Lee Guhrke
CLAIMING THE COURTESAN by Anna Campbell
TWO WEEKS WITH A STRANGER by Debra Mullins

SARA BENNETT

MISTRESS OF SCANDAL

AVON BOOKS
An Imprint of HarperCollinsPublishers

AVON BOOKS
An Imprint of HarperCollins*Publishers*
10 East 53rd Street
New York, New York 10022-5299

Copyright © 2007 by Sara Bennett
ISBN: 978-0-06-079649-5
ISBN-10: 0-06-079649-9
www.avonromance.com

First Avon Books paperback printing: April 2007

Avon Trademark Reg. U.S. Pat. Off. and in Other Countries, Marca Registrada, Hecho en U.S.A.
HarperCollins® is a registered trademark of HarperCollins Publishers.

Printed in the U.S.A.

10 9 8 7 6 5 4 3 2 1

MISTRESS OF SCANDAL

Prologue

London
Aphrodite's Club
1849

"**I** need you to go back to a time many years ago." Madame Aphrodite sat forward in her Egyptian-style chair, her black silk gown rustling, her long fingers, heavy with rings, gripping the sphinx carvings on the armrests. Her beautiful, haggard face was intent, while her dark gaze was fixed upon Sebastian Thorne. "I need your help," she said hoarsely.

"Of course," Sebastian murmured. He was used to overwrought clients—it was something he had seen a

1

lot of in the past eight years—but there was something about this one that was different. "I will do what I can, Madame."

Aphrodite must have decided she was playing her hand too openly, exposing her raw feelings, because she leaned back, forcing her clenched fingers to relax, one by one. "So you *will* help me?"

"Yes, if I can."

"You are the best . . . or so I have been told." She gave a little smile.

"I am flattered." Sebastian bowed his head.

"Don't be, *mon ami*! I was also told that you are a dangerous opponent and give no quarter to those you hunt; that there are those who glance over their shoulders and look for you in the shadows and shiver. But I am not one of them, so that does not concern me. I want results, and I do not care how they are obtained. If you are ruthless, then so much the better."

Sebastian raised an eyebrow. "Then explain to me what it is you want, Madame, and I will tell you honestly whether or not I can obtain it for you."

"Very well." She smoothed her skirts. "Let us begin."

Beyond the room Sebastian heard laughter—women's voices. He knew that although Aphrodite's Club offered many forms of entertainment to its patrons, it was actually a high-class brothel. Such things did not bother him; for the past eight years he had walked through the darkest streets in London and seen some nightmare sights, so he doubted he could be shocked. Besides, Aphrodite's Club had a better reputation than most. The owner was the mysterious Madame Aphrodite, and although there were plenty of stories and rumors about her, no one knew the truth. Whatever it was she wanted from him, he needed to hear it from her own lips.

"You called me here to help you, Madame," he prompted her now. "I am at your disposal."

She looked amused, as if she knew his gentlemanly good manners were nothing more than the veneer over something far more dangerous. But then her face grew serious once more, her eyes full of painful memories.

"Twenty-four years ago my three daughters were stolen by a woman called Mrs. Slater. She was one of those evil creatures known as a baby farmer, and she came to my country home in the night, and bundled my poor children into a coach. I was here, in London, and the servants were asleep. I do not blame them, for how could they know what was about to happen? How could any of us have known? Besides, it seems likely she had an informant, someone who knew which door would be unlocked, and where the nursery was situated."

For a moment she seemed to brood on the perfidy of that someone, and then she drew a deep breath and went on.

"Unknown to me, Mrs. Slater took my daughters north, to the Greentree estate in Yorkshire, where she had leased a cottage. For a time they lived there, unharmed, although they were left very much to fend for themselves." Aphrodite blinked back tears. "Imagine it, *mon ami*, three little girls—Francesca no more than a baby—left to feed and dress and care for themselves?

Vivianna was six years old . . ." She managed a smile. "I dread to think what would have happened to the two tiny ones without my sensible and clever Vivianna. Then Mrs. Slater's husband came to live at the cottage. He was in his cups most of the time, shouting at them. They were afraid of him—they had never been shouted at before. They were left alone more than ever, locked in one room, cold and hungry. Frightened. And then one day the Slaters left, abandoning the cottage . . . and the children."

"They were left entirely alone?" Sebastian found his jaded senses could still be shocked after all.

"*Oui*, all alone, until Amy Greentree rescued them."

"And you want me to find Mrs. Slater and her husband?"

"That is part of it. While she was living in the cottage, Mrs. Slater would visit the village inn, and she was heard to boast about how clever she had been, and that she was expecting to be well paid for something she was hiding. Of course she meant the children. Someone was paying her to do what she did. *That* is why I need you to find that monstrous woman, Mr. Thorne. Mrs. Slater is the key that will unlock the truth."

Sebastian's voice was tempered with caution. "You don't know that Mrs. Slater is still alive. These events happened many years ago. She may have drunk herself to death by now."

"*Psht!* Creatures such as she do not die so easily. They cling to life, no matter how miserable, because they are afraid that their evil will be punished in the hereafter."

Sebastian thought she might well be right.

"Go to Yorkshire," Aphrodite was instructing him in a firm voice. "Go to the Greentree estate and visit the village. After Mrs. Slater and her husband fled, they must have hidden themselves somewhere. People notice. There was much talk at the time the children were found. Someone must remember something. Start there, Mr. Thorne, and follow the trail. I will pay your costs. How much do you require to begin?"

He smiled, and bowed his head to hide it.

But Aphrodite saw, and raised her slim dark eyebrows at him. "I amuse you, *mon ami*?" she said tartly.

"It is just that I'm not used to such plain speaking, Madame. Most of my clients prefer to pretend I am doing their bidding out of the goodness of my own heart. They do not discuss money. It is impolite; it is beneath them. Besides"—and he shrugged to show he didn't care—"they prefer to despise me for what I do."

Aphrodite waved an impatient hand. "*Psht!* I have no time for such foolishness. I do not care who you are, only that you will do this job for me, and for that I will pay you very well."

"I will try—"

"Come now, you are the best! You found Lady Harmer when she shot her lover and fled her home, and you discovered Sir Marcus Grimsby when he ran off with the parlormaid and his family's fortune. You have a reputation, Mr. Thorne."

She was right; he was the best at what he did. He was a hunter, and once he had the scent of his prey he followed the trail wherever it led. "A veritable human bloodhound," he murmured.

She laughed, but sadness lingered in her eyes and about her mouth.

"If it becomes necessary to speak with your daughters, Madame . . . ?"

"Vivianna is presently in Derbyshire, and Marietta is in Cornwall. Francesca remains in Yorkshire, at Greentree Manor." She sighed, as if Francesca were a source of concern to her.

"And will you take your daughters into your confidence in this matter?"

Again she leaned forward, her expression deadly serious. "Under no circumstances should you reveal your true quest to them, sir. I do not want them to know. They will pester me into telling them, and . . . and I cannot be pestered about this matter. It is dangerous. Even you, Mr. Thorne, must tread very carefully. The persons you are seeking will harm you if they think you might threaten their anonymity."

"I am not afraid, Madame, but I am not a fool. I will be careful."

"Good, that is good."

"May I ask what you hope to accomplish by this search? And why you have waited so long?"

Aphrodite's dark eyes took on a feverish quality. "A name. I need to hear a name spoken aloud. I thought I could put it behind me but I can no longer live with this terrible fear. I begin to think that he will strike again," and she pressed her hand to her heart. "It is making me ill. I want to know that my daughters are no longer in danger from him. I want to enjoy their company and not be always *afraid*."

"You want to put an end to it, Madame. I understand that. What about punishment? Justice? Do you want this person brought before the law? Or do you prefer to deal out your own brand of retribution?"

She blinked, but he could see that she understood exactly what he was saying. "You have done this before?" she whispered. "You have punished people for their crimes?"

"You said you knew the sort of man I was," he reminded her quietly. "Madame, it is clear that you suspect someone else to be the general behind Mrs. Slater. Can you tell *me* his name?"

But she shook her head violently. "*Non, non!* Not yet. I want you to discover it for yourself. I want to hear it spoken on your lips. I want to know I am not the only one who believes it is so."

She was frightened, and it was a fear that had been with her for a long time.

"Very well, Madame, I will do as you wish. I am very discreet. And, as for justice, we will discuss it when the time comes, *oui*?"

Aphrodite took a shaky breath and nodded jerkily, strands of her curling dark hair loosening from its pins. "Thank you, *mon ami*. I feel better now. I am afraid, oh yes, I am afraid, but this is the right thing to do. This is the thing I *must* do."

Sebastian rose and took her hand, pressing his lips lightly to her elegant ringed fingers. "I will return to you when I have news, Madame."

She was distracted, but she smiled as he moved to leave the room. "Thank you, Mr. Thorne."

Sebastian's steps were quick and light, and as he opened the door, the woman outside stepped back with a gasp. Dark hair, a pretty face, a mouth that was designed to smile. "Oh, I do beg your pardon," she said in an attractive Irish lilt. "I have a message for Madame, and I wasn't sure if I should interrupt."

She was watching him, a combination of wariness and flirtatiousness in her gaze. Sebastian had that effect on women—they liked what they saw, but at the same time they sensed he wasn't easily tamed.

Aphrodite spoke behind him. "Maeve? Is something wrong?"

"The champagne, Madame. I think it has gone bad—the guests are complaining."

Aphrodite clicked her tongue in annoyance. Sebastian bowed again and left them to domestic matters, but the Irishwoman's face remained with him. Perhaps what Maeve had said was true; she was simply being polite by waiting outside the door. But Sebastian had learned to be cautious, and he suspected she was eavesdropping. That in itself was not a serious offense—she might simply be curious, with nothing sinister in her actions—but he promised himself that he would be far more vigilant the next time he visited Aphrodite's Club.

Right now he had work to do.

His blood began to stir as he contemplated the chase. The role of hunter came naturally to Sebastian. It amused him, too, that those high-society types who treated him with contempt and refused to speak to him in everyday life were forced to be polite to him when they wanted to hire Mr. Thorne.

Dancing with the devil, he called it to himself, and while none of them enjoyed it, plenty of the highborn rich had been his partners. Mr. Thorne was useful in a difficult situation, and no one remembered that he had another life, had been another man, eight years ago. Why should they care? They simply wanted him to do their dirty work for them and then disappear into whatever alleyway he'd crawled out of.

And that was fine with him, because he'd lost the ability to be the man he'd once been. That man had gone forever. And Sebastian had no intention of bringing him back.

Chapter 1

Yorkshire
Several weeks later

Sebastian settled himself more comfortably upon his hired hack. In the bracing cold he followed his companion across the bleak Yorkshire moors, hoping he was getting closer to whoever had planned the kidnapping of Aphrodite's daughters.

He always found the northern light different. More diffused and atmospheric, in a way that made him think of worlds beyond this one. Or perhaps that was just because of the landscape; miles of lonely moorland and rocky outcrops and not a sign of habitation. He glanced sideways at his companion. The man—Hal—was dressed in rough clothing that was none too clean, but he rode as if he knew where he was going. Hal was the village blacksmith, and Sebastian had found him in the village inn, eager and willing to talk. His eagerness had increased when Sebastian offered him the chance to earn ten guineas, five before and five afterward. He'd be a fool, Sebastian thought, to renege on the deal and lose out on the second portion, and Hal didn't look like a fool.

"T' Gypsy camp is over the hill," Hal called out now, his unshaven face flushed from the cold. "The man you want'll come out to meet us. As I told you before, Mrs. Slater and he were as thick as thieves. Every day they'd be in the inn, whispering, plotting I called it. If anyone knows owt of where she's gone, sir, then it'll be that Gypsy."

"And Mrs. Slater's husband?"

Hal shrugged. "Didn't see much of him."

"Was there anyone else she associated with, apart from her husband and this Gypsy fellow?"

"No, but sometimes she got letters. Letters all the way from Lon'on."

Sebastian nodded. It was as he thought. Mrs. Slater was taking her orders from someone else. He was hoping that the Gypsy he was on his way to meet was another link in the chain that would eventually lead him back to the real mastermind behind the kidnapping of Aphrodite's daughters. The name that the courtesan already knew but couldn't tell him.

"Not far now." Hal's voice drifted back to him. "Aye, there he is!"

They had climbed a rise, and below them lay a verdant green valley. Sebastian admired it a moment, before following Hal's pointing finger to the horseman waiting on the far side, on top of another bleak, limestone tor. It crossed his mind that there were no birds about—this part of the moor was very quiet indeed—but it was only a passing thought. He was more concerned with the meeting ahead of him; his heartbeat quickened with anticipation.

They started down into the valley at a trot, and then suddenly Hal drew up, cursing, and dismounted. "Damn me, my horse's lame," he said, when Sebastian circled back to see what was the matter. "Could be nowt more than a stone in his shoe." He prepared to inspect the animal's hooves. "Don't you worry about me, sir, you go ahead. The man you want is waiting."

Sebastian met his eyes, trying to read them, but there was nothing to read. Either Hal was a practiced liar or he was telling the truth. Whichever it was, Sebastian had come too far now to go back. "Very well," he said. Then, just in case there was something devious afoot: "If you're not being true with me I will come after you."

Hal's gaze shifted nervously, but his voice was firm. "I am true to my principles, sir. You can't ask more than that of a man."

Sebastian nodded. "Fair enough." He left Hal struggling to lift one of his restive mount's hind legs and set off again. He was watching the dark silhouette of the horseman atop the crags—if it was a trap, then he wanted to be ready. He was so busy observing the horseman's every move that it was a moment before he realized the danger did not come from there. It came from below.

The ground beneath him had begun to shake and quiver in a most alarming way.

Sebastian drew up with a shout, trying to turn his horse around, but the ground was sucking at the animal's hooves like quicksand. That was when he remembered some passing comment he had heard at the inn. Something about a mire or a bog, where the unwary wanderer could be swallowed whole and never seen again.

I must get out of this, he thought frantically, but the horse was in a total panic and reared up and threw him. As he lay, stunned and winded, he heard it struggling to find a footing, and then galloping off triumphantly.

His horse had escaped but it was too late for Sebastian. He was sinking. He tried to scramble out, shouting to Hal to help him. The other man was already running toward him. "Get me out of here!" Sebastian called.

But Hal stopped at the very edge of the mire, and the expression in his eyes was unmistakable. "Can't do that, sir."

It is a trap then, he thought bleakly. But he was not beaten yet. "You want your money, don't you?" he cried angrily. "It's not much good to you if I sink to the bottom."

"Some things are more important than money," Hal replied forebodingly, and crouched down on his haunches, watching closely as Sebastian sank up to his waist. "You don't want t'struggle too hard, Mr. Thorne," he said helpfully. "Makes you go under quicker. Stay nice and still and you'll live longer."

"You mean I won't sink if I don't struggle?"

"No, you'll still sink."

Sebastian gave a breathless, bitter laugh.

"I'm sorry about this, sir," Hal added surprisingly.

Sebastian tried to read the irony in his face but there was none. Hal was telling the truth; he was genuinely repentant. "But you're not going to save me, are you?" he snarled.

"I can't do that. As I told you, I have to be true to my principles, see. My family comes first. You're a threat to them, sir." He nodded toward the tor, which was now empty. "We had no choice but to stop you. I reckon you'd do the same."

"Spare me your homespun philosophies and get me out. Whatever you're being paid, I'll double it."

"It isn't owt to do with money," Hal said sincerely. "If it was I'd pull you out, for I've got nowt against you, sir. Believe me, this isn't personal. I have to do as I'm told or *my* life is in danger. These people . . . they're serious folk. Dangerous folk." Abruptly he straightened up and took a step backward. "Good-bye, Mr. Thorne," he called out. "I won't stay to watch you die. I hope for your sake t'end is quick."

Shaking with fury, Sebastian watched as Hal walked back to his horse and rode away, leaving him to die.

It didn't seem real, but the cold mud and sour smell of rotting vegetation were real enough. No matter how still he tried to be, he was sinking, slowly but surely. There was something truly horrible in the thought of dying in such an inevitable manner. To have so much time to think about his own end. This was far, far worse than the quick death he'd dreamed of—a dark alleyway, a knife in the back.

He turned his head, seeking help that wasn't there, and caught sight of something nearby, poking up out of the mire. It was a dead branch, rising up like a spear . . . or an outstretched hand. He reached out, his fingers trembling, and touched the wood, wrapped his hand around it. The branch was still strong enough for him to grasp it and use it to drag himself closer. He threw one arm over it, half expecting to hear it snap, but it didn't. He hung on, wriggling upward every time he started to sink again, trying to keep his head and chest above the mire.

Sebastian drew a shaken breath. He was certain there was no Gypsy camp over the hill—Hal would not leave him within reach of help—but he shouted anyway, as loud as he could for as long as he could. He shouted until he was hoarse. But no one came.

It would be night soon, and he was alone. And although Sebastian Thorne was a man who was used to his own company, this was different. He didn't want to die here all by himself. There were questions in his head clamoring for answers, questions he rarely asked himself. Did he really deserve such an ignominious end? Sebastian wasn't the sort to give in easily, and he wasn't going to let Hal and his masters rid themselves of him without a fight. He told himself that he would escape, and after he had dealt with them, he'd complete his assignment for Aphrodite, and then . . . perhaps he'd go home.

Home. The ramshackle manor house in the New Forest, his brother's pained expression when he left. A longing that he hadn't felt for years rose up within him. He stifled it. He couldn't go home; he could never go home.

As the darkness began to fall, and freezing night closed over him like a fist, he found his mind drifting. Suffering from exhaustion and cold, Sebastian clung to the branch, and sometimes he slipped into a doze through sheer exhaustion. But the sinking motion that followed always brought him to his senses again, sending him struggling up through the mud, terrified his face would go under.

Then he began to feel as if he was being watched. He'd peer into the night and think he could see shadows, darker than the rest, one moment there, the next gone. He knew it was his mind playing tricks on him, but as the long hours dragged by, it gave him something to think about other than his own death.

It was a woman, he decided, the woman of his dreams. She had fine, straight red hair, and blue eyes, and a well-bred nose, and lips as ripe and red as cherries. Those lips looked sweet, too, and when she smiled at him . . . He smiled back, although it was more like a grimace, his teeth white in his muddy face. He'd had plenty of women, from serving girls to society ladies, but it all meant nothing, because none of them had touched his heart.

As the long night continued, Sebastian wondered if his dream woman was out there somewhere, and if she was, whether he would ever find her.

The ground was spongy underfoot. It could be treacherous, but Francesca knew the ways of these wild and desolate moors. She had lived here all her life; the country was a part of her. Only here could she truly be herself.

Climbing onto higher ground, her steps firm and sure, Francesca paused to look about her. Her cloak flapped in the cold wind, and the hood fell back from her curling dark hair. A gust of rain-filled wind stung her cheeks, and she narrowed her dark eyes against it.

Wolf, her lurcher, began to bark. Francesca murmured reassurance to him, her gaze upon the horizon. There were clouds coming in, but she had time enough before the weather closed down. She had already walked a long way this morning, and really she should be turning back. There was packing to be done. Lady Greentree, or Mrs. Jardine as she now was, would be worrying and wondering where she was. Her adoptive mother was soon to embark upon a journey to London . . .

And Francesca was going with her.

That was why she was out here in the cold and the rain, walking upon her beloved moors. Soon there would be nothing for her to see from her window but houses and rattling vehicles and people, lots of people, all crowded into the confines of the smoky, dirty, and ever expanding city of London.

Already she felt the ache in her heart at leaving, the loss of her freedom. She would put on her smart traveling outfit, the one her mother had purchased in York, and the façade that went with it. Respectable, restrained, proper Miss Francesca Greentree—everything that deep in her heart she knew she wasn't.

Wolf barked again. He ran higher, to the very top of a limestone outcrop, and stood with legs stiff and wiry coat bristling, staring intently down the other side. Francesca knew that over there lay the green and deceptively beautiful Emerald Mire, and that the mire was the last resting place of many a wandering sheep, or an unwary stranger.

Quickly she climbed up to join the lurcher, ignoring the splatters of rain falling about her. A strong gust of wind caught at her clothing, and she tugged her cloak closer around her. Her skin tingled with the cold, her blood was coursing through her veins, and her body felt alive, and at one with the elements.

At that moment she reached the summit. Her hand resting on Wolf's head, she drank in the view, storing it away in her heart for the long months ahead.

Wolf took off, loping down the other side, straight for the mire. Francesca called him to come back, but he ignored her. Worried, even though she knew he was familiar with the dangers, she caught up her skirts and ran after him, her old boots slipping and sliding on the rough ground.

"Wolf!"

He turned and gave a series of barks, as if to say, *Can't you see him!* before he set off again.

Francesca stared out over the green shimmering surface, and she *did* see him. The man.

He was lying awkwardly, trapped, with his arms wrapped around a branch that had somehow found its way into the mire. His head was turned away from her.

Was he alive?

A shiver of horror went through her and she slowed her steps. He was so still. He must be dead. She told herself that she should go and fetch help to remove the body, but her feet wouldn't move.

Aware that Wolf was still barking, she hushed him. And then she saw one of his hands move, just a twitch, and the man lifted his head and turned his face toward her. It was pale, mud-smeared, with eyes so dark and burning that for a moment Francesca was frozen to the spot, her gaze locked with his.

And, the strangest thing, he smiled. "It's you," he said, his voice deep and hoarse.

As if he'd been expecting her.

Chapter 2

~~~
⌒⌒∞⌒⌒
~~~

Francesca felt her heart give a painful jolt. He was alive and there was no time to be lost! She picked her way onto the outer edges of the treacherous mire, until her boots began to sink. Wolf ran ahead of her, knowing instinctively where it was safe; he was showing her the way.

Cautiously Francesca followed until she reached the spot where the big dog stopped. There was a patch of ground about a yard across that was solid and safe, but all around the mire shimmered treacherously. "Good Wolf," she murmured gratefully, ruffling his coarse coat. "You're far too fussy to get your feet wet, aren't you, boy?" For a moment her fingers clung to his warm, wiry body, seeking comfort.

How was she going to save the man? He was closer now, but still out of reach by several feet, and there was nothing lying about that she could use. She needed a rope or a pole, something for him to cling to so that she could drag him to safety.

He was watching her, probably wondering if she was going to join him in the mire. "My dog knows the safe path," she explained.

"I hope you're right." He wiped his face with the sleeve of his jacket, smearing the mud. He had a gentleman's voice, he'd been to a good school, but other than that and the fact that his hair was as dark as his eyes, Francesca couldn't tell what he looked like.

"How long have you been here?"

"All night."

He moved, grimacing with pain. Was he injured? Francesca could see that he was holding on to the half-submerged branch with the crook of his elbow. It didn't look very secure. Something needed to be done, and soon.

Wolf made a whimpering sound in his throat and Francesca patted him again, soothing him and herself, while her gaze remained on the man. His head had dropped down, but now he lifted it again and his gaze fastened hungrily on to hers, as if he was afraid that if he blinked or looked away she might disappear.

"Are you injured?" she called out to him, feeling shaken. "Can you move at all?"

"You're not a dream, are you?" he said.

"No, I promise you I'm no dream."

"And is there a Gypsy camp over the hill?"

"No. There's nothing between us and the manor house in that direction." She pointed. "Or the village in that direction." She swung her arm around.

"Fool, bloody *fool*. I should have realized. The birds, that was it, when there were no birds, I should have—"

Because the conversation he was having appeared to be with himself and had nothing to do with her, Francesca ignored him. She bent down, and by testing the ground in front of her with her hands, she was able to creep slowly forward. Wolf was whining anxiously at her back, clearly of the opinion that she was pushing her luck, but she ignored him, intent on getting as close as possible to the stricken stranger. She'd remembered seeing a boating accident once, when she and her family were holidaying in the Lake District. A child had fallen from a boat, and one of the men stripped off his jacket and used it as a sort of rope, so that the child had something to grasp.

Francesca didn't have a jacket, but she did have her woolen cloak. It was old but it was made of stout Yorkshire wool, and Francesca thought that it would do very well.

The stranger was still muttering to himself, so Francesca interrupted him. "Sir?" He swung his head around, eyes narrowing, as if he was surprised to find her there. "Can you move at all? If I were to twist my cloak into a rope and throw it toward you, could you use it to try to pull yourself free?"

He was watching her mouth intently, as if he was trying to read her lips. Perhaps he was delirious.

"Sir?" she repeated desperately. "Did you understand what I said?"

"Cherries," he said, as if he'd come to some important decision. "Ripe cherries. But the hair is wrong, and the nose . . ."

Crouching on the edge of the mire, her skirts muddy, her face frozen, and her hair damp from the soft falling rain, Francesca wavered in her determination to rescue him by herself. "I'm going back for help." She spoke loudly and clearly. "I don't want to leave you here, but I think I must. It will not be for long."

He blinked, and clarity returned to his face and focus to his eyes. "No," he said with hoarse desperation. "Don't go. I promise you I am unhurt, just very tired from a night spent trying to keep myself from being swallowed up by this infernal muddy soup."

Francesca hesitated.

He could see the doubt. "Please," he repeated. "If you go, I won't be alive when you get back. Don't desert me." He was tired and close to the end of his strength. She read it in his eyes as they stared at each other, and knew that this man's life was in her hands. She felt a trembling deep inside her as she acknowledged the responsibility, but it was one she was willing to accept.

"I will do my best," she agreed. "I won't desert you."

"Thank you." He smiled, and despite his state, there was something about his smile . . .

Francesca busied herself by removing her cloak

and twisting it until it resembled a bulky rope. One end she wound as tightly as she could around her hand, and then she tossed the other end toward him.

It fell short.

He tried to reach it anyway, stretching out his free arm, scrabbling with his fingers. The branch cracked sharply, and the mire made a horrid sucking sound, as if it wasn't prepared to give him up. Wolf began barking hysterically, dancing in tight circles. Quickly Francesca pulled her cloak back, trying not to panic at the sight of him grappling with the branch to keep himself from being swallowed.

"This . . . bloody . . . thing . . . will . . . not . . . hold . . . much . . . longer," he gritted.

"You swear a great deal," she said, flustered, struggling with her cloak.

He laughed wildly.

Francesca prepared to toss him the makeshift rope once more.

He tried to alter his position so that he had a better chance of catching hold of it when she threw it, and then swore again, abruptly. "Damn and blast it! I can't feel my legs. It's the cold, curse it."

Francesca prayed it was not something worse. If he could not help her with the task ahead, then they were both lost.

He struggled, and ominously the branch cracked again. "I'm sinking," he said grimly.

"Hold on!"

"If I stop talking you'll know I've gone under."

"At least you'll stop swearing."

"It's . . . not . . . unreasonable . . . to . . . swear . . . in . . . the . . . circumstances."

Ignoring him, on her hands and knees, Francesca began to creep closer still, feeling her way, and although she sank a little, she didn't stop moving until the ground began to tremble violently. "That's far enough." Behind her, Wolf showed his concern by whimpering.

Francesca stretched out on her front, trying to spread her weight evenly over the quivering ground. She secured one end of her cloak beneath her. "Are you ready?"

His hand was outstretched, fingers spread wide. "Do it."

She flung it.

He caught it. Just as the branch finally snapped in two. He clung to her cloak with both hands. With a grunt of effort, he twisted the woolen cloth around his arm, so that it was tightly drawn between them.

He grinned at her without humor. "My life is in your hands."

Francesca tried to think of some clever retort, but she was beyond it. Besides, she wasn't sure she *could* save him. She was tall and strong for a woman, but he was a big man. Then Wolf tugged at her skirts with his teeth, doing his best to pull her back to safety, and she knew this was the moment. It was now or never.

"Now!" Francesca shouted, and began to haul on the makeshift rope, moving back as she pulled him in like a huge fish.

Dear God, he was heavy! Her muscles burned; her arms felt as if they were being torn from their sockets. The mire made that awful sucking sound again, as if it were loath to give up its prey.

"I'm moving," he gasped, and when she looked into his face she saw the strain, a mirror of her own, his lips drawn back into a snarl. His dark eyes glittered. "Pull harder!"

Francesca, who was sure she couldn't pull any harder, pulled harder. She came up onto her knees, and then her feet.

His hips came free. He wriggled wildly, and now his thighs were free, and then his knees, and he was crawling toward her. Francesca gave a last tremendous heave and found herself stumbling backward, onto the area of solid ground that Wolf had found for her. The stranger was moving toward her, so quickly that there was no possibility of his sinking.

His body knocked hard against hers. As she fell, he fell on top of her. They landed together, and all the breath went out of her. He was heavy and warm, and he was covered in wet mud. She was aware of his chest heaving up and down, violently, pressing to hers. He'd dropped his face to her shoulder, and now he began to shake. In the back of her mind she could hear Wolf barking, crazy with excitement, but he seemed far away. Everything seemed so far away.

That was when Francesca realized she was going to faint—there were black dots forming in front of her eyes. Perhaps she said it aloud, because abruptly his weight was lifted from her. She drew in a great gulp of air. A large hand gripped her chin, holding her face up.

"Better?" he asked, examining her with an intensity that unnerved her.

Francesca looked up into his eyes. She still felt light-headed, and the question just popped into her head. "What did you mean?" she said. "When you said, 'It's you'?"

"When I said . . . ?"

"The first time you saw me, you said, 'It's you.'"

He shook his head. "I don't know why I said it. I was dreaming, I think. I've been imagining things alone here in the dark. I thought I'd imagined you."

He was telling the truth. She read it in his eyes. Dark eyes, black as pitch, whereas her own were a warm brown. He lifted his face to the sky, and she realized it was raining lightly, washing the mud away. He helped it along by scrubbing his hands over his skin, and then shaking his hair like a dog, sending droplets of mud and water in all directions.

"That's better," he said at last, and looked down at her again.

His hair was longer than the fashion, and stuck out wildly from the shaking he'd just given it. He was so close that she could see every feature, every line, from the scratch on his unshaven jaw—the sort of strong, uncompromising jaw that a man who had kept himself alive all night in Emerald Mire would have—to his blunt nose, and the dark brows that slashed so boldly across his forehead. His mouth was thinned, tightly closed, as if he kept secrets, but there were faint lines at the edges, as if he had once smiled a great deal.

Energy and vitality seemed to spark from him. Francesca thought he was one of the handsomest men she had ever seen in her life, but he would not be to everyone's taste. He was far too dark and dangerous. If he were a character in a novel, he wouldn't be the hero, oh no.

This man would be the villain.

It occurred to her that neither of them had spoken a word for some time. Was he examining her as she was him? The idea made her squirm. Francesca valued personal privacy, and she had the sense that this man's bold dark eyes could strip her bare.

Naked.

As if the word was a switch, she became aware of the heavy heat of him on her. Although he was using his forearms to take some his weight, there was barely any space between their upper bodies, and his legs lay half on hers and half on her skirts, pinning her beneath him. It was the closest she'd ever been to a man, and she should be protesting and demanding he remove himself at once. But the words wouldn't form in her head; she couldn't summon up the will to speak them. She felt languid, sensual, as if she might reach up and slip her arms around his neck, and pull his mouth down to hers.

A tingle of dismay made her catch her breath.

To kiss this dangerous stranger in the middle of a storm on the moors was surely the ultimate in shocking behavior? Worthy of Aphrodite herself! And that was why Francesca couldn't let it happen . . . *must not* let it happen.

"We need to find shelter before the weather gets worse," she blurted out, trying to wriggle out from under him. "You'll catch your death."

"After what I've been through, a little rain doesn't seem worth worrying about," he said, not moving an inch. There was a glint in his eyes, and she knew then that he was thinking of kissing, too. She licked her lips, and his gaze narrowed. His breath was warm and slightly ragged against her skin. "I'm alive, thanks to you."

He swooped, and she turned her face to one side. Francesca felt the scrape of his unshaven jaw against her cheek, the tickle of his unkempt hair. Shocked, she realized her hand was now resting on his shoulder. How did it get there? Had she done that? She must have, and yet she didn't remember. She knew she couldn't risk another second of his closeness.

"Please, let me up."

The pause seemed to last forever, and it was only as he moved away, slowly, as if he was acting against his inclination, that Francesca knew she was safe. Not just from him, but also from the dangerous hunger he stirred within her.

He swayed as he stood up, before he found his footing.

Francesca's gaze traveled over him—she couldn't help it. He was still wearing his riding boots. Long, well-muscled legs in breeches caked with the muck of the mire, narrow hips, and a shirt that had once been white beneath a brown jacket. His chest and shoulders were wide and strong, his throat manly, his face wickedly handsome.

He's a spinster's dream, and I'm a spinster.

She felt dizzy, but she knew that must be from her exertions. It was no easy matter to pull such a big man from the mire—he must stand over six foot.

Wolf was whimpering. Francesca reached out and drew him against her, pressing her face against his warm, rough coat, murmuring praise. He licked her cheek.

"Damn and blast it, my legs feel boneless," the stranger's deep voice interrupted.

Francesca gave him a wary look.

"You didn't see my horse about?" Although he spoke the words with his mouth, his eyes were saying, *I want to kiss you and I know you want to kiss me.*

"No." Francesca stood up, shaking out her muddy skirts. "I didn't." The light was even gloomier than it had been a moment ago, and it was only a matter of time until the storm struck. She rested her hand on Wolf's head. "Take us out of here, boy. Show us the way." A quick warning glance at the stranger. "Follow my footsteps exactly."

With Wolf leading the way, they made the journey through the edge of the mire to safety. Wolf loped off excitedly, and Francesca took several long strides—putting a safe distance between them—before turning to face him. She needn't have bothered. He'd found a good-sized rock to sit on.

"How far is it back to the village?" he said, with a hint of impatience.

"Three . . . nearly four miles."

"Not so far."

"You'd never get there in this weather. It's far too dangerous, even for those who know their way."

He didn't argue, although she sensed he wanted to. "What do you suggest then?" He climbed stiffly to his feet.

"It depends if you're able to walk," she said cautiously. "It might be best if you wait here while I go and fetch help."

But she already knew he was the sort of man who would refuse to wait for anything. "No, damn it, I won't wait here!" He wrenched a handful of heather from a bush, using it to clean the mud off his clothing. He stamped his boots, wincing. "This manor house you mentioned, is it far? I need a horse. Can they supply one?"

"You are in no fit state to go riding!"

She sounded sharp, and when he turned to her, his dark brows were drawn down and his eyes were glittering. He was angry—no, he was furious—but not with her. "I have unfinished business in the village, and it can't wait."

The way he said it . . . For a moment Francesca felt as if she had been transported straight into a novel, and a thrill ran through her.

Dangerous.

She gave him the kind of look an adult gives an unruly child. "Isn't the fact that you're alive enough to be getting on with? You can finish whatever it is you have to finish tomorrow. Dastardly deeds can be committed in sunshine as well as rain, can they not?"

He laughed, and now his black eyes gleamed with

admiration. "'Dastardly deeds.' I like that. I see you have my measure, my lady."

Her skin prickled.

"I don't find the situation funny."

He looked contrite, but it was all an act. His eyes gave him away. They were speaking to her again, with words like *seduction* and *temptation* and *indiscretion*. He made her feel exposed, vulnerable and afraid.

Francesca put a hand to her hair, which she knew was wild and unkempt from the wind and rain. Her gown was old and unfashionable, with a darn in the skirt and a lighter inch of cloth at the hem, where it had been let down. She wasn't wearing a corset, and her stockings were coarse, her boots muddy and, though comfortable, very worn.

She was herself, and it had never bothered her before, but now she found herself wishing she was wearing the magenta taffeta she'd seen in York last month, with the matching parasol and slippers. The preposterous image of herself dressed in such an outfit, walking in the rain on the moors, made her smile.

His gaze was roaming her face. "Last night, when I was trapped in the mire, I was dreaming of a beautiful woman. I thought I was dreaming of you, but I see now it wasn't you."

Francesca stiffened. "I'm so sorry I don't measure up to your feverish imaginings!"

He realized he'd insulted her, and shook his head impatiently. "But you do. That is my point."

"I do?"

"My 'feverish imaginings'—I *do* like your turn of

phrase—didn't do you justice. I can see that now. Who needs blue eyes and a perfect nose and—" He stopped hastily. "You are my dream."

"I think you must be delirious, Mr. . . ." She laughed angrily. "I don't even know your name!"

"Sebastian Thorne." He bowed like a gentleman. "From London."

"Then, Mr. *Thorne,* I think you've mistaken me for someone else." Her voice was chilly and formal, her "proper" voice. "I am Miss Francesca Greentree, of Greentree Manor. And I do not make appearances in men's dreams, especially not yours!"

He was staring at her blankly. And then, slowly, his dark eyes lit up with an unholy amusement, and his mobile mouth was smiling again.

"Miss Greentree," he repeated. "Miss *Francesca* Greentree. I feel as if I know you already."

Chapter 3

The woman of his dreams was watching him as if she wasn't at all certain of his sanity. She was right. He was wondering about it himself. She was Aphrodite's daughter—his client's daughter—and although he hadn't known that at first, he did now. It made no difference. Just as it made no difference that she wasn't strictly the woman of his dreams. Her hair was too curly and unrestrained, her eyes were brown and not blue, her nose was tip-tilted, and her mouth was lush and too wide, although the color was right. But none of that mattered.

He wanted her.

Wanted her with a feverish single-mindedness he

usually reserved only for his prey. Perhaps he had lost his mind as well as his scruples during the night in the mire? Death had breathed upon him and left him with an unquenchable thirst for life. And Miss Francesca Greentree *was* life.

He took off his jacket, every muscle and sinew tired and aching, and shook it hard. Clumps of mud rattled to the ground. He reminded himself that he was a sensible man, most of the time anyway. A practical and hardheaded man, with no time for romantic fairy tales. With gritted teeth he put his jacket on again, straightening the cuffs and the lapels with determined tugs.

And all the time he was aware of *her*, like the sun at his back. The softness of her flesh beneath him, cradling him, was burned into his brain. No corset. He couldn't remember a woman of her class not being properly tucked in and turned out, but he wasn't shocked, far from it. He wanted to lie down upon her again and feel every inch of her responding to him, while he kissed those luscious lips. How was it that such a proper woman had such an improper mouth . . .

His practical voice said, *This is lust, Sebastian. The sort of lust that makes fools of the rich and powerful, the sort of lust that topples governments. The sort of lust that can cause Mr. Thorne to lose his focus. Hal and his cohorts are out there somewhere and they must be found.*

"What is it that brings you onto the moors, Mr. Thorne?" Miss Francesca Greentree questioned him in her melodious voice. Ah, that voice. It sent a tingle all the way down to his groin.

Sebastian turned to look at her. She had the same unruly dark hair as Aphrodite, and the same wide, dark gaze that seemed to pierce him as if he were an insect on a pin, but she was also different in ways that were entirely her own.

"Mr. Thorne? I asked you what you were doing out on the moors? How did you come to be here in the first place?"

Sebastian ran an impatient hand through his matted hair. "I was lost. I thought I'd take a shortcut, and the next thing I knew I'd fallen off my horse. If not for that branch I would be dead now, with no one the wiser."

He was watching her carefully to see if she believed him.

She didn't, but she was clever enough not to say it aloud. Apart from a quick upward flicker from the corners of her eyes, she did not give herself away. If he hadn't been adept at reading faces he wouldn't even have noticed.

"Emerald Mire has a reputation for swallowing up everything and everyone who wanders into it," she said, staring ahead now. "Sometimes they come up again—days, even months later—sometimes they don't."

"You paint a grim picture," he replied.

She gave him a frowning look, making him wonder what he'd said wrong. But all she said was, "We must hurry," and looked up at the sky.

He, too, stared up at the darkening heavens. The energy he had used to escape from his muddy prison had taken its toll, and he only hoped he could persuade his aching body to carry him to shelter before the storm broke. Suddenly he wanted nothing more than to sit in a comfortable chair in front of a roaring fire, with a glass of brandy in one hand and a cigar in the other. His rooms in Half Moon Street, and his manservant Martin, were his one indulgence, his one concession to the past.

But he couldn't go home, and he couldn't collapse in his bed at the inn. There was Hal to deal with. He and his conspirators would be imagining him dead and themselves safe, and Sebastian must strike while they were still laboring under that delusion. There was no time to be lost.

As if on cue, lightning streaked from the glowering clouds, turning the moors a sickly yellow. It was frightening and elemental, and wonderfully invigorating.

"Greentree Manor isn't far." Francesca was eyeing him as if she was afraid he might fall over at any moment. Thunder rumbled threateningly. "Are you certain you can walk, Mr. Thorne?"

"Of course I can walk!"

She lifted an eyebrow in disbelief.

In reply, he strode off up the hill, just to show her. She followed, and for a time they carried on in silence. When his steps began to lag, she slipped his arm over her shoulders to support him.

He sighed. "I can manage, blast you."

"No, *blast you*, you can't manage," she retorted. "I have better things to do than rescue you from the mire again, Mr. Thorne."

She was tall for a woman, but he was taller. He

must be a burden to her, although she did not say so. Sebastian thought about protesting and pulling away, but frustrating as it was, he knew she was right. He needed her help.

Several times he had to pause, and once he found himself leaning on her shoulder, his head bowed, breathing hard. But when she asked him again, her own voice breathless, whether he would prefer to wait while she fetched help, he gruffly refused her and began to walk, muttering curses under his breath to disguise his discomfort.

"You really do swear a great deal," she said, not in the least shocked.

"It helps."

"How?" she asked curiously.

"It makes me feel better."

"How can behaving in such a childish manner make you feel better?"

Sebastian took the opportunity to stop for another rest. He looked down at her, tucked beneath his arm, wiping the dripping rain from his eyes so he could see her better. The rain was causing her hair to curl even more wildly and the cold had turned her skin white, apart from two red circles on her cheeks.

She blinked, and he saw that her lashes were clubbed together. He had the urgent desire to reach out and touch them with his fingertip.

"This is ridiculous." Francesca tugged him forward, her wet cloak flapping around them, her boots slipping on the sodden ground.

He leaned down so that he could whisper in her ear. "You feel it, too, don't you?"

She gave him a suspicious glance and leaned away as far as she was able. "Feel what?" she said.

"Francesca," he murmured.

"I beg your pardon?"

"It makes me think of the sun and hot days and nights, and passion. Oh yes, definitely passion."

She blinked. "Stop it."

"Desire, Francesca. Lust . . ."

"Mr. Thorne!"

"What do you want me to say? Do you want me to lie to you and pretend we are two halves of a whole? Two sides of the same coin? Two souls amid a sea of—of . . . ?"

"Run out of metaphors, Mr. Thorne?" she mocked. "No, I don't want you to lie to me. I know we are nothing of the sort. Let us just say we are strangers in a storm, and our acquaintance, I hope, will be mercifully brief."

He laughed. "Then we agree on something, Miss Greentree. Neither of us believes in destiny. But desire . . . now that's another matter."

Francesca made a sound and turned away. But her foot slipped on the wet ground, and she stumbled and began to fall. He caught her and swung her around, and she cannoned into him. The sensation was like fire. Somehow he kept his feet. For a moment they stood clasped together, both too shaken to move, and then she lifted her head, her eyes very wide.

"I want to kiss you, Miss Greentree," he said.

The acknowledgment flared in her face. She wanted to kiss him, too, and he knew it in that instant. She desired him as much as he did her. It was all the permission he needed.

Sebastian bent forward, savoring the moment, controlling the urge to plunder. Her lips were soft, trembling, and cold. He let his own breath warm them, and ran his tongue gently around them. She gasped. He caught it with his mouth, pressing closer. Flame licked at him, burning, a desire such as he had never known. And suddenly she was pulling away, shaking her head, pushing at him. He let her go, stunned by what he had felt as much as from any belated gentlemanly instincts.

There was fright in her eyes. The knowledge sobered him into remembering that he was seducing her, not forcing her against her will. Whatever her birth might be, this was a respectably brought-up young lady.

"My apologies, Miss Greentree," he said, and didn't try to hide the regret as well as the apology in his voice. The desire to feel her lips under his again was a powerful one.

She turned away, presenting him with her flushed cheek.

Just then lightning flashed dangerously close to them. A heartbeat later thunder roared. The rain was back and heavier than before, sweeping across the moors, drenching everything in its path. Sebastian could hardly see more than two feet before him. Francesca seemed to have forgotten about the kiss as she hurried along beside him.

Francesca Greentree, Aphrodite's natural daughter. Did the heart of a courtesan lie buried beneath Francesca's plain—and now decidedly damp—bodice? He wondered what she thought of being the daughter of a courtesan. Did she revel in the decadence of it, or was she appalled by her own birth? Sebastian considered the questions as he trudged along beside her, trying hard to ignore the exhaustion in his body and mind, and the appalling weather.

"How can anyone live in this bloody place?" he grumbled.

"You are not seeing it at its best," she said, pausing to wipe the rain from her eyes. She sneezed.

"Bless you," he muttered.

"There!" Her voice was ragged and she was bedraggled, but when she turned to him, her eyes were burning with joy. Sebastian followed the direction of her pointing finger, peering through the rain. Lights. A house, and a comfortably large one.

"Greentree Manor," she said. "Come on, Mr. Thorne, only a little farther!" At that moment the wind strengthened, blowing her wild hair about her. She seemed completely at home in this hostile world. Dear God, but she was beautiful, he thought in astonishment. This was no respectable spinster, although she might try to pretend she was. Francesca was a creature of the storm.

"I still want to kiss you," he gasped, and he didn't know whether he was shaking from exhaustion and cold, or Francesca Greentree. His blood was drumming in his ears.

"Oh look, the servants coming to help us! Thank goodness . . ."

"I said, I still want to kiss you, Francesca."

"Mr. Thorne—"

"I mean to have you."

She stared at him a moment in astonishment, and then she turned abruptly to the approaching men and cried out, waving her arms. Voices shouted in reply, and lanterns bobbed in the gathering darkness.

He watched her rush toward them, thinking she was saved.

She wasn't. Sebastian Thorne had her in his sights, and nothing but complete surrender would save her now.

Chapter 4

Francesca wriggled as much of herself as possible down into the hip bath. Lil had lined it with towels to make it more cozy, scented the warm water with something sweet and restful, and she was gradually beginning to feel like her old self.

It must have been the shock. I couldn't possibly have felt what I did.

But, uncomfortable as it was, she knew that it wasn't simply an illusion due to the circumstances she had found herself in. There was more. Something she had sworn never to feel. Oh, she had fantasized through her poetry. Byron in particular. The darker side of love attracted Francesca, and she enjoyed dreaming about dangerous heroes, but she'd certainly never felt anything like the wild attraction she'd experienced when she looked into Sebastian Thorne's eyes.

He was cursing the storm one moment and trying to seduce her the next. He was very possibly unstable. She didn't know why he was wandering around the moors, but she thought it was probably something illegal. As they had said about Byron, he was "mad, bad and dangerous to know," but Francesca found herself hooked and wriggling, like a fish on a line.

He'd kissed her!

She could hardly believe it. He'd kissed her, and she'd let him. Francesca supposed she could pretend that she hadn't known what he was about to do until it was too late, but that wasn't true. She'd seen the desire in his eyes, and she'd wanted him to kiss her. Wanted it as much as she'd ever wanted anything.

A shiver ran through her now at the memory of his lips on hers, of his body pressed to hers. Oh yes, it had certainly lived up to expectations. And it wasn't as if she'd never been kissed before—several times she had been the unwilling recipient of the attentions of smitten young men. But nothing could compare to Sebastian Thorne's kiss. She felt as if he'd opened up a door inside her, and she was having difficulty closing it.

But close it she must.

Because of her heritage, Francesca had long ago sworn an oath to herself that she would never allow any man to stir in her the passions she feared were sleeping just below the surface. She didn't want to end up like her mother, tossed from lover to lover, without any control over her own destiny. Ruled by her emotions and her desires. The truth was, it had never been a problem, until now.

She'd have to find some other way to persuade Mr. Thorne that she was exactly what she seemed, a respectable spinster who enjoyed walking and painting, and spent her spare time doing good works for those in need. And she was not the slightest bit interested in playing a part in any man's life, especially *his*. She had long ago resigned herself to spinsterhood.

I want you and I mean to have you.

She shivered again at the memory of his words, with that delicious mixture of fear and excitement.

" 'Ave you caught a chill, Miss Francesca?" Lil was using a soft cloth to wash her back and shoulders. "You shouldn't've been out in that weather. The moor's no place for a lady."

Francesca leaned forward to allow Lil better access to her back, enjoying being pampered. "You know I've been wandering the moors since I was a baby, Lil. They don't frighten me."

"Well maybe they should do," Lil retorted, unstoppable as ever.

Francesca smiled into her folded arms. Lil was Lil and they all loved her dearly. It was sad that she hadn't married the balloon aeronaut she'd met at Vauxhall Gardens, but for some reason Lil had broken off with him and returned north to Greentree Manor. She'd married Jacob Coachman a year later, and they'd been happy until Jacob was killed in an accident ten months ago. It was tragic, and Lil still wore her widow's weeds, but secretly Francesca wondered whether she ever regretted making the safer choice. Not that she'd ever ask; Lil kept her personal feelings very much to herself, and wouldn't appreciate any unsolicited prying.

"That man you was out there with . . ." Again Lil's voice broke into her musing.

"Mr. Thorne?" Francesca's voice was muffled by her arms. Even saying his name gave her a sense of stepping outside her boundaries.

Lil paused in her ministrations. "That's him. He's no gentleman, miss. I've seen his like before."

"Lil, you don't even know him!"

"I don't need to know him. I seen the way he looked at you."

"Mr. Thorne spent all night in the mire, remember? He was too weak to walk without assistance. What harm could he possibly do to me?"

"Men are men," Lil said, as if that was an end to the argument. "Now lean back and I'll wash your hair, Miss Francesca. Tsk, such a wild mess it is! I don't know how we're ever going to get a comb through it."

Francesca leaned back. "He said he was here on business."

"Who did?"

"Mr. Thorne. But what sort of business would bring him here? We have no mills or mines, we live in a part of the county where there are few villages and fewer people."

"Could be he's a robber. Or a smuggler. Or he's on the run from the authorities."

Francesca smiled. "Dear me, Lil, you have a vivid imagination," she said, pretending she hadn't thought of those very things herself.

"I've been packing your trunk for the journey to London," Lil went on, changing the subject again. "It's just as you wanted it. Though why you want to take all those tatty old dresses with you when you'll be in London where you can buy the latest fashions, I don't know."

"I like myself the way I am," Francesca said stubbornly.

Lil's hands gentled. "A new dress don't mean you'd be any different, miss."

But Francesca didn't believe that. She'd seen how easy it was to be drawn into the fashionable world. Look at Vivianna and Marietta, and how they had changed! London changed people. Tempted them. And before you knew it, you were being led down paths you'd sworn never to tread. Like Aphrodite. And it was all the more dangerous when you were secretly aware of that little hidden part of you that wanted nothing more than to be let loose. To run completely and utterly wild.

Restraint, that was the thing. Self-restraint. Francesca had made it her mantra. The only place she allowed herself to be herself was here, on the moors. Anywhere else she kept a tight rein on her emotions.

"Are you looking forward to seeing London again, Lil?"

"Whyever not, miss?" Lil shot back. "Is there some reason I shouldn't?"

Clearly the subject was a touchy one. "Never mind."

Lil's voice gentled. "Come on now, let's get you out

of there, Miss Francesca, and you can have a nap before dinner."

Francesca sighed. "Really, Lil, you make me sound like a child just out of the schoolroom."

"Sometimes I think you have no more sense than one!"

"I'm glad you're coming to London, too," she said, and meant it. "I think my mother has plans for me. I know I can always rely on you to talk good sense."

Lil smiled, her severe expression softening. "Thank you, miss, but I fear Lady Greentree . . . eh, Mrs. Jardine, has a great deal on her mind at the moment."

It was true. These days her adoptive mother seemed to have much to contend with. Not that Amy wasn't very happy in her everyday life, because she was. She and Mr. Jardine were still like newlyweds, although it was now three years since they had been married in the village church. Francesca often found herself smiling in their presence, if for no other reason than that their happiness was infectious. For so long Amy had mourned her husband, Sir Henry Greentree, and for so long Mr. Jardine, her secretary, had worshipped her in silence. Francesca had despaired of them ever overcoming the obstacles, but they had, and all because William Tremaine, Amy's brother, had made a fuss about Mr. Jardine's partiality for her. In trying to keep them apart—he didn't consider Mr. Jardine good enough for a member of his family—he had actually brought them together.

But it wasn't all happily-ever-after. William Tremaine had been being difficult ever since the engagement was announced. He'd refused to come to the wedding, and continued to treat Amy as if she were a naughty four-year-old instead of a grown woman with a mind of her own. Amy, although never one to be browbeaten by William, found it irritating to be at odds with her brother and the head of her family. Worse, she was well aware that her sister, Helen, was suffering. Helen craved harmony within her family—she had troubles of her own with her feckless husband, Toby—and living in London, she relied heavily on her brother William's support. Recently there had been a marked increase in the tearstained letters arriving at Greentree Manor.

Francesca knew that Amy was quietly furious with William, and she had decided that enough was enough. For poor Helen's sake, she was going to London to speak with her brother and settle the rift between them once and for all.

It promised to be a stormy visit, and Francesca hoped there would be no time for frivolous things like new clothes or balls or matchmaking. Amy didn't seem to realize her youngest daughter was on the shelf and relieved to be there. That was the trouble with newlyweds; they thought everyone should be in love, and didn't understand that some people were better off avoiding such excessive emotion.

She supposed she would just have to deal with London when they got there. But first there was the urgent matter of dinner with Mr. Sebastian Thorne.

"Lil," she said. "I'll be wearing my green wool to dinner. The sensible one. With the narrow lace collar."

"The ugly green wool, do you mean, miss? The one that hangs on you like a sack?"

"Yes, Lil, exactly."

Lil nodded, her mouth pursed, and Francesca could almost hear her thoughts: *Very wise, miss.*

Sebastian straightened his cuffs, giving them a good tug, but they still weren't quite long enough. The jacket had belonged to Mrs. Jardine's first husband, Sir Henry Greentree, and although it fit in width and length, Sir Henry's arms were rather shorter than Sebastian's. Still, it would have to do. The servants were dealing with his own clothing, he'd been told, and it would be returned to him as soon as possible.

The alternative was to skulk in his room, and he had no intention of doing that. He wanted to see Francesca again. Considering what he had been through, he felt reasonably fit and well. He'd bathed, eaten, and rested, and apart from a few bruises, he felt restored to almost new. He was looking forward to dinner with the Jardine family.

Sebastian couldn't remember the last time he'd sat down with a respectable family. Usually, in houses like this, he would be let in the back door and asked to wait in some out-of-the-way corner until he was given his instructions. The master of the house would be loath to allow him close to his womenfolk, in case he contaminated them, and if he was introduced it was usually because the women had insisted on meeting the infamous Mr. Thorne. More than once, the wives of his clients had invited him back when their husbands were out. There was something very daring and exciting, evidently, in taking a man of his reputation to their beds. And who was he to argue?

It would be different here at Greentree Manor. For a start, no one knew who he was, and second, he had every intention of leaving as soon as possible. He had Hal to deal with. He should be on his way now. But for the first time in years, he didn't seem able to concentrate on his job. For a man with such a fearsome reputation to maintain, his indifference should be worrying. But he didn't care. His powerful hunting instinct was focused on Francesca Greentree.

She was a puzzle. Had he really looked into her eyes and seen that passionate woman lurking behind the proper façade? Someone as untamed as the storm they'd battled together? Had she really lit that spark deep within him . . . or was he completely delusional?

Well, he would soon find out.

With a final wry glance at his ill-fitting clothes, Sebastian made his way out of his room and down the stairs toward the drawing room he had been directed to earlier. Since he was naturally stealthy of foot, his hosts didn't hear him approaching, and he was outside the door when he heard Mr. Jardine speak.

"If Mr. Thorne is a gentleman then I am a buccaneer!"

"My dear, he speaks like a gentleman."

"That doesn't make him one, Amy. Toby speaks like a gentleman, too, and look at him!"

"Surely there's no harm in offering him a place at our table after the terrible time he's had? It is only charitable."

"I know you always prefer to think well of people,"

Mr. Jardine said musingly, "but I don't entirely trust our Mr. Thorne. For goodness' sake don't let him inveigle his way into Francesca's affections. He's exactly the sort of man we *don't* want her falling for."

"Francesca is far too sensible to give her heart to Mr. Thorne," Amy reproved him gently. "Besides, once we are in London, there will be any number of suitable gentlemen for her to choose from."

Mr. Jardine made a doubtful sound. "My dear, don't raise your hopes too high."

"Well, I think I can raise them higher than Mr. Thorne!" Amy replied complacently. "After all, her sisters have done so well, and what have they that she has not? I'm certain that the reason she has not settled down yet is that there are so few eligible men here. In London it will be different."

"My dear, I don't think it is the lack of eligible men that—"

"I want to see her happily wed, is that so awful?"

"Of course not, Amy."

"Even if she doesn't love the man she chooses, she can be content. And there are some good matches to be made."

"Logically, yes, but the heart is not always a very logical organ, is it? If it was, I fear you would never have married me."

Amy laughed softly, and there was a hush, broken by a contented murmur.

Sebastian backed away from the room as silently as he'd come. Normally he would be amused by the Jardines' dismissal of him as a suitor for their daughter. He knew he was far from husband material and he didn't pretend otherwise. Besides, he was not a man who contemplated marriage—in his occupation the future could mean waking the next day with a dagger between his ribs . . . or not waking up at all, as the case may be.

No, it was not marriage he had in mind for Francesca Greentree.

Chapter 5

Francesca hurried down the stairs. No doubt everyone else was already gathered in the drawing room, awaiting the call to dinner. She knew she was late, but the unflattering green woolen dress had taken some time to get just right—the enormous charging-boar brooch pinned to her breast was a masterstroke—and then there was her hair, pulled back so tightly into a roll at the back that it looked like a cap. She touched her hand to the austere style, pleased with the result. If Mr. Thorne had ever really desired her, he would be cured now.

With a little smile of triumph, and some anticipation, she made her way toward the drawing room door.

"Miss Greentree?"

Startled, Francesca stopped and turned. Sebastian Thorne was standing there, staring at her as if he wasn't at all certain who she was.

"Hell and damnation! It is you . . ." A frown drew down his heavy brows as he strode toward her, and then around her, circling her with all the caution of a gunner facing an unexploded cannonball.

Calmly Francesca stood with her hands folded at her waist. "Mr. Thorne."

He was still pale, with a dark bruise to add to the scratch on his jaw, but otherwise he was smoothly shaven, and his hair was combed back from his brow and clubbed at his nape. They'd found him some borrowed clothes, and by their old-fashioned cut and style, Francesca suspected that they must once have belonged to Sir Henry Greentree. But they fit him, more or less, even if they gave him a slightly disreputable air.

"What in God's name are you wearing?" he said, still clearly in shock. "Did you pay a visit to the church jumble sale? Or was it the ragbag?"

Francesca achieved an outraged expression. "I beg your pardon?"

"What is this?" He brushed her sleeve with his fingers. "And this?" He pointed at her hair. "You've turned yourself into someone else."

"I don't know what you mean," she said primly. "This is my usual mode of dress."

He put his hands on his hips and glared at her. "You're a beautiful woman, Miss Greentree, but you've managed to make yourself almost ugly." He began to prowl around her. "This must have taken quite a bit of achieving. Congratulations!" He moved closer, and she felt his warm breath on her cheek. "But if it was done for my benefit, then you needn't have bothered."

"*Your* benefit?" she retorted, arching her brows.

He was going to tell her he didn't want her. Perhaps all this hard work had been for nothing? What a relief! Then why did she feel so unaccountably depressed at the prospect of not having to fight him off after all?

"I." He reached out, and digging his fingers into the thick roll of hair at her nape, he dismantled it. "Know." Her thick, curling tresses sprang free and tumbled down, like a dark cloud, about her face. "The truth." He smiled at the effect he had created. "You want me as much as I want you. But you're afraid to admit it. You're afraid to *be* yourself!"

"You are deluded," she gasped, reaching up with both hands to gather up her curls again. "What would you have me be?"

"The woman I saw on the moors."

She wouldn't look directly at him; she couldn't. With shaking fingers, she refastened her hair, but it wasn't the same. Her cheeks were flushed and her eyes glittered, but she couldn't help that, even though he was smiling at her with his villain's smile, as if he was more than pleased with what he'd done.

"I'd remove that ugly dress, too, if this spot wasn't so public," he murmured.

Startled, she met his eyes. "You would not dare!"

she hissed, but even as the words left her lips, she knew they didn't sound like a reprimand. They sounded like a challenge.

One long finger stroked her cheek. "I would dare anything, Francesca. When you come to know me better, you'll realize that."

"I don't know what you thought you saw on the moors, but you were mistaken."

That long finger pressed firmly against her lips. "Keep your voice down, my sweet liar. Do you want the entire household to hear? I know what I saw."

It was a measure of her compliance in his game that she obeyed without giving it a thought. "What did you see?"

"A passionate woman. I want to set her free."

Francesca stared at him, her heart pounding, wondering wildly how she could escape his pursuit. Casting around, she said the first thing that came into her head. "Well, you can't. I—I am engaged."

He went still, eyes searching hers. "You have a fiancé?"

"Yes."

"Where is he?"

"He's away."

Sebastian smiled. "Away where?"

He'd believed her at first but now he was doubting her. She had to convince him. "He's been asked to help out. A—a tiger has escaped from a traveling circus, and they need someone to shoot it. He's an excellent shot."

"I see . . ."

"My fiancé will shoot you if you don't stop this . . . this nonsense. After he's finished dealing with the lion."

"I thought it was a tiger."

"It—it is both. A freak of nature. That's what makes it so dangerous."

He allowed his skeptical gaze to run all the way down to her hem and back up again. "Is this how you dress for him? Keeps him at arm's length, does it? Pretty Polly could teach you a thing or two."

"Pretty Polly?" she repeated indignantly. "Who is she? Your amour? I gather that she works at the cheaper end of the market."

He laughed. "You've a tongue like a dagger, Francesca, sharp and quick. But I don't believe you."

"That Pretty Polly . . . ?"

"Not Polly, damn it! I don't believe you have a fiancé. You're like a flower, just waiting for spring to unfurl you."

"Oh *please*," she groaned. "Our groom could write better poetry! My fiancé certainly could. He writes and—and sings, and paints, too."

He smiled, that seductive villain's smile that promised her everything that she wanted, and was most afraid of.

At that moment the drawing room door opened and Mr. Jardine stood there, his instinctive smile wavering. "Francesca?"

It occurred to Francesca that all she had to do was tell Mr. Jardine that Mr. Thorne's behavior was inappropriate and he would be gone within the hour. All her troubles would be over. But the words stuck in her throat. It was because she didn't want to explain herself to others, she told herself. She wanted to handle this herself, in her own way.

But somehow her inner protestations didn't quite ring true.

Admit it, you're enjoying yourself! It's like a game, and although it frightens you, you don't want it to stop. Secretly you might even want him to win . . .

"I'm sorry I'm late," she spoke brightly.

Mr. Jardine said, "Come in and join us. A drink, Mr. Thorne?"

Francesca led the way. Inside the drawing room, Amy Jardine, elegant in lavender silk, was seated on the sofa. Her pale eyes grew round when she saw what her daughter was wearing. "Good gracious, my dear!" she blurted out, and then bit her lip as Francesca's own gaze narrowed warningly. She rushed on. "You're wearing that brooch you found in York. So . . . so . . ." She fumbled for the right word to describe the hideous thing.

Mr. Jardine was pouring brandy into two glasses, but came swiftly to his wife's aid. "I think Francesca would look beautiful in whatever she chose to wear. And perhaps this style is all the fashion in London?"

Oh dear, Francesca thought. "I don't know what is fashionable in London and what isn't," she said loudly. "I am far too countrified for London."

Was Mr. Thorne smiling? There was something about his mouth . . . curse him! Didn't he care if she was gauche and unattractive? He was from London; surely he preferred the sort of women who knew their way about? Like Pretty Polly.

"To my mind country girls are always so refreshing," Mr. Jardine went on gamely.

"I'm hardly a girl," Francesca retorted. "I am five and twenty. How old are you, Mr. Thorne?"

Mr. Thorne made a sound that could have been a cough or a laugh. "I am nearly thirty, Miss Greentree."

"Londoners are so pale and wan, and the children so dreadfully skinny." Amy was trying to wrench the conversation out of the hands of her headstrong daughter. "Country folk are so much more . . ."

"Strapping?" Sebastian said. "Buxom?"

Buxom! How dare he? Did he really think her buxom?

"Rosy-cheeked and strong of limb," Amy finished reprovingly.

Mr. Thorne took the drink his host was offering him. "In my experience," he began, and Francesca knew by the glint in his black eyes that he was going to say something rude and impertinent, "a man wants a woman he can hold without fearing she will break."

"You mean a Toby jug as opposed to a Dresden shepherdess?" Francesca asked sweetly.

"I was thinking more of a Valkyrie. A Boadicea in her chariot."

"They are very warlike examples of our sex, Mr. Thorne," Amy said doubtfully. "Don't you think it would be more appropriate for a female to pour your tea and listen to your troubles than throw thunder and lightning bolts?"

"Perhaps Mr. Thorne prefers thunder and lightning bolts," Francesca said slyly. "Did you enjoy the storm on the moors that much, Mr. Thorne? Should I have left you in the mire?"

"Francesca," Amy reproved her. "I'm afraid Mr. Thorne won't understand your teasing."

He smiled at Amy, a truly attractive smile, and it was only when he turned it on Francesca that it lost its innocence. "I don't mind," he said. "Tease away, Miss Greentree."

It was the smile that did it. There was something very intimate in it, something wicked and wanton. Something that spoke of heat and . . . and naked flesh. What was happening to her? Francesca's blood seemed to be pounding through her body like a runaway coach, turning her hot and a little sick. Sebastian was doing this to her. She must not allow him to see her weakness. He already knew far too much about her, and she knew he would use that knowledge against her, to take what he wanted.

Self-restraint. Self-control. The room was spinning . . .

She felt his hand, clasped about her elbow with a ironlike grip, and realized he was holding her upright. Her knees seemed to be buckling.

"Don't swoon on me, my Valkyrie," his deep voice said in her ear.

Fainting was for debutantes and expectant mothers. Francesca was not the sort of woman to faint. She straightened up, clenching her teeth until her jaw ached. "I . . . it is very warm in here," she said in a small, husky voice.

Amy was on her feet. "Francesca? Are you well? You are not yourself, are you? I knew it the moment I saw you in that . . . that dress. Oh, I do wish you would not prowl the moors! I'm sorry, Mr. Thorne, I am grateful my daughter found you, but she will make herself ill one day, if she hasn't already . . ."

"I am perfectly well, Mama," Francesca said. "The room is overheated, that is all."

"You must go straight to bed," Amy insisted.

Bed. I do want to go to bed. I want to go to bed with Sebastian Thorne and make love to him all night, and when the dawn comes, I want to awake in his arms and make love again.

Oh dear God! Her thoughts shocked her witless. What was happening to her? She was truly losing her mind, and it was all his fault. Francesca looked up, full of fear and guilt, and found herself staring directly into his black eyes. His own widened, and something sparked deep within them—an acknowledgment of what she was feeling? The same thought? Whatever it was, Francesca knew she had just succeeded in making things worse.

"Nonsense," Mr. Jardine was arguing gently with his wife, "the girl needs a sip of brandy, that's all. Here you are, Francesca. Drink up."

The cool glass was pressed into her hand and she lifted it to her lips, doing as she was told because she wasn't capable of doing anything else. Her mind was numb, suspended. She choked as the alcohol burned her throat, the room blurred. And then Sebastian was leaning toward her solicitously, and everything came into her sharp focus. She was aware of his clean, masculine scent.

What was happening to her? She knew he was

dangerous; she knew she must stay away from him. Why was she being drawn into his orbit like a moth to a flame? And like a singed moth, she felt raw, her emotions stripped bare so that she was finding it difficult to breathe.

"I'm perfectly all right," she insisted, edging away. "I have been out on the moors in far worse weather, as you well know, Mama. Besides, if I am ill then I won't be able to go to London with you, now will I?"

Amy's brow wrinkled. "Perhaps you *should* stay here."

She looked so worried that Francesca was swamped with guilt. She was being selfish. "Mama," she said gently, moving to take Amy's hand, "I couldn't possibly allow you to go on your own. I won't. To face Uncle William without me? Certainly not!"

Amy Greentree smiled. "I admit it is a somewhat daunting prospect."

"Then you must let me come, too," Mr. Jardine insisted.

"No. You know that would make it worse."

Sebastian was absorbing their conversation with interest, and realizing it, Amy was apologetic. "Family difficulties, I'm afraid, Mr. Thorne. No matter how much we might love our relatives, they can still give us heartache."

"I wouldn't know." His smile turned chilly, and the black eyes that had been so alive turned blank. It was as if he had shut himself away, or closed them out. Whichever it was, it was very effective, and an awkward silence fell.

Thankfully, just then the bell rang for dinner.

* * *

Sebastian was remembering now why he preferred to spend his time with thieves and murderers. Mr. and Mrs. Jardine reminded him painfully of his own past, and he did not want to revisit it. He wished now he'd made his excuses, but then he wouldn't have been able to sit across the table from Francesca, would he?

The golden candlelight softened the somber effect she'd created with the hideous dress. He'd been right. Instead of putting him off the scent, as she'd obviously intended, she'd revealed the truth to him. She was afraid of him, of herself . . . He watched her hand tremble as she lifted her wineglass to her lips. She looked flushed and feverish and utterly captivating.

Mr. Jardine asked him a polite question, and he answered, but he didn't take his eyes off her for too long. He couldn't. He was drawn to her like a thief to gold. She hadn't looked at him once since they sat down, studying her plate with an unnatural fixedness, but he knew she felt the same.

Should he leave her alone? Forget whatever obsession had taken hold of him? Walk away? But then he reminded himself that the Jardines were saving her for some respectable worthy, so that she could be petted and pampered by a gentleman who saw her as a necessary possession, like his fine house in Belgravia and his matching grays. Was that really what she wanted? Sebastian couldn't see the woman he'd met in the storm enjoying such a tame and tedious situation. She was a thunderbolt kind of girl. If she was to have a tedious future, then let her have at least one exciting memory. One passionate encounter with a man like . . .

Well, like him.

The meal limped along. Sebastian answered their questions politely but briefly. Yes, he was from London, yes, he was here in Yorkshire on business, private business.

"Do you know the Braidwoods?" Amy Jardine was trying to draw him out. "They have ties to one of the mills in Manchester."

"I do not know the Braidwoods."

"Sir James Friswell lives beyond the village. Do you know of him?"

"No, Mrs. Jardine, I don't know Sir James Friswell. Oh, but wait a moment . . ."

His pause fixed their attention to him. Slowly, suspiciously, Francesca's eyes lifted to his. "Is he the gentleman who shoots?" he asked silkily.

Scarlet flooded into her cheeks. She dropped her knife with a clatter.

"There is a great deal of shooting on the bigger estates," Mr. Jardine began.

"Oh? I had heard . . ." Sebastian went on, drawing it out. He could see Francesca fumbling with her napkin, a frown between her brows. "I had heard that there was a tiger escaped from a circus."

Amy gave a gasp. "A tiger? Is this true?"

Mr. Jardine shook his head. "Not to my knowledge. I think someone has been having a game with you, Mr. Thorne. Some of the locals think it sport to make fun of strangers. There are no tigers in Yorkshire."

"How disappointing," he said.

Francesca lifted her chin. Their eyes held, clashed, and then she rose to her feet. "I am weary, Mama," she said. "I think I will retire. Good night, Mr. Thorne, and . . . *good-bye*."

Mr. Thorne bowed his head, but his smile remained.

She might believe that.

But he knew otherwise.

Chapter 6

~~~~~~~~

Somewhere in Greentree Manor a clock was chiming midnight. Sebastian sat up and rubbed his eyes, forcing himself awake. There was work to be done. He needed to pay a visit to Hal. He needed to see the expression on Hal's face when he realized Sebastian hadn't perished in the mire after all, but had returned to take his vengeance.

The cold water in the basin helped, and he splashed it over his head, then proceeded to dry himself vigorously with the towel. Of course he was tired, he was still recovering from the mire, but he couldn't afford to stop now that he was well and truly on the trail of his prey.

Sebastian's own clothing had been placed at his

bedside, cleaned and pressed by meticulous servants. He dressed and slipped through the door, onto the narrow landing, aware of the stillness around him. The Jardines had put him at the farthest end of the house, far away from the family, and that amused him. Mr. Thorne was not respectable. Did they fear he would creep into Francesca's bedchamber in the night and ravish her?

For a moment he was overwhelmed by the images he'd conjured. Francesca, all warm and rumpled with sleep, turning over and smiling at him with her deliciously sensual mouth. He'd take down the bedclothes, so that she'd be lying there . . . Would she be naked? Reluctantly he abandoned that idea. She'd be in her nightdress, and he'd undo the tiny buttons one by one, opening it over her breasts and belly and thighs, and bending his head to kiss every inch of her.

He groaned, then instantly froze, glancing around the landing. This was madness! He must stop it immediately, or the next time he met up with Hal he wasn't going to survive the encounter.

The oil lamp on the hall table flickered in the draft, as he made his way down the stairs. He turned left. He'd made a quick survey of the layout of the house before he went to bed, and now he moved without hesitation to the back door and reached to draw the bolt.

His hand stilled. The bolt was already drawn. For a moment surprise paralyzed him, and then he gave a soft, relieved laugh. He was deep in the countryside here, where doors were rarely locked. After all,

Sebastian mocked himself, who would be foolish enough to be abroad at this time of night? He cracked open the heavy door and slipped through, closing it noiselessly behind him.

Outside the wind had dropped and the rain had ceased, the storm having given way to a cold, clear night. He looked up, and acres of stars shone down on him. He should be able to see well enough to traverse the moors without blundering into any more mires. If he could borrow a horse from the stables—grooms, he had found, were always open to a bit of bribery— then he could ride to the village and see Hal.

Sebastian made his way toward the stables, taking a circuitous route via the lawn so that his boots didn't crunch on the gravel path. Ahead of him the buildings appeared dark and deserted, and he was thinking that perhaps he wouldn't need to bribe anyone after all, when he felt a prickling at his back.

Someone was watching him.

Sebastian turned slowly, already plastering a false smile on his face as he ran through possible excuses for being out here so late.

Francesca Greentree stood a little way off, her curling hair like a dark halo in the starlight, and her eyes pools of shadow.

"Mr. Thorne?" she said, as startled as he. "Whatever are you doing?"

He strolled toward her—her voice had been loud and he didn't want to wake anyone. "What am *I* doing? I might ask the same of you, Francesca. It is past midnight. I thought countryfolk went to bed with the sun."

She'd been watching him approach, as if she might turn and run, but his words fired up her temper, as he knew they would. "Some of us countryfolk have the stamina to stay up beyond dusk," she said drolly. "I was checking on Wolf and his family." Her voice softened. "He and his mate have four puppies."

He couldn't help but smile at the doting way she said it. "You love that dog, don't you?"

"More than most people."

"Why is that, do you think?"

"Because he's loyal and he will never leave me."

In the silence that followed, he sensed she had disconcerted herself. "Is that what you demand from a lover, too, Francesca? Loyalty and staying power?"

She looked away, hesitated, and then said candidly, "I've never had a lover. And before you offer to step into the breach, I don't want one. I have resigned myself to a life alone. No, not *resigned*. I look forward to it. Believe me, Mr. Thorne, I have seen too much unhappiness to allow myself to sail into *those* dangerous waters."

"In case there's a shark?" he mocked.

"Exactly."

"And I am the shark, is that it? You would prefer to die miserable than experience all that life can give you, just in case you get hurt?"

"You make it sound as if being hurt by a man is a small thing," she said angrily. "For a woman it is the end of her. Unhappiness, misery, abandonment. I know what 'love' does, and I do not want any part of it." She drew a deep breath. "Now, I will ask you again, what are you doing here, Mr. Thorne?"

He considered her. "I have unfinished business in the village. I need to complete it as soon as possible."

She was horrified. "You're planning to go to the village now? You are not fit!"

"I'm fit enough and this cannot wait. I wonder if I might ask you for the loan of one of your horses, Miss Greentree, if I promise to bring it back when I am done?"

She shook her head, her eyes still on his.

"I am determined to go," he said, quite gently, "and I am arrogant enough to think you cannot stop me."

"You intend to ride across the moors? After what happened?"

He waved an impatient hand. "Isn't there a road around it?"

"Yes, but it will take you many more hours."

"Ah . . . then I will just have to risk it. Unless you can find me a guide, Francesca?" And he smiled.

She read his mind. "No," she breathed.

He peered at her, sensing a tangle of emotions in her stillness. She didn't want him to go alone. She was concerned for him. But he thought it was more than that: He was heading off on an adventure and she wanted to come, too.

"Will you guide me?" he asked abruptly, to test his theory.

"No!" she gasped, but the violence of her refusal only gave him more hope.

"Why not? It will be fun, Francesca. An adventure. You like adventures, don't you? You enjoy creating fantasies. I can't give you an escaped tiger, but I can give you a midnight gallop across the moors."

"I'm not wearing my riding habit." But she sounded as if she'd already given in.

He folded his arms and inspected her green dress. "Is it anything like what you're wearing now?"

Her mouth curled up at the corners. "Are you insulting my taste in clothing, Mr. Thorne?" Then her smile faded. "You knew why I was dressed like this, didn't you? How did you know?"

"Because I understand, Francesca. I understand *you*."

I know you are living your life as something you are not, just like me.

She stared beyond him, toward the stables. "You're a dangerous man, Mr. Thorne. I shouldn't be here with you. You will be leaving tomorrow, won't you?" with a searching look. "Do you promise?"

"I promise. So you can't refuse my offer for an adventure. This is your one and only chance. After tonight you can return to being the respectable Miss Francesca Greentree—I do like that name!—if you still want to."

Sebastian knew, for so many reasons, that he shouldn't be encouraging her to come with him. But that didn't stop him, any more than her own doubts were going to stop her. It was a moment when the usual considerations didn't count.

"Very well."

He grinned. "It could be dangerous."

She smiled back. Damn and blast it, she smiled, and he saw the wildness in her. The caged passion. "Dastardly deeds, Mr. Thorne?"

He took a step nearer and she tilted her head, her

eyes glinting in the starlight. "I call it dancing with the devil," he said quietly.

There was a moment when he thought she might change her mind, turn and run, but then she said recklessly, "I always excelled at dancing. Perhaps I can show the devil some new steps?"

They galloped across the moor. Francesca rode astride, like a man. She thought she might have shocked him when she swung herself into the saddle, although her skirts preserved her modesty, but he laughed. He was the only man she knew who would laugh at such a moment.

How could he know that she often rode at night, alone? Even Mama didn't, and if she did she'd give Francesca one of her despairing looks—"Francesca, for goodness' sake, you should know better!" And she did know better; it was just that sometimes she couldn't help herself. Something inside her needed to break free, so that she could feel *alive*. She thought of it secretly as her mother's inheritance. The blood of Aphrodite running in her veins. Surely it was far better to ride about in the dark with the wind in her hair than to go from lover to lover?

"Who is it you wish to see?" she asked him, as they approached the dale where the village was set.

He peered down into the valley at the dark shapes of cottages and the white daubs of sheep on the hillsides, and said, "I can find my own way from here."

Disappointment gripped her. "Is the adventure over then?" she asked, breathless, anxious. She didn't want it to be over.

"The danger increases from here, Francesca." His voice was serious.

"Good," she said. "What's an adventure without danger? Where are we going?"

He seemed to be considering her request. "We're going to the blacksmithy," he said finally.

"Hal?" She was surprised. "Is it Hal you want to see?"

"Francesca, please don't ask questions."

But she wasn't a servant, to be told when to be quiet. She was Francesca Greentree, and she had been brought up to speak her mind. "It's a strange sort of business that brings you out in the middle of the night to visit the village blacksmith. Is it legal business, or are you a smuggler? The tax on tobacco is very high, and I have heard that there are men who seek to profit from contraband. Are you one of them?"

"Ah, you have me there," he said, sounding like an actor in a bad play.

"Rubbish," she retorted. "I don't believe it. What are you up to?"

He sighed. "No, I am not a smuggler, but that's all I can say. Now, please, can we find Hal before dawn breaks? Do you want to be discovered?"

Without another word she led him down through the village. There was a lantern outside the inn, put there to guide late-night travelers. The blacksmithy was down a narrow lane. Small dark windows stared at them from the upper rooms.

"Hal lives over his shop," she explained. "He's probably asleep."

"His son?"

"Jed left years ago. Why are you—"

"He has no wife or . . . or mother?"

"No one. He lives alone." He was so serious, so intent, that she was beginning to get more and more anxious. "You're not going to hurt Hal, are you? I can't allow that," she added firmly.

Sebastian dismounted, and when he looked up at her she couldn't read his face very well in the shadows and the starlight, no matter how she tried. "Stay here and wait with the horses."

Suddenly Francesca knew she shouldn't have come. She didn't trust him. This was a mistake, and she would live to regret it.

He hadn't waited for her reply, and was making his way toward the dark bulk of the building. Soon Francesca lost sight of him. Above her head the stars wheeled in the dome of the sky. Such a beautiful night, a night made for the sort of adventure that wasn't in a book. She told herself that she should be savoring every moment of it instead of worrying about what would happen next. Tomorrow he'd be gone and she'd never see him again.

She heard a cry.

Francesca froze, listening intently, but there was nothing more. Could it have been Sebastian? Was he hurt? She'd never thought of Hal as being a violent man, but perhaps she was mistaken.

Francesca urged her horse forward, hooves clipping on the cobbled lane, Sebastian's mount following behind.

The upstairs windows had been dark a moment before, but now a low light flickered. She became aware of loud voices.

"But bugger me, you're dead!" Hal yelped.

"And I've come back for my revenge!" declared Sebastian.

There was a thump, the sound of someone falling, and then nothing.

Chapter 7

⟨∽᪵∾⟩

Upstairs, Sebastian stood over Hal, breathing quickly and looking as menacing as possible. It wasn't difficult. He'd come upon Hal, asleep, slumped in a chair. Just as he'd moved to shake him awake, Hal had lurched to his feet, swinging his fists and roaring like a bull. Sebastian had enjoyed stopping him. Now, with Hal subdued and a candle lit, he was looking for answers.

"Who told you and your son to deal with me?" he demanded.

Hal, wiping the blood from his nose with the back of his hand, muttered thickly, "You don't understand—"

"How can I understand if you won't tell me?"

"These're dangerous people, Mr. Thorne."

"Damn it, tell me your master's name!" Sebastian shouted, losing patience.

"*His* name?"

There was a pause. "Do you mean it's a woman?" Sebastian couldn't keep the excitement out of his voice. "Mrs. Slater is your master, isn't she? She's the one who told you to make me disappear? Tell me I'm wrong, Hal!"

Hal looked away and said nothing.

"Is she here in the village? Where can I find her?"

Hal's face looked pale and wretched in the gloomy light. "She's not here. She's in Lon'on, safely hid, and I can't tell you where, so don' ask. She's my cousin, Mr. Thorne," he went on, in genuine misery. "I didn' want to leave you in t'mire, and that's the truth, sir."

"Then why did you, Hal?"

"She told us we was t'make it look like an accident."

"By 'us' I presume you mean you and your son?"

"Aye."

"Where is he now?"

"Jed's gone back to Lon'on. He only come up here to give me orders from her . . . Angela. He followed you," he added, with a hint of his old spark, "and you never even knew it. I thought you was a man with eyes in the back of his head, Mr. Thorne? He showed you, eh?"

"I'll congratulate him when I see him," Sebastian said, icily.

He tried to think, but his head was buzzing. Mrs. Slater—Angela Slater—was alive! And she was on his home turf, in London. That made it all so much easier. And perhaps it also explained why she had brought the children here to Yorkshire all those years ago—because she had family in this area and felt safe.

More worrying was the fact that Hal's son had followed him here. How did Jed know that Sebastian was planning to come to Yorkshire? And more importantly, what he meant to do once he got here? Who had told Mrs. Slater that, after all these years, someone was looking for her? As far as Sebastian was concerned, only he and Aphrodite knew the details of his assignment. The first thing he'd do when he returned to London was visit her and ask her who else knew.

"I despise that woman," Hal muttered, and Sebastian realized he meant his cousin. "Do you know she has houses where she brings girls, young girls, and sells them to men? She makes money from misery. I always warned Jed against being drawn into that world, I told him it were no good, but in the end it didn' stop him. The thought of being rich lured him, like a fox to the lamb, and last year he left. I know'd he'd gone to work for Cousin Angela. Some days I still hope to persuade him to come home, sir. 'Twas for Jed's sake I lied to you and took you to the mire. Whatever he's become, he's my son. He's my flesh and blood."

Sebastian sighed. He'd been so looking forward to a good bout of fisticuffs, but Hal was making it difficult to hate him unreservedly.

"Tell me where Jed is. Perhaps I can persuade him of the error of his ways."

"And what'd Angela do to us if she found out I'd told?"

"Isn't the risk worth it? Anyway, it's not Jed I want, it's her. I can stop her. I can have her arrested and jailed. Isn't that what you want? You said you despised her and wanted to save your son? This way we both win."

"She'll know!" He looked terrified. "She'll send her creatures after me."

"Why should she? I'm not going to tell. But if you're worried, then go away somewhere and keep your head down until it's over."

"You asked me before what happened to her husband," Hal said, glancing over his shoulder as if he expected to see Angela Slater leering in the shadows. "He called himself her husband, at any rate, though no one remembered seeing a preacher say the words over them. Anyway, this was back when she was farming babes in Lon'on, years ago. Too many of t'bairns were dying, and there was nasty talk. Folk said she was letting the babes die, and keeping t'money she was paid for their upkeep for herself. Some even said it went further than neglect. Well, her husband, he gave her up to the magistrates to save his own skin. But she had friends—she has friends everywhere, Mr. Thorne, never forget that. The court let her off, and next thing her husband was dead, dragged up out of the river, with his tongue cut out. Some folk said the fishes ate it out, but we knew it was her revenge on him, to show he'd blabbed." He fixed Sebastian with staring eyes. "If she'd do that to her man, imagine what she'd do to us."

"All the more reason why she needs to be stopped, Hal. You have to help me, or you'll be frightened of shadows for the rest of your life. Do you want that? I don't think you're a bad man, Hal. I think you're loyal to your son, and that loyalty has forced you into an intolerable position. But that doesn't change the fact that you tried to murder me. I could go to the constable now and have you arrested. You'd hang for it, or else see out your days at Botany Bay."

"I didn't want to trick you into t'mire," Hal said sullenly. "I told you—"

"Then prove it. Save yourself. Save Jed."

Hal slumped in his chair, accepting that Sebastian was right, and that there was no other way.

"She has a house in Mallory Street. That's the one Jed's in charge of, or so he boasted to me. Turned my stomach, it did." He took a deep breath. "Number forty-four Mallory Street. There are other places, but that's the only one I know about."

"Thank you, Hal. You've done the right thing. I'll keep Jed out of it if I can." Excitement rippled through him. He had an address, a starting point!

Hal was watching him anxiously. "What're you going to do now?"

"Better you don't know."

"I hope you know what you're getting into," Hal said. "Angela's a murderous bitch, Mr. Thorne, the sort would kill anyone to save her own skin. You need to find her and deal with her, before she deals with you."

"Don't worry, I can handle her."

"Can you?" He shook his head.

Sebastian got to his feet. "One last thing, Hal. How did Jed know that I was coming up here? Who told him?"

Hal shook his head. "Jed doesn't mention any names. I don't reckon he trusts me. If someone is telling secrets, you'd better look to your friends and acquaintances, Mr. Thorne. Angela has spies everywhere . . . and they'll be more afraid of her than of you."

Francesca paused, resting her hand on the stair rail. It had been a simple matter to walk in through the front door, but she wasn't at all sure about continuing on up the stairs. That was where the voices were coming from, and her plan had been to burst in and discover what Sebastian was up to.

"Private business," he'd said, but what could he possibly have to say to Hal the blacksmith that it had brought him all the way from London? She was dying of curiosity. He wouldn't appreciate her breaking in on them, but it was her adventure.

Feeling her way in the darkness, Francesca moved up the stairs. There was a faint light spilling out from under the door on the landing, and as she drew closer it helped her to see her way. Something made a scuffing sound below her in the shadows, and she came down on the next step more heavily than she'd meant to. It gave a loud creak. Francesca held her breath, listening, but the voices in the upstairs room continued without pause, while downstairs there was only silence. Probably mice, she thought with a shudder.

Go home. This is madness, her inner voice castigated her, but it didn't seem to matter. Good sense might tell her she should be running as fast as she could in the opposite direction from Sebastian Thorne, but good sense had little to do with it.

". . . has friends in high places," Hal the blacksmith's voice was slightly muffled by the closed door. "You'd be surprised, Mr. Thorne, what sort of thing some great men fancy. And once she has 'em in her web, that's it. She never lets 'em go."

"She blackmails them?" Sebastian sounded cool and collected, but Francesca heard his suppressed excitement.

"Aye."

She? Who was she? Francesca put her eye to a knot in the wood. She saw a candle on a table, flickering and smoking, but other than that only shadows.

"You said her husband was dead, Hal. Is there anyone else?" Sebastian's voice went on.

"She has a daughter . . ."

"Where is she now?"

"I don' know," he muttered, "I haven't seen her for years." But there was something in his voice that suggested he did know.

Sebastian heard it, too. "You've come this far, Hal. If I'm to stop her, I need to know everything you know."

Francesca pressed closer. Distracted, she heard the creak of the stair behind her. A rough and sweaty hand closed over her mouth, and stopped her from screaming. The door in front of her was wrenched violently open, and Francesca was shoved inside.

She shrieked as soon as he let her go, careering full on into an immovable object. It had a muscular chest and hard arms that wrapped around her, while her nose was pressed hard into a clean-laundered shirt with a familiar scent. She said something like "Oomph."

"Damn and blast you, Miss Greentree," Sebastian said with quiet fury. "I told you to wait."

"Ah, women! They never do as they're told, Mr. Thorne, you should know that." The new voice was young and cocky.

Francesca tried to extricate herself from Sebastian's arms, but he kept a tight grip on her. She turned to look over her shoulder, and the first thing she saw was that the other man was holding a pistol in his hand. The next thing was that she knew him.

"Jed?" she cried. "Is that you?"

Jed cursed beneath his breath. "Now see what you've done, Da," he said to Hal, a trace of a whine in his voice. "She knows me."

"Of course I know you, Jed," Francesca retorted. "You used to help in the stables when I was a girl." She felt Sebastian's arms tighten, as if she'd said something wrong.

"Aye, well, I've better fish to fry these days," Jed said, full of importance.

"I thought you was gone." Hal rose to his feet. "You said you was headin' back to Lon'on."

"So I was, but I met someone on the road who knew of a gen'leman who'd just been saved from Emerald Mire. So I come back."

Hal eyed his son with a mixture of doubt and fear. "What are you going to do, lad?"

Jed's angry gaze turned to Sebastian. He was of only medium height, but thickset, with big shoulders. There was something of the bully in him, Francesca decided, and wondered why she hadn't noticed it before. "I'm going to have to kill him myself, seeing as you didn't do the job properly, Da."

His father and Francesca gasped, and Jed smiled, pleased with the effect of his words.

To Francesca, standing in the warm circle of Sebastian's arms, the moment didn't seem real; it was as if at any time she would wake up.

"What about Miss Greentree?" Hal was saying. "You gonna kill her too, lad?"

Jed glared at him, his hand clenching on the pistol, as if he was trying to make up his mind.

"Stop it," Francesca said. "I can't believe what I'm hearing."

Jed curled his lip at her. "You always was too good to be true. Maybe I'll enjoy wringing your neck, miss."

"Jed—"

"Always handing out your charity, always visiting the poor folk. You visited us. Da here was over the moon, but I hated it. I hated you. Well, now I don't need your charity."

Francesca was shocked. She hadn't known Jed felt this way. It had never occurred to her that her good works might be resented by those they were meant to help.

"Jed, you know that if anything happens to me, or my guest Mr. Thorne, there will be a hue and cry all over the county. You will be hunted down. Is that what you want?"

"This has nothin' to do with you," Jed snarled.

"She's right." Hal moved toward his son. "Leave them be, Jed. I'm asking you as your da."

His impassioned plea was enough to distract Jed, just for a moment. Francesca didn't even see Sebastian move, but suddenly she was brushed aside, and he launched himself at Jed. They clung to each other, toppling over the chair and falling to the floor.

The pistol clattered across the bare wooden boards. Francesca went for it a moment too late. Hal knocked her to one side, and she fell heavily against the table, bruising her shoulder and her leg. The candle teetered in its holder and fell. The flame was extinguished, and suddenly everything went dark.

As Francesca lay, momentarily stunned, she was aware of the men still rolling and fighting on the floor nearby. The next moment there was the sickening crack of something hard striking flesh and bone. She tried to move, but she was disoriented. Where was he? Then, from the blackness, Hal's voice: "Come on!" Jed was cursing softly. They stumbled to the door, one of them limping, and it slammed shut behind them.

A moment later Francesca heard horses galloping away, and silence. They'd gone. But where was Sebastian? She climbed to her feet and stood perfectly still. It wasn't really pitch dark. There was some starlight from the window, but not much.

"Mr. Thorne?"

He didn't answer. She felt dizzy. What had they done to him? What if he was dead?

That just wasn't possible, she told herself with rising alarm. The villain didn't die, at least not until the very end, when the hero bested him, and so far there were no heroes in this story. She shuffled forward, creeping across the room, feeling for him. She was praying, but she didn't know for what. It couldn't be a happy ending, could it?

That was when she smelled it.

The smoke.

At first she thought it was the candle, and that when it'd fallen over, it had caught alight on some piece of furniture. But then she realized this had nothing to do with the candle. Jed really had meant what he said about killing them.

He'd set fire to the blacksmithy before he rode away.

Chapter 8

He was dreaming again, and a very nice dream it was, too. Francesca Greentree was holding him in her arms and caressing him. He could feel her trembling hands on his chest and shoulders, her fingertips touching his face. That was nice. But then she began calling his name in a shrill voice that pierced right through him, and suddenly she grasped him under the arms and attempted to haul him to his feet.

Her seduction technique certainly needed some refining, he thought muzzily. And then nausea curled in his stomach as she jolted his head forward, and his brain felt as if it was jumping up and down inside his skull. He thought about protesting, but the next moment she sat down on the floor, cradling his poor aching head on her lap. She leaned over him, and he felt her breath, tickling his cheeks and jaw, the tip of his nose, his eyelids . . .

He wished she'd kiss him. He wanted to feel those luscious lips on his again. You could keep your resurrectionist remedies, a kiss from Francesca Greentree would bring a dead man back to life.

He sneezed.

"Oh!" She nearly leaped out of her skin. "You're alive!"

"Unfortunately," he said, trying to sit up and groaning aloud with pain. "What the hell happened?"

"I think Hal hit you." She sounded breathless. "He and Jed are gone, but they've set the building on fire."

He could smell the smoke now, strong and growing stronger. They probably didn't have much time. He lurched dizzily to his feet, knocking against her as she also stood up. She gasped. Visions of Jed hitting her, too, filled his pounding head. An icy rage flooded him.

"What is it?" he demanded, more shaken by the possibility of her injuries than his own. "Are you hurt?"

But her voice was strong. "Just a bruise. By the way, they bolted the door when they left. We're locked in."

Sebastian began feeling his way over the framework. It wasn't all that sturdy. He used his boot against it, kicking hard, but it didn't do much damage, apart from his aching head. He took a breath, gave himself a run up, and tried again. This time there was a cracking and splintering of the wood. The third time the door broke off its hinges and hung drunkenly onto the landing.

Downstairs was a chaos of flames and smoke.

Francesca started to cough. He caught her hand in his and squeezed it hard, to gain her attention. "Follow me," he said. He didn't wait for her to answer, quickly moving down the stairs, feeling the heat of the flames as the fire licked at the banister. Sparks landed on them and all around them. With streaming eyes he ran for where he thought the door should be.

Fortunately Jed hadn't thought it necessary to lock it, and they staggered out into the night, gasping in the cold, fresh air.

He spied the horse trough on the opposite side of the yard and, dragging Francesca protesting after him, went to plunge his head into it. The water was icy, but it did the trick. He was alert again, and thinking. He shook himself like a dog.

"Your head . . ." Francesca was watching him with streaming eyes, her face flushed and streaked with soot.

He reached up cautiously and discovered a tender lump at the back. "It's too hard to break," he said wryly. "He must have hit me with the butt of the pistol."

She shuddered and half turned away, and that was when he realized the hem of her green dress was smoldering. In a moment, he thought, she'd be alight. Burning. He reached out and grabbed her.

"Sebastian?" she said uneasily, her voice rising on a wail as he swung her up and around and dropped her into the horse trough. She sank, completely.

"Are you sure no one saw me?"

Her teeth were chattering; she was drenched, hair and clothing wringing wet, but all Francesca could think about was being discovered in Sebastian's room at the inn. She knew there would be a terrible scandal and she'd be ruined, like her sister Marietta.

He was working on the small fire, building it up with curses and slivers of wood. "The blacksmithy is burning, and the innkeeper, and everyone else in the village, is trying to put it out. So to answer your question, no, no one saw us come in."

They'd crept around buildings and cottages, avoiding the crowd headed in the direction of the fire, and found the empty inn. Now here she stood, dripping, in the middle of Sebastian's room. He'd dunked her in a horse trough.

"You do realize," she said, with as much dignity as she could muster, "that wool is very slow to burn. You could have put me out without resorting to such drastic measures."

"So you've said . . . several times. There," he added, as the fire crackled. He frowned at her, then tugged the coverlet from his bed and wrapped it around her.

"I—I suppose you thought you were saving my life," she said, between violent shivers, "but I'm finding it difficult to feel grateful."

"I've apologized," he said evenly. He began to rub

his hands over her arms and shoulders. "Would you like me to kiss you better?" he added, his voice dropping.

"No, thank you," she said, trying not to blush.

"Pity."

She winced when he touched her bruised shoulder. A glint shone in his eyes. "Did they hurt you?"

She pushed her wet hair back from her face. "I don't think he meant to. Hal, I mean. We bumped into each other when we went after the pistol. He won," she added ruefully.

"Where does it hurt?"

"My shoulder."

"Show me," he demanded.

"I don't think—"

"Which shoulder?"

Francesca sighed. "The left."

He began to peel down the coverlet with quick, impersonal movements. She was still dressed, of course, so then he moved to the back of her, and started unfastening the long line of buttons. About halfway down he had enough slack to draw the garment over her left shoulder and down her arm, so that he could examine her for any injury.

Francesca was still shivering. She supposed she should be horrified at her situation, and his actions, but she'd gone beyond horror. All she wanted was to be warm again.

"You have the beginnings of a fine bruise," he said levelly. He stroked her skin lightly with his fingertips. "Can you lift your arm?"

She did so, carefully. He grasped her elbow through the woolen cloth and manipulated it in a professional manner. "No pain?" She shook her head. He rewrapped her in the cover, leaving her dress half undone. "I have some brandy here somewhere," he said, moving away.

"I hate brandy." She crept closer to the fire, holding out her hands. A long, wet strand of hair fell forward. "Mr. Thorne . . ."

"Sebastian," he corrected her, finding the brandy and uncorking it. "I think we've gone beyond formalities, don't you?"

"What are you doing here? Why did Jed want to harm you . . . us? I don't understand."

He handed her a glass with a bare inch of liquid in it. "Adventures don't always make sense," he said, and took a swig out of the bottle with his eyes closed and his head tilted back. When he looked at her again, the firelight flickered on his face, making shadows. She thought how strange it was that she should feel as if she knew him so well, when she didn't know him at all.

Why, he could be a . . . a highwayman, and she could be a tavern wench. He might find her alone in his room, and before she knew it . . . She swallowed and tried to halt her imagination before it led her into danger.

"Why did Jed want to kill you?" she repeated. "Are you from Scotland Yard?"

He smiled. "No, I'm not from Scotland Yard, although my profession is of a similar nature."

"Your profession?" she said. Her clothes were beginning to steam and her hair to curl. Finally some warmth was starting to pierce her frozen state.

"I investigate. I find missing people. I solve mysteries."

Her lips parted. "Oh?"

"I am here on a private commission." Sebastian seemed to stop himself. He shook his head. "In a moment I'll be telling you everything, and that wouldn't be professional. But there's something about you that makes me feel . . . safe, and that makes me think the situation is very unsafe." He laughed softly.

The heat was making her sleepy, and her wet clothing was so heavy. She swayed, and Sebastian pulled the shabby armchair closer to the flames, and she sank into it with a sigh.

He was still musing. "If I were sensible I'd get as far away from you as possible, as soon as possible," he said, bending to remove her sodden boots. "But I'm not feeling very sensible." He tossed her boots over by the hearth, and stared down at her stocking-enclosed toes. "The truth is, I haven't felt like myself since I first saw you."

"You said this was an adventure," she murmured, her eyes growing heavy. "I don't think I've ever had such an—an interesting time. I don't want it to end, either." The coverlet slipped, and she saw his gaze go to her bare, rosy skin and the soft curve of her shoulder. He was looking at her, and she liked it. "This doesn't seem real," she said dreamily. "I feel like I can do whatever I wish."

"What is it you wish to do?" He was holding her feet in his warm hands, the firelight behind him.

Francesca was feeling very peculiar. There was something about his eyes and his voice; she felt like a silly rabbit held by the eye of a snake, except this was a far more pleasurable experience. *Pleasure*, that was the word. Sebastian Thorne was a man who could give her unlimited pleasure, and he fascinated her and frightened her at the same time. Or perhaps she was more frightened of herself.

What was it like to kiss a man like this? In her life she had kissed, of course she had, but usually bumbling boys who slobbered on her cheek before she pushed them away. She'd never let herself imagine how it must feel to kiss a real man, an attractive man, and one she was attracted to. She had been too afraid she might not be able to stop.

But now here he was, the man of her dreams, and suddenly desire outweighed fear. Impulsively she threw her arms about his neck and placed her lips on his.

Surprise gave way to passion. He grasped her roughly in his arms, and he was strong. Lovely. She felt caught up in something she mightn't be able to stop and she was afraid, but only for a moment, before his mouth proceeded to plunder hers.

An explosion of sensation. Her sense of touch and taste and smell were all focused on him. There was no escaping this, and she didn't want to.

Francesca groaned beneath his mouth.

"Francesca," he whispered, and now his breath was

on her hair, his lips caressing her temple. She felt her blood beating and her skin tingling, and knew this was desire. The breathless, soaring sort of desire she had only read about in books. She turned her face, but toward him rather than away, and felt his mouth on hers once more.

His kiss was tremendously and excitingly dangerous. Irresistible.

Again heat flashed through her, turning her bones to liquid, and she knew she couldn't fight him even if she'd wanted to. His mouth was on her throat, hot, tasting her, making her squirm. She gave another little moan, tilting her head back to give him better access.

He was kneeling before her, unwrapping her like a present. Her dress, still sodden beneath the coverlet, was clinging to her. She gave a violent shiver.

"Poor sweet," he murmured, and began to strip the garment from her, peeling it away from her cold flesh. She might almost have believed he was doing her a favor, if it wasn't for the hungry expression on his face and the glitter in his black eyes.

Underneath the dress were her chemise and stays and petticoats—the impossible world of Victorian undergarments. He groaned when he saw her. Francesca giggled. "Are you beaten already?" she teased, and wondered at herself. He was seducing her, and she had never felt more at ease. Or perhaps she was seducing him.

"Not me," he said, and promptly swung her up into his arms, before lowering them both onto the chair. He arranged her onto his lap, and Francesca rested her head on his shoulder. He murmured soothingly, without words, but there was nothing soothing in the way his hands were caressing her shoulders. He explored the plump swell of her breasts with his fingertip, where her stays had pushed them up.

She trembled, but it was no longer with the cold.

He cupped her breast, slipping his hand down the front of her undergarment, her flesh filling his palm to overflowing. An ache formed between her legs. As if he could read her mind, he reached down and laid his hand there, against her petticoats.

"You're not a child, Francesca," he said, his voice hoarse. "You know what will happen if you do not tell me nay. I am giving you one last chance to say it."

She supposed she'd been hoping he would just go on, seduce her, and she'd never have to make a conscious decision. But he was forcing her to choose. He was giving her the responsibility of continuing with her adventure, or bringing it to an abrupt end.

She closed her eyes and felt the heat of him, the heavy rise and fall of his chest. He was here, right now. The man she had dreamed about all her life— her handsome villain—and if she stopped she knew she would always regret it. This might be her only chance to experience something she had dreamed about for years. And where was the danger? He would be gone tomorrow, back to whatever world he inhabited in London, and their paths would never cross again. There was no fear she would lose her heart to him, grow attached, except perhaps as a fond memory. There was no comparison between this and Aphrodite's many lovers.

She turned to look at him, so there would be no mistake.

"Yes," she said.

The bedsheets were chill, but he didn't feel cold. Usually when he came to a woman's bed she was already naked and prepared for him, but this time it was different. Francesca expected him to undress her.

He'd never seen so many buttons and hooks and ribbons. She was like a gift, waiting to be unwrapped, and his fingers trembled as he removed layer after layer. And then, after each garment was tossed aside, he had to stop and explore. The swell of her breasts, the curve of her thigh, her rounded hip. But then finally there she was, Francesca Greentree, the woman of his dreams. He groaned as he reached for her, tumbling her over, her hair heavy and damp about her face and shoulders.

There would be regrets; he knew it. And repercussions, when the truth about his reasons for being here came out. But right now he didn't care.

He groaned again, pressing his body to hers, feeling her respond with passion. With his hands stroking her back, he found the curve of her waist and the soft globes of her bottom. She was nuzzling against him, her breath warm as she explored his throat and the hollow there. Then she licked him, tasted him, and lifted her face so that he could kiss her, deeply this time. A lover's kiss.

Her lips clung; she felt hot and eager. He cupped her breast, feeling the hard nub of her nipple, and bent to take it in his mouth. She arched against him, her legs tangling with his, and he felt the sensitive length of his cock brush against her thigh. He nearly lost control, but he held on, knowing the more she wanted him, the better it would be for them both.

A moment to remember forever.

But she'd discovered his weakness, and her eager hand was upon him, tentatively at first, exploring his hard length, and then as he pressed against her soft core, impatiently. She was hot and moist, and he couldn't wait any longer. He slid inside her.

She went still. Perhaps he'd overestimated her state of arousal? But no, it was simply that it was new to her. He looked down into her face and saw the surprise in her eyes. She was a virgin, of course she was! He'd never taken a virgin before. For a moment he felt disoriented, confused as to his real reasons for doing this, and then she smiled up at him, and all doubt left him.

"It feels strange," she murmured, "but nice. I think . . . yes, I think I am going to like it very much . . ."

The blood rushed to his head. He began to move against her, no longer trying to hold back. She was obviously enjoying this as much as he, and he let her actions rule him. They clung together, riding the storm, and at the end she gasped and shuddered, and he lost himself in his own pleasure, and hers.

"So that's what it's like," she said dreamily.

And, as they lay in each other's arms, he felt as if he'd given her something very precious, and it was perfect, but then in a heartbeat it all changed.

It grew awkward.

Sebastian wished he could fall asleep. He deserved it, by God, but Francesca wouldn't let him. She wriggled out from his grip, and when he tried to hold on to her, murmuring soothing words, she wriggled the harder. It was over, and no amount of hoping would bring it back again.

Giving up, he threw back the covers and rose, and striding naked to the fire, he stretched the tired, aching muscles of his body.

Behind him in the bed she went still, staring. Of course, she hadn't seen a man in all his glory before, he thought wryly. Let her have her fill! He turned to face her with only a smile.

Her eyes slid over his chest and stomach, dropping to his groin.

But her staring at him was igniting desire again. She was half propped up against the pillows, her wild hair curling around her, her improper mouth swollen from his kisses. She was like a dream come true—she was his dream come true—and he wanted her with a fierce ache.

Her eyes widened at the evidence of his feelings. Perhaps, he thought, he could have her again, before it was over. Was twice too greedy? Sebastian knew he was willing to take what he could get.

"Francesca, you were made for love," he murmured huskily as he moved toward her. And realized it was the worst thing he could have said. He might as well have told her that she was her mother's daughter, and for a woman like Francesca, struggling against her bloodline and her nature, it was setting a match to tinder.

She sat bolt upright. "I need to leave now," she said in a hard little voice.

"Francesca . . ."

But it was no use; he could see she'd made up her mind. Her clothing had hardly dried, but she began to dress, and with a sigh he did the same. "Wait here," he said when he was done. "I'll try and get us some horses."

When he had gone, Francesca stood by the fire and wondered how she could feel so empty after what she had just experienced. She'd enjoyed what they'd done, yes, and she didn't regret it, but suddenly she could see how it was possible for a woman to become like her mother. Sebastian had made her feel like a goddess, and she already wanted more. It was addictive. She knew she would never be with Sebastian again, but she could also see it might become possible to begin searching for him in every man who looked at her, every man who touched her. Always searching and never finding.

The idea made her sick and dizzy with disgust and terror.

Oh so very easily, she could become another Aphrodite.

The door opened softly and he returned. "There's only one horse in the stable."

So she would have to ride pillion, pressed against him, reliving the moments they'd spent together. Francesca dreaded it and longed for it at the same time. *It will be a test*, she told herself as she followed him down the stairs. *If I can bear this without showing my true feelings, then I can do anything.*

But the journey was surprisingly swift, and they hardly spoke until the lights of Greentree Manor came into sight. She meant to jump down and run, but he was too quick for her, reaching to help her. She fell against him, and for a moment she was enveloped in the scent and feel of Sebastian Thorne. One last time. And then she was pulling away.

Running. As if he really were the devil.

She heard him call her name, but she didn't turn. Her head was filled with just one thought, and one regret. She wanted him.

But she couldn't have him.

The next morning Francesca waited until the hour was late before coming downstairs, and as she had hoped, he was gone. It was as well they were traveling to London after all. She told herself she would be able to forget Sebastian Thorne in the bustle and rush that was the capital, and by the time she returned to the manor, all thought of him would have been washed from her mind.

So very neat and tidy.

She could only pray it was true.

Chapter 10

London
Late summer

As they passed through the newly completed Euston Square Railway Station, Francesca looked up at the grand Euston Arch. The metropolis was changing and growing at an amazing pace. It had been four years since she'd last visited London. That had been when Marietta married her Max in a grand ceremony at St. James's Church. Since then her sisters had visited Greentree Manor often enough that Francesca had not been obliged to travel south to London. Besides, Max and Marietta spent much of the year in Cornwall with their daughter, while Vivianna and Oliver were currently at their estate in Derbyshire with their two sons.

Her sisters had their own lives to lead, and if sometimes Francesca felt the loneliness of her own solitary state, it was what she had chosen, and she told herself she was content. Better to be alone than prey to her emotions.

I have had my dance with the devil. Why should I need another?

The reminder was meant to comfort her, but it seemed to have the opposite effect.

A railway porter fetched them a hansom cab and loaded their luggage aboard. Amy held up a handkerchief to her nose as the smoke and grime of the city swirled around them, complete with an amazing collection of smells. At least summer meant there were not so many coal fires burning, so there was less chance of the impenetrable fogs that frequently smothered the capital.

The vehicle soon rattled its way into the thick stream of traffic, jostling with carts, omnibuses, carriages, and pedestrians. They were on the final leg of their journey. While Amy fidgeted and Lil sat bolt upright in her corner, looking frighteningly neat, Francesca closed her eyes and tried to picture herself far away from this man-made chaos.

"It seems ages since I was last in London," Amy said. "I am looking forward to seeing the new London bridge, and the statue of Nelson in Trafalgar Square, and the work on the Houses of Parliament in Westminster. And the shopping. Perhaps I can persuade Helen to come with me, although she never needed much persuading to shop. And you must come, too, my dear. It will do you good to freshen up your wardrobe."

Francesca opened one eye. "I am happy with the wardrobe I have."

"Oh Francesca, I do hope you will indulge me! That dreadful green monstrosity you were wearing when Mr. Thorne sat down with us to dinner . . . I hardly knew where to look. It was one of your charity dresses, wasn't it?"

Francesca sighed and gave up on calming thoughts. "Mrs. Hall has four children and an invalid husband, Mama. She needs the money. And I find her sewing quite adequate to my needs."

"You only say that to make me feel guilty," Amy retorted. "She could be employed making clothing for the servants, or darning the household linen. But please, never ask her to make you another dress!" Their vehicle rattled around a corner, veering to make way for a trolley bus. "I wonder if we will ever see Mr. Thorne again?" she added idly.

"Who?" Francesca exclaimed, as if she truly had forgotten.

Amy smiled. "Mr. Thorne, our gentleman in distress, or perhaps not quite a gentleman. Mr. Jardine seemed to think he was not a man whose acquaintance we should pursue, and I am sure he is right. He usually is."

"Whatever he was, Mama, he is gone and we will never see him again."

Amy did not reply, not even to argue that since they were in London and Mr. Thorne lived in London,

might they not run into each other accidentally . . . ?
Francesca, who had several replies ready, to show just
how indifferent she was, felt her spirits sink. Her life,
she admitted to herself, seemed very tame now Sebastian was no longer part of it. He had arrived so suddenly, stayed so briefly, she couldn't believe she could
miss him so much. It was to do with the sense of
excitement and danger he had brought with him, of
course, that was it. Burning buildings and men with
pistols and . . . and other things, she thought hastily,
stealing a glance at her companions.

They were deep in their own thoughts.

That was just as well, because the guilty pleasure
was probably there on her face for the whole world to
see. Scandal, ruination, disgrace—take your pick. She
could become the center of any one of them.

"Good heavens, what is that smell?" Amy pressed
her handkerchief firmly to her nose. Her eyes were
watering.

Lil's nose gave a brief twitch. "Tannery across the
river in Bermondsey," she said knowledgeably. "And
the soap factory in Southwark."

"Oh," Amy murmured faintly. "I'd forgotten how
Londoners live. Factories, rookeries, mansions, all
within a short stroll of each other. Rather dreadful,
really."

"Perhaps we should forget all about Uncle William
and turn around and go home?" Francesca said hope-
fully.

Amy met her eyes, and with an air of determination, set aside her handkerchief. "Certainly not. We

are here now. I'm sure we will soon get used to the—
the miasma."

"Eau de London," Francesca murmured. They had
turned into Wensted Square and were approaching
the Tremaine house. She could see Amy's agitation
growing with every turn of the wheels. Perhaps she
was more afraid of her brother's temper than she let
on, and like Helen, she didn't enjoy scenes. William
was always very good at scenes, in fact he seemed
to thrive on them, and he was intimidating when
angry.

"He won't turn us away," she went on, staring up at
the houses lining the square. "But he *can* be dreadfully
unpleasant, my dear, and I think we should prepare
ourselves for that until I work him around. I always
was able to win my brothers around to my way of
thinking; we must hope I haven't lost the knack."

"Such a shame Uncle Thomas died so young,"
Francesca said, knowing that he had been her favorite brother.

Amy's smile held sadness. "Thomas and my husband Henry died together in India. They were the best
of friends from childhood. I fell in love with Henry
when I was still in the schoolroom, and Thomas was so
pleased. He was a very pleasant man. William and I
have never been close. I used to think he was jealous of
Thomas, even when he would so loudly disapprove of
him. Of course dear Thomas laughed and took no notice. 'William will never be happy,' he'd say, 'no matter
what he does.' I think, in a way, Thomas pitied him his
lack of joy in the world around him."

"William *should* be happy now. He's head of the family and can order us all about."

"To give him his due, William has always been most diligent and meticulous when it comes to family matters. I know he can be overbearing and—and difficult, but he is also a man respected by his peers."

That was all very well, thought Francesca, but Uncle William was such an unpleasantly prickly man, it was sometimes difficult to feel comfortable in his company. He had a morbid dread of some scandal attaching itself to the Tremaine name, and that hadn't helped his relationship with Amy when she adopted Aphrodite's daughters.

They had come to a stop outside the Tremaine house. Lil hurried off to find someone to inform that they had arrived, and to help them with their luggage. It was August, late summer, and the sky was hazy over the trees in the garden that graced the center of the square. A young boy was busy sweeping a path for two gentlewomen with parasols, who were crossing the dusty cobbles. As Francesca and Amy ascended the front steps, the door opened.

"Mrs. Jardine?"

It was a nasal-sounding voice, with a thin layer of ice. The woman stood in the doorway, almost as if she was blocking their entry. She was dressed in gray silk, with the skirts so padded out with petticoats and horsehair stiffening that they brushed the door frame on either side. Her hair was so fair almost to be white, and had been caught up and curled into ringlets. It was a style more suited to a young woman, and this woman was thirty at least.

"I am Mrs. March," she said proudly. "Mr. Tremaine's housekeeper." Her eyes were cold, and there was certainly no smile lurking in them. "Your servant tells me that you have come to stay. We were not expecting you, Mrs. Jardine."

Her tone suggested that she found Amy's conduct wanting, and it stung Francesca to her mother's defense.

"This is Mrs. Jardine's family home, Mrs. March. Surely it isn't necessary for her to make an appointment?"

Mrs. March's cold, haughty gaze lingered on Francesca. "Mr. Tremaine rarely has visitors," she said, more like the mistress of the house than a mere housekeeper.

"Then this is an occasion for celebration."

Mrs. March pursed her mouth. For one awful moment Francesca wondered whether she was going to refuse to allow them to pass, and they would have to wrestle with her on the doorstep. But perhaps she only wanted to give that impression, because suddenly she stepped back, her skirts swinging.

"This way," she said, with a mirthless smile. "You may have to wait a moment or two while your rooms are prepared. Mr. Tremaine does not like to have rooms in use when there is no need, so parts of the house are closed up most of the year. I'll have tea served to you in the second-best parlor."

" 'The second-best parlor'?" Francesca repeated, feeling cross.

But Amy laid a warning hand on her arm and shook her head. "Thank you, Mrs. March," she said, to the woman's ramrod-straight back, her voice falsely bright.

"Mama," Francesca whispered her protest. "She's being insufferably rude!"

"That may be true, but I still don't think we should commence our stay in London by coming to blows with my brother's housekeeper, no matter how much we might be tempted. My dear, you know you're inclined to accept first impressions far too hastily. Perhaps Mrs. March is shy ... overwhelmed by the occasion ..." Amy waved her hand, seeking inspiration.

"Mama, the woman is a nightmare," Francesca retorted.

"Here we are." Mrs March had stopped at one of the doors and was waiting for them to catch up.

"Thank you, Mrs. March." As usual Amy's manners were impeccable. "I remember this room when it was my dear mother's sitting room," she added, gently reminding the housekeeper of her family's long association with the house, and her right to be there. "Do you know what time this evening my brother will be home?" Amy went on, stripping off her gloves.

"The master is in Oxford," said Mrs. March, with satisfaction. She watched their faces fall, and allowed herself a smirk. "If you had let him know you were coming, I'm sure he would have been here to greet you, but as it is he won't be home until the day after tomorrow."

"Oxford," Francesca repeated woodenly.

"William has friends in Oxford," Amy explained, but her voice was full of disappointment. "Oh dear, I suppose I should have written to inform him we were arriving today, Mrs. March, but I so wanted to surprise him."

Even the housekeeper wasn't proof against Amy's sweetness, and her chilly expression thawed slightly. "He's asked for leg o' lamb for his dinner day after tomorrow. It's his favorite and he won't miss that."

Amy smiled. "Well, that is a relief. I suppose we can occupy ourselves until then."

"Ma'am?" Lil was hovering in the hall. "Do you have any further instructions for me?"

"No, it's all right, Lil," Amy said kindly. "You go and have something to eat. I'll send for you when you're needed."

"The servants' quarters are this way," Mrs. March moved briskly across the hall. Lil fell into line, and her back was, if possible, even straighter than the housekeeper's.

In the second-best parlor, Amy sat down and stared at the shabby and depressing decor. "I am missing Mr. Jardine already," she said in a woebegone voice.

"At least we will be able to visit the theater, Mama. And the opera. And Madame Tussauds. Maybe there is a wax effigy of Mrs. March in the Chamber of Horrors."

Amy chuckled. "Terrible child! I beg you don't upset her, Francesca. Helen did mention in one of her letters that William relies on her a great deal."

"You don't think they are—?"

"No, I don't."

Francesca thought of the housekeeper's cold, unsmiling face and steely eyes, and decided there was little likelihood that Uncle William would want a woman like that sharing his bed. Surely his preference—if he had one—would be for someone soft and sweet and pretty? One of the soiled doves whose only way of surviving was to find a protector who would house and care for her . . . until boredom set in, and she was once more adrift.

Francesca shuddered. Aphrodite had once been such a woman . . .

"Do you wish to visit Madame Aphrodite while we are in London?" It was almost as if Amy had read Francesca's mind.

"No," she said shortly.

The subject, she hoped, was closed.

Aphrodite was busy with the evening entertainment, gliding about the room, making certain that her guests were being entertained and that their glasses were full of champagne. She seemed to know just what to say to each of them.

Years of experience, Sebastian supposed, watching her as he half listened to the pretty girl at his side. Her smile was seductive, promising more than conversation, if he was interested. He knew she'd be knowledgeable in the giving of pleasure without emotion—no need to think beyond the moment—which was what most men here tonight were seeking. But Sebastian wasn't. Passionless encounters bored him, even more so now that he'd known Francesca.

He wondered whether she was thinking of him. Thinking of Mr. Thorne, the dangerous, wicked Mr. Thorne. If she knew the truth . . . would she be interested then?

"Mr. Thorne." The soft, French-accented voice brought him out of his musings. Aphrodite, in a cloud of sweet perfume, was standing at his side.

"Madame." He bowed over her fingers, heavy with rings. "I have news."

Her hand trembled, but her beautiful face gave nothing away. "Very well. If you will wait for me in my sitting room, I will join you as soon as I am able. Dobson!" A straight-backed man in a red military-style uniform, with the battered-looking face of a pugilist, approached them. "Show Mr. Thorne into my private sitting room, Dobson," she said, and then leaned close, resting her hand on his shoulder to murmur something in his ear. Dobson nodded and proceeded to lead the way from the salon into the quieter, private areas of the house.

"Madame won't be long," Dobson said, showing him into the sitting room. His gray gaze swept Sebastian, assessing him, and Sebastian wondered if this was the spy who had given information to Aphrodite's enemies. Dobson didn't look like a spy, but then Sebastian had learned that in life nothing was as it seemed.

With the door closed, the gaiety was muted. The sitting room was furnished very differently, too, from the flamboyant air of the public areas of the club. The colors here were soft and restful, and there were some beautifully rendered miniatures arranged on a small table. Sebastian inspected them and recognized Aphrodite's three daughters. Vivianna, Lady Montegomery, was the eldest, a striking woman with chestnut hair and hazel eyes. Marietta, Lady Roseby, was more conventionally pretty, with fair hair and blue eyes and an angelic smile. And then there was Francesca, resembling her mother to a striking degree with her dark hair and eyes. But there was something elusive in her smile, as if she were here under protest.

Sebastian knew she expected never to see him again, but that was her misconception. He'd promised to leave Yorkshire the morning following the fire, and so he had. How would he arrange their next meeting? A chance encounter? A surprise visit? Or should he simply climb through her window at midnight? It might be worth it, just to see the expression on her face . . .

The door opening startled him, and he turned, Francesca's likeness still in his hand. Maeve smiled as if she was genuinely pleased to see him.

"Mr. Thorne, Mr. Dobson said you were here. I came to ask you if you'd like something to drink. Champagne, coffee, tea?"

"Thank you, no."

"I'm Maeve," she babbled on, strangely nervous.

"I remember you, Maeve," he said, and waited.

Maeve gave him another smile, as well as a searching glance from under her lashes that took in the miniature in his hand. "Well, then, if there's nothing I can do, Mr. Thorne . . . ?"

"There's nothing more, thank you, Maeve. Perhaps another time . . . ?"

She smiled, and the door closed softly behind her.

Sebastian stared after her, thinking. Had the invitation really been there? Was Maeve willing to lie with him, and was it because she was attracted to him, or because she wanted to know what he was up to? Was Maeve, with her penchant for listening at doors, his spy?

When Aphrodite joined him, and before she could begin to speak, he put his finger to his lips and went to the door, opening it to check that the entrance hall was empty this time. When he turned back, Aphrodite was watching him with a crease between her arched brows. "You do not trust my staff?" she queried, and she wasn't pleased.

Sebastian, who had been considering telling her of his doubts concerning Maeve, changed his mind. He'd just have to think of another way of keeping a watch on the Irishwoman. "Habit," he reassured her with a smile.

"Mr. Thorne, I promise you we cannot be overheard in here. Now, please, tell me what it is you learned in Yorkshire?"

There was no easy way to break the news. "Mrs. Slater is alive."

Her face lost all color. "You *spoke* to her?"

"No. Not yet. She's here, in London."

"Do you know . . . ?"

"I've yet to discover her whereabouts, but never fear, I will."

She stood, frozen, staring beyond him into the past. "I knew she was alive. I felt it. Here," and she pressed her closed fist to her breast, above her heart.

"I *will* find her, Madame."

"Yes, you will," she said grimly. "And when you do, she must be made to name the one who planned the kidnapping of my children. I must hear that name, Mr. Thorne."

Gazing into the courtesan's face he could see Francesca—her determination, her spirit, and her passion—and for a moment he was mesmerized. But Aphrodite wasn't finished.

"I fear for my daughters, Mr. Thorne. I fear particularly for Francesca . . . because of her—her father." She struggled with the words.

"Her father?" he echoed sharply. "Madame, if there is something I need to know . . . ?"

But Aphrodite shook her head. "I can say no more, not yet."

"Have you warned Francesca she might be in danger?"

A bitter twist of her lips. "Mr. Thorne, my youngest daughter does not speak to me. She prefers to pretend I do not exist. Any fears I have for her must be kept secret. She is quite likely to rush into that danger if she discovers I do not want her to do so, just to defy me."

Sebastian smiled. Yes, he could see her doing that.

"I thank God she is in Yorkshire and far away from all of this!"

He realized what she'd said, and what it meant. "But Madame, I thought you knew? Frances— your daughter is in London. She and Mrs. Jardine traveled down by railway train. They are presently staying at the home of Mr. William Tremaine in Wensted Square."

If she had been pale before, she was white now. *Mon Dieu!* She is *here*? And Mrs. Slater is alive and in London, with her . . . her master . . ." She began to pace back and forth in the small sitting room, very agitated. "He will strike to save himself, I know it. He has no soul. Mr. Thorne, I beg you to protect my daughter!"

He thought of protesting, but he could see she was in earnest. Besides, the request suited his own plans. "Would she agree to that?" he asked curiously.

"Don't tell her!"

"She does not like me, Madame." Suddenly Sebastian felt uncomfortable as Aphrodite's penetrating gaze turned on him. "I should have told you straight away; we met while I was in Yorkshire." He explained briefly, leaving out the physicality of their encounter.

Aphrodite fell quiet. "My daughter is in danger. I thought she was safe at Greentree Manor, and all along she was living among those who wished her ill. *Mrs. Slater,*" she spat the word, "a buyer and seller of children."

"She was safe," he assured her. "Until I arrived. It was me they were trying to stop."

She sighed. "You did not know, but in a way it is a timely lesson. Now you see why I have been so afraid all these years. These people have tentacles reaching everywhere, just waiting to pounce."

Her sentiments were heartfelt, despite the mixed metaphors. "Look at it this way, now we both have reasons to seek revenge."

"Yes." Suddenly she smiled at him, and her dark eyes were curious as they assessed him. "I cannot believe my daughter does not find you attractive, Mr. Thorne. Most women would."

"Your daughter is not most women, Madame."

She laughed. "My daughter is *my* daughter, no matter how she chafes against the fact. Believe me, she is a woman well and truly. You must protect her, Mr. Thorne, whether she wants you to or not. I must insist upon it."

He bowed. "As you wish, Madame."

"Francesca is her own worse enemy," she murmured. "She fights against her nature. When she learns to be true to her nature, then she will be happier. We all must learn to be true to our natures, Mr. Thorne."

"Sound advice, Madame, thank you." But he already knew his true nature, and he didn't like himself very much.

"You will keep me informed?" Aphrodite was brisk now, her fears set aside.

"I will."

She nodded, but the lines about her eyes had deepened. Her secrets were wearing her thin. Why, Sebastian wondered, was Francesca in especial danger? What was it about Aphrodite's youngest daughter that put her at extra risk? *Who was her father?*

Aphrodite wasn't about to tell him, but Mrs. Slater was the key. He'd find her and unlock the secret, and save the damsel in distress.

He smiled. Mr. Thorne as the hero—what a novel idea.

Chapter 11

William arrived home exactly when Mrs. March had said he would. Amy and Francesca were already seated for the evening meal, and they could hear voices in conversation outside the dining room door, too low to make out the words but lengthy enough for Francesca to wonder if she'd been mistaken in her assumption that her uncle and the housekeeper were not romantically involved. Or perhaps Mrs. March just had a lot to tell him.

When William finally entered the room, his expression was every bit as irritable as she'd expected. There was also an element of the henpecked male about it.

"My dear Amy," he said, "why can't you stay with Helen?"

Amy's lips twitched at his lack of tact, but she answered him with her usual unruffled calm. "Helen has little enough room as it is, and you know that Toby gambles away her housekeeping. How would she feed us? Whereas I know that you, William, as head of the family, will always make us welcome. It is your duty, and you are famous for your diligence to duty." She gave him a sweet smile. "It is good to see you, brother."

His mouth opened and closed again. Francesca bit her lip to stop herself from laughing aloud, but perhaps she made a sound because her uncle fixed her with a disapproving, beetle-browed stare, before shifting his attention back to his sister.

"Is *he* here?"

"If by 'he' you mean my husband, then no, he is not."

"Well, at least you had the sense to leave him in Yorkshire where he belongs."

Amy's back went rigid and her eyes lost their warmth. "William, if you continue to speak of my husband in that rude manner, then I'm afraid we will have a serious falling out. And you do not want to fall out with me, you really don't. Remember, I am not Helen, and you cannot frighten me."

He glared at her a moment more, while she returned his look, and then, to Francesca's astonishment, he grinned. "You always were a headstrong girl, Amy," he said admiringly. "You refused to listen to me once before and went ahead and married Sir Henry Greentree."

"And very happy I was, too," Amy replied mildly.

She sighed and shook her head at him. "William, must we fight like children? I make my own decisions, you know that . . . or you should by now. Helen has nothing to do with it. To make her miserable just to punish me is unforgivable, especially when she depends upon you so."

With a shrug he sat down and gulped his glass of wine. "Helen is weak," he pronounced impatiently. "She always was."

"Marrying Toby hasn't helped her state of mind."

"Toby," he snorted in disgust. "Please, let's not talk of that fat wastrel. Last time I saw him he was laced so tightly into his corset, I thought his eyes might pop out. I wish they would—I would pay to see it." He flung himself back in his chair and observed them a moment in silence. "Did you have a pleasant journey?"

"Yes, thank you. The first-class compartment on the train was extremely comfortable."

"Smelly, noisy things. Give me a horse any day."

"You're being old-fashioned, William. One must be progressive."

"Progressive? What's progressive about it? I prefer as little progress as possible when it comes to my life. As you can see, I haven't rushed to have gas lighting in this house—candles were good enough for our father and they're good enough for me!"

"I wonder if Mrs. March agrees with you, William?"

"Why should I care what she thinks?" he demanded belligerently. "She's my housekeeper. She takes her orders from me."

"She seems most efficient, William."

"She was recommended by one of my acquaintances." He sounded smug, as if he'd gotten himself a bargain.

At that moment the servants brought the meal in, and conversation waned. It wasn't until the apple pie that it resumed.

"Did you enjoy your stay in Oxford, William?"

"It was well enough. Always glad to get home, though." He eyed his bowl greedily, reaching for the cream jug.

"You must get lonely, here on your own? I always thought you'd marry and have an heir, to carry on the Tremaine name."

This time Francesca truly believed William was about to have an apoplexy. His face went the color of beetroot, and his hand was shaking so much, he spilled the cream on the tablecloth. "Good God, is there no end to your interfering, woman!"

"William, really, I was only—"

"I have no intention of saddling myself with a wife. I only have to cast a look at the choices my sisters have made to strengthen my resolve never to wed."

"I didn't know you felt like that," Amy said, flustered.

"Well, I do," William retorted, his eyes flashing. "I won't have you interfering in my life. I cannot abide interference."

"William, you're behaving like a child. I didn't mean to interfere. Even though you seem to think it your right to interfere with Helen and me."

"I am going to bed!"

And he was gone, the door slamming behind him.

"Mama," Francesca breathed in amazement, "I have never seen him so angry. What did you say?"

Amy looked shaken. "I don't know."

"I thought he might throw us out into the street."

"I underestimated how much work it is going to take to restore ourselves to my brother's good graces."

Francesca rose and slipped an arm about her. "Poor Mama. I don't envy you."

"He is family, I'm afraid, and it is a terrible thing to fall out with one's family. Speaking of which . . . Francesca, now don't bite my head off like William, but you really should visit Aphrodite."

Francesca stiffened. "No," she said. "I will enjoy seeing Aunt Helen again, despite Toby's awfulness, but I do not wish to see Aphrodite. I have nothing to say to her, nor she to me."

Amy patted her hand. "Very well, Francesca, I won't make you go. But it would be polite to send a note and give her the chance to call on you. She is your mother."

"No, she isn't," Francesca retorted. "*You're* my mother. I don't need two. I don't *want* two. Now I think I will retire. Good night, Mama."

Francesca closed the door, relieved to escape further probing and questioning. If Vivianna and Marietta were here, they'd pester her to see Aphrodite, but she was determined to stand firm. From the moment they discovered Aphrodite was their true mother, Francesca refused to have any sort of relationship with her, and over the years nothing had changed.

Soft footsteps sounded from the head of the staircase. Francesca looked up and saw Lil, cloaked and ready to go out. The maid obviously hadn't realized she was there, because when she saw Francesca she froze, her expression full of guilt and dismay.

"Lil? Where are you going?"

"Nowhere," Lil said quickly. "I . . . It's nothing."

There was something odd about her. Beneath the neat, respectable Lil she knew so well, there was a person Francesca had never seen before.

"What is the matter, Lil?" she said impulsively, climbing the stairs toward her.

Lil's blue eyes met her own, and to Francesca's surprise they filled with tears. The maid looked away and bit her lip.

"Lil," Francesca said gently, "do tell me what's the matter. You know I'll help you if I can."

"Oh, miss," Lil breathed. "I don' know what's wrong with me. Ever since we got here, I've been thinkin' about things."

"Things?"

"It's like the past has risen up to swallow me whole, and I can't escape it."

"You never speak about your past, Lil," Francesca said gently. "I know you're from London, of course I do, but other than that you've never confided in me."

"They ain't . . . aren't the sort of memories a respectable woman confides in anyone, miss."

"Come, Lil, you know me better than that!"

Lil sighed. "I had a family once. I haven't seen them in twenty years, miss. I don't suppose they're still living in the same street as they was. Perhaps they're dead. So many folk who die in London are buried in paupers' graves, without names."

"Oh Lil, is that where you're going now? To find them?"

Lil nodded, and her tears overflowed. "I—I know it's stupid, miss. You don't have to tell me. But ever since Jacob died, and I've been alone again, I've been thinking of my family and wondering . . ."

"It must be difficult, being all alone in the world, Lil. But you know we think of you as part of our family."

Lil looked as if she was going to dissolve completely, but then she took a deep breath and gave a sniff, and pulled herself together. "I know that, miss," she said huskily.

"But you still need to go and look?"

"I know it's not logical, miss, but it's like I hear their voices in me head, calling out to me."

"Emotions are not always logical," Francesca murmured wryly. "Do you want me to come with you, Lil?"

Hope shone in her eyes, mingled with a tremendous relief. "Oh, would you, miss? I don't think I can do it on me own."

"Of course I'll come. Just let me fetch my cloak."

"The places I'll be going to aren't very nice," Lil warned anxiously.

"Then no one will recognize me, will they? Not that I would care if they did."

"You don't want to cause a scandal, miss," Lil warned, with something of her old self.

Francesca laughed a little wildly. If only Lil knew. Scandal seemed to be her middle name!

Sebastian threaded his way through the crowd. Even this late at night, the streets in the poorer parts of London were awash with the homeless, the unemployed, the drunkards and the urchins, as well as the gents out for a good time and the thieves who preyed upon them.

He'd been watching the house in Mallory Street Hal had told him about. Knowing that Jed might well have been warned, Sebastian exercised caution. Mrs. Slater's bully boys might be waiting for him to show up so they could finish him off once and for all.

Mallory Street was a busy thoroughfare, all the more so since many of London's slums had been demolished to make way for train lines and new stations. The poor and the dispossessed had to go somewhere, and Mallory Street was better than some of the other areas. He proceeded along at a leisurely pace, dawdling outside the gin palaces and the drinking dens, ogling the tarts as if he were enjoying himself mightily. He'd dressed himself up as just another inebriated toff, slumming it, with his top hat askew, cane swinging erratically, and cigar planted firmly between his lips. He was playing a part.

"You make a good toff." Martin, his valet, had grinned at him as he set out.

"Nothing good about this toff," Sebastian had said.

"Do you still want me to watch over Miss Greentree?"

"Yes, Martin, I do."

"I thought maybe I could come along with you instead. Keep a lookout for suspicious characters."

"That's what you'll be doing in Wensted Square."

"Right you are, sir."

Martin could be a little overenthusiastic, but he was good in a crisis and Sebastian knew he was loyal and honest, at least where his master was concerned. But it was Martin's unfailing cheerfulness and optimism that always impressed Sebastian the most, even while it drove him to distraction.

He paused across the street from number 44, and while pretending to stagger drunkenly, adjusted his hat brim so that his features were all but hidden by the shadow it cast. All London streets were lit by gas lamps now, even Mallory Street, but many of the courtyards and alleyways were still as dark as ever. Unfortunately for Sebastian there was a lamp right next to where he was standing, opposite the house.

A passerby bumped against him, and he felt the questing hand of a pickpocket. Quick as a flash he caught the nimble fingers, bending them back, saying gruffly, "Keep away from me if you know what's good for you."

There was a grunt of pain, and the fingers fluttered in his grip.

"It's me, guv'ner. Dipper."

Sebastian turned to face his captive. A thin man who looked about fifty but was probably at least twenty years younger, his face lined and drawn from a lifetime of poverty and graft, his eyes sly and watchful from a lifetime of staying one step in front of the law.

"Yer asked me to meet yer, an' 'ere I am."

"So I see. What have you to tell me?"

Dipper was busy pulling thick woolen gloves onto his hands. "Got to look after 'em," he explained, wriggling his fingers. "They's me tools of trade, Mr. Thorne."

"Dipper . . ."

"All right, I know, yer always in a rush. Here's what I've got for yer, sir . . ."

Sebastian listened carefully. Dipper had asked, but no one had heard of Mrs. Slater. The house across the street was taken by a man called Jed Holmes, and he paid for the use of other premises, too, dotted throughout London. He had a reputation for dealing in the darker areas of prostitution."

"Jed Holmes," Sebastian said. "No mention of a woman's involvement at all?"

"Well." Dipper gave him a sly look. "I did hear somethin'."

"Come on, Dipper. I don't have all night."

"There's a woman been seen off and on, but she's a cripple. Gets carried about in a chair. Might be Jed's mother, the way he treats her, awful polite."

"You don't know who she is or where she lives?"

"He keeps her hidden away, I reckon."

"Ask, will you? Try and find her. There's money in it for you, Dipper."

The little man gave him a toothless smile, taking the coins Sebastian handed him. "Thank you muchly, guv'ner."

"And tell Polly I may have some work for her, too. She needs to look respectable, mind. A lady."

Dipper chortled. "I'll tell her."

"And don't get caught with your hand in anyone else's pocket. I mightn't bail you out of Newgate next time."

Dipper chuckled and vanished into the crowd.

Sebastian leaned back against a brick wall, pretending to warm himself beside a smoky brazier. Across the street, the shabby house looked innocent enough. But God knew what went on behind that door . . .

Just then the door opened, and a short, thickset man came into view. He was speaking to someone just out of sight, but by moving closer to the brazier, Sebastian was able to get a glimpse inside the house.

A woman, soberly dressed, holding on to the hand of a child. The little girl was around nine or ten years of age. She, too, was neatly dressed, but the very fact that she was there, in such a place, boded ill for her. Sebastian felt his heart sink. He didn't like this; he didn't like it at all.

Chapter 12

Francesca huddled deeper into her cloak. Lil had told her that the trick to not seeming out of place was to pretend you were at home, but she didn't feel at home. This part of London was beyond squalid, and the shadows had a sinister air to them that she'd never felt on the moor. And there before her was another of those horrible narrow gateways to another horrible dark courtyard where who knew what was waiting.

But this was the place where Lil had been born and lived as a child. Francesca knew that Lil had worked hard to become what she was, but she hadn't realized quite the depths from which she'd sprung.

And now it seemed that Lil was being haunted by a past she'd tried to hide from for twenty years.

Was there a warning in that for Francesca? Perhaps the cold, hard truth was that no one could escape her past.

"The smell of this place," Lil whispered. "I remember it. I feel like a prisoner, miss, struggling to breathe. I feel like I'm a child again, frightened and hungry. That awful gnawing hunger that used to eat away at my very bones, until I'd do anything to sate it. Thieving, lying, selling whatever I had to sell . . ."

She glanced sideways at Francesca and bit her lip, as if worried she'd said too much. Francesca wrapped an arm about her and held her tight, not commenting, just listening.

"Do you know the sad thing? This part of London used to be respectable. Toffs built these houses and lived here, but as time went on, they moved away and their big houses were carved up for cheap lodgings."

"Lil . . ."

"When I left here I went as far away as I could, and I always promised meself I'd never come back."

Just then something scuttled across the ground in front of them and they both jumped and squealed. Francesca covered her mouth with her hand, staring at Lil with wide eyes, and saw the maid's own lips quiver. She giggled.

"Big and tough we are, miss, afraid of a mouse."

"It looked too big to be a mouse," Francesca said with a shudder.

"You should see the rats. Around here they use them to pull carts, they do."

They both dissolved into slightly hysterical laughter.

"I never expected to find my family," Lil admitted as they made their way back through crowded Mallory Street. "But I had to look, miss. I'm glad we came."

Garish light from a gin palace shone out as the doors opened on reeling patrons. Francesca tried not to stare.

"Don't give up hope, Lil."

"They probably wouldn't want to know me anyway," Lil muttered.

"Whyever not!"

"I was a poor wretch when Miss Vivianna found me, different to what I am now." She flicked a glance at Francesca. "You won't judge me, miss?"

"Of course not. Who am I to judge you? You know my story, Lil, and it's hardly a moral example to hold up to others."

"I was sold," Lil said stiffly.

Francesca was too overwhelmed to speak.

"To one o' them places that men go to."

"Oh Lil, that's awful. That such a thing could happen in England!"

"It happens all the time, miss. Even now. Look around you and you'll see what I mean. Look, over there . . ."

Francesca looked in the direction Lil was pointing. The scene before her didn't really register, not at first. There were lots of people and noise, and then she saw the young girl, a child really, standing on the steps of a house. The door to the house was open and there was a man inside. The child stood, hands clasped before her, eyes downcast, while a soberly dressed woman bent to speak to her. She was small, probably nine years old, with her fair hair brushed out over her shoulders. She was wearing a pinafore over a cotton dress, and petticoats with lace edging that reached to mid-calf, and on her feet were ankle boots. Someone had dressed her up in her best clothes.

Someone must love her, Francesca thought. Then why did she feel such a sense of dread?

The man came out of the house and seemed to be saying something to the woman. He gestured at her, telling her to go. She backed away, down the stairs toward the street. The child went after her, but the man grabbed at her, to stop her. The little girl began to cry.

"Oh dear Lord," Francesca breathed.

"She's sold her," Lil said woodenly, "that's what she's done."

Francesca saw then that the girl's lips had been colored with rouge, and there were circles of it upon her cheeks, so that she looked like a little doll—or a caricature of the unfortunates who were shrieking outside the inn farther down the road.

"She knows no one's gonna help her." Lil sounded outraged and sick. "No one cares."

The sober woman was gesturing, too, now. She looked frantic. She was shaking her head. Then she snatched something she'd tucked into the bosom of her dress and threw it at the man. Coins rattled on the stairs, rolling and tumbling. As if it was a signal, street urchins came running from all sides, a melee of desperate, shoving bodies.

Francesca didn't remember making any conscious decision, but suddenly she was moving forward, pushing through the crowd that had gathered from nowhere to watch the fun. The little girl was jammed against the wooden stair railing, and Francesca slipped in beside her, grasped her around the waist, and swung her up and over the railing and the backs of the squabbling urchins. The next moment she was running, the child clasped in her arms.

Behind her someone began to shout. Francesca ran faster. The girl was clinging around her neck, her arms squeezing so tightly, her body pressed so close, that Francesca could feel her heart's rapid beating.

"They'll catch us," Lil gasped, and that was when Francesca realized the maid was running beside her.

"No, they won't."

"Where we going with her?" Lil cried, wild-eyed. "What's your plan, miss?"

"I don't have a plan."

"Then Gawd help us!"

The raised voices were a little distance behind them, mixed with the heavy pounding of boots. A woman was screaming, "Run, run!" Was it the child's mother? Had she changed her mind?

"They're coming, they're coming!" the child shrilled in Francesca's ear, staring behind them. "Don't let him have me, please."

"I won't," she panted, and tightened her grip on the girl, telling herself that only brute force would separate them.

"Look out!" Lil shouted a warning. "He's just behind you, miss!"

Francesca had time for a quick look over her shoulder. Lil was right, he was there. She tried to run faster, but her skirts clung to her legs, trying to trip her, and there was a stitch in her side. With a sob of despair she realized it was already too late. Her pursuer was only inches away from capturing her and returning the child to her new owner.

Wildly she twisted and turned, attempting to evade his outstretched hand, but he anticipated her movement. His fingers fastened painfully onto her shoulder.

"Let me go!" she screamed, spinning around, prepared to fight.

He was tall, big, and she was so frightened that it was a moment before his words registered. "Damn and blast you, Francesca, I'm on your side!"

She knew that voice; it was *his* voice.

"Sebastian?" she gasped. "What—"

"Do you want to get away or not?" He grasped her arm and gave her a shake. She could see his eyes, black and gleaming, just as they'd been during their last adventure. It really was he.

"I want to get away," she said.

"Then let's run!" He set off, propelling her with him.

Suddenly she wanted to laugh for joy, but she didn't have any breath to spare. They rounded a corner and then another, and it was dark and smelly. To their left was one of those horrible narrow gateways, and when he said, "This way!" she followed, and instantly found herself in the stygian black of a courtyard. Tall buildings surrounded them, but they were either unoccupied or the occupants were asleep, because there wasn't any light or sound. Apart, that is, from her breath rasping in her throat and her heart pounding in her ears.

They stood still, waiting. The child was clinging to her, face hidden in her neck, and she could feel Lil hovering almost as close. Sebastian was in front of them, but she heard his breathing as he waited. Shakily, Francesca listened to the approach of the pursuers. Their running steps passed the gateway without even a pause, and quickly faded into silence.

"Thank Gawd," Lil gasped.

"Shhh," Sebastian hissed. Silently, like a wraith, he moved into the gateway and peered down the street outside, first one way and then the other. He took his time about it.

"How'd *he* get here?" Lil whispered. She sounded cross, but that was just Lil's way of hiding her fear.

"I don't know." Francesca was dazed, not sure what she was feeling. The wild joy that had gripped her when she first saw him had faded, and all her fears had returned.

"Don't you trust him, miss, you hear me?" Lil wasn't helping.

"He's just come to our rescue. I think we need to bear that in mind."

"We could have done it without him. I'm sure you would've come up with a plan, miss."

The child stirred, lifting her head, and Francesca knew she was peering at her in the darkness. "What's your name?" she asked gently.

"Rosie," the girl murmured.

"Where's your home, Rosie? Where's your mother and father?"

"They're dead. My auntie, she sold me to the gentleman at that house. Then she changed her mind, but he said it were too late, and that I belong to him now."

Lil made a sound of furious disgust, but Francesca's throat was closed. It was too dreadful for words.

"It's safe." Sebastian had returned, and his voice made her jump. "Now, Miss Greentree, would you mind telling me what in the bloody blazes you think you're doing?"

He was angry. More than that, he was furious. When he saw her strolling along the street he thought he was hallucinating. But when she grabbed hold of the child and ran off . . . He thought he was going to explode on the spot. The looks of shocked surprise and delight on the faces of the crowd had been of less importance than the look of murderous fury on the face of the thickset man. He'd shouted for help, and several more like him had come from the house. Sebastian knew they weren't likely to stop Francesca and ask her polite questions. She'd taken what was theirs and they wanted it back, and they'd enjoy making her sorry.

An image flashed into his mind: Francesca with her dark eyes and wide mouth, all bloodied and broken.

He couldn't have it. He *wouldn't* have it.

"I didn't mean it to happen," she said now, lifting her chin. "It just did." She wasn't going to apologize, of course she wasn't. Francesca Greentree had probably never apologized for anything in her life.

"You know you're in grave danger? These people will kill you if they catch you."

"I very much doubt that! When I tell them who I am—"

"All the more reason to do away with you, before you can draw the attention of the Metropolitan Police down on them."

"You're exaggerating."

He wanted to shake her until her teeth rattled. He wanted to squeeze her in his arms and curse her for her courageous and thoughtless foolhardiness. And he wanted to kiss her, because she was like no other woman he'd ever known.

"What are *you* doing here, Mr. Thorne, if it's so very dangerous?" He knew she was fixing him with her direct look, while that needle-sharp mind was searching for the truth. And the last thing he needed was for Francesca to find out the truth.

He sighed, as if he had better things to do. "I was working. I was watching someone. And now you've frightened them off."

"You look like you're out on the town," Francesca accused him. "Another gentleman with more money than sense."

"That's how I'm meant to look," he said between gritted teeth. "I am in disguise."

"So am I."

"I knew the moment I saw you that you were a gentlewoman wandering where she shouldn't be. Your clothing is wrong. If you want to fit in you should wear your scullery maid's clothing, or else buy from a shop that sells corpse clothing."

There was a pause, and he thought he'd probably gone too far. Just as he began to wonder what she'd say in return, she spoke, and as usual she surprised him. "I'll bear it in mind for next time," she said evenly.

He laughed. He wanted to kiss her, and in a moment he might have done so.

Lil must have thought so too, because she cleared her throat noisily. "Miss, where are we going to take Rosie? She needs to be made safe. If these people are so dangerous, then we have to hide her."

"We'll take her home," Francesca announced confidently, making her way out of the narrow gate, and back to the street. "Just until Vivianna returns to London and I can arrange for her to take Rosie in. My sister," she explained frostily to Sebastian, "runs a charity school."

"I don't want to go to no charity school!" Rosie wailed.

Francesca cast him a look, as if this was his fault, and then lifted the child so they were eye to eye. Instantly her manner changed, and she was all gentle and reassuring. "My sister's name is Vivianna, and she's a lady. You'll love her, Rosie. Everyone does. And she will love you just as she loves all the children in her school. You see it's a very special school."

"No slops?" Rosie whispered.

"Definitely no slops. When you arrive my sister will ask you to choose a color, and you will be given a smock of that special color, your color. Because she believes every child in her school is different and special."

Rosie gave a tentative smile, her eyes growing thoughtful. "I want to wear pink," she said with certainty. "Pink is my color."

"I'm sure they will have pink. I like pink, too."

"Bloody hell, can we get on?" Sebastian burst out.

"You are swearing in front of a child, Mr. Thorne."

"I'm so sorry. But they'll be back to find us. Do you really want to wait around?"

"If you're frightened, Mr. Thorne, we will excuse you," Francesca said, but her steps quickened.

He gave an angry laugh. "I just saved your neck."

"Nonsense. I was perfectly capable of saving my own neck."

"This is not Yorkshire," he went on, aware he was beginning to rant, and yet unable to help himself. "You're a stranger here, and as far as these people are concerned, you've strayed into their territory, so you're prey. They'll take your money and every stitch of your clothing, and leave you for dead."

"You forget that it was I who saved you from the mire. And without a lecture, I might add."

Lil stepped between them. "Stop it!" she burst out. "This is my fault, Mr. Thorne, not Miss Francesca's!

I wanted to come, and Miss Francesca insisted on accompanying me. She did it as a kindness to me."

Francesca threw him a burning look, before reassuring Lil. "It's not your fault. I came because I wanted to, and I'm very glad I did."

Sebastian said nothing. Ahead of him he could see the line of waiting cabs, and it was tempting to rush out and hire one, and bundle Francesca into it. But the danger was far from over. He held up his hand, forcing them to halt, while he surveyed the situation with narrowed dark eyes.

An old woman approached with a basket of violets tied up with ribbon. "Posy for the pretty lady," she asked with a gap-toothed smile. "Come on, sir, buy your wife some flowers."

"She doesn't deserve them," he muttered, but he was already reaching into his pocket and taking out a shilling.

The old woman's eyes lit up. "Thank you, sir!"

The violets were pressed into Francesca's hand, and the next moment he was urging her forward toward the cabs. "Come on, damn it!" He felt her stiffen, but for once she bit her tongue.

He soon had the two women loaded into the cleanest of the cabs, with Rosie tucked in between them. He gave the address in Wensted Square to the driver, with the fare. When he turned back to Francesca she looked worried, although she was trying to hide it.

"Mr. Thorne . . ."

But he wouldn't allow her to wind her spell around him, not now. Better if she stayed angry.

"Go home," Sebastian said forcefully, "and stay

out of trouble. I may not be here to rescue you next time."

Oh yes, that did it. Her eyes flashed.

"*Good-bye*, Mr. Thorne. And I did not ask for you to rescue me this time."

"Someone had to, and I look upon you as mine, Miss Greentree."

"Yours?"

"Miss!" Lil hissed.

"Because I want you in one piece."

Francesca was oblivious to her maid tugging on her sleeve. "You want me . . . ?"

"Yes," he said quietly.

The color burned in her cheeks. She was looking into his eyes, and he knew she'd seen his desire for her. Did she also see what he already knew? Their night at the inn had been the start, not the end. Francesca opened her mouth, but he never discovered what she would have said.

Lil cried out shrilly, "Drive on! For Gawd's sake drive on!"

The cab lurched forward, just as there was a shout from behind them in the street. Their pursuers had found them. The cab clattered across the road and into the traffic, which was thankfully light, with Francesca's pale face turned back to him. Sebastian gallantly tipped his hat to her.

"Sebastian," Francesca groaned. Her hands were clenched, mangling the violets, their sweet scent enveloping her. She watched, helpless, as he turned away and began walking down a side street. The group of running men paused, looking one way and then the other, before they plunged into the shadows after him.

"He can look after himself, that one," Lil said knowingly. "You shouldn't fret about him, miss."

Francesca turned to stare straight ahead. "I'm not fretting."

But it was a lie. Francesca knew she wouldn't be able to forget him, not really, not deep inside, until she saw him again and knew he was safe.

Chapter 13

"What happened last night then?" The voice strained and slurred its way through the sentence, as if the speaker was losing the ability to channel her thoughts into words.

"They got away," said Jed. "Two doxies took the girl in a cab, and the gen'leman took off on foot. Our men went after them, but it were no use."

The woman cursed foully. "You should have been there." She reached out to grab Jed's sleeve, but her hand was shaking too badly. Cursing again, she tucked the useless hand back into the folds of her shawl, out of sight.

Warily, Jed watched her to see which direction her

mood would take. With her ailing body and trembling limbs, she had all the appearance of a pitiful old woman, but Jed knew better. He thought himself immune to the darker sights of London, immersed as he was in those shadows, but he still felt his guts clench whenever he was in his cousin's presence. There were stories of some of the things she was supposed to have done, and he wouldn't be surprised if they were true. His father'd warned him against her, and he'd scoffed, taunting the old man with: "You're scared of a woman, Da?"

But he understood now.

"I'll get the girl back," he said. "I'll find out where she is and—"

"I know where she is." She smiled at his expression, showing yellowed teeth.

"But . . . how can you know? We haven't even found the driver of the cab yet."

She chuckled. "I have my ways," she said. "I haven't reached the stage where I'm ready to hand over the reins to you, Jed. Patience. Your time will come."

Jed, who was counting the days until she died, shrugged as if the thought had never crossed his mind. "I'm happy with the way things are," he lied.

"Of course you are," she mocked.

"So where is the girl then?"

"She's being looked after in a gentleman's house, but not for long." She grunted. "I knew there'd be trouble. I told him to do them in straight off. Hold a pillow over their faces—nothing to it. But he was squeamish. And now, all these long years later, he's paying the price."

Jed was silent. She was rambling of the past.

"*He's* coming to see me," she said abruptly. "I don't want you here. You hear me?"

"I hear you."

The man who visited her was an old friend, or so she said. His visits were meant to be secret. Jed wondered whether he might be able to use the information one day, but he'd have to be careful. Angela was quite capable of having him killed if she thought he was becoming a threat to her.

She might be sick and crippled, but she was still a very dangerous woman.

Francesca woke to the sound of Lil's urgent voice and her none-too-gentle shaking. "Miss Francesca, please . . . wake up!"

"Lil? Whatever is it?" She opened her eyes, trying to rearrange her thoughts. She'd been dreaming of dark streets and a man with black eyes. She'd been running desperately . . . but was it toward him, or away from him?

"Miss, we need your help."

Francesca sat up, pushing her hair out of her face, and said the first thing that came to mind. "Is it Mr. Thorne?"

"Bless you, no! As far as I know, he's well."

"Then what . . . ?"

"It's Rosie, miss."

Lil was twisting her hands in a frantic manner. It was so unlike her that Francesca reached out and grasped them hard to make her stop. When they'd arrived home the night before, Lil had decided Rosie would be more comfortable sharing her room, and after they'd washed her face and found her a night-dress that was more or less her size, they'd tucked her into the truckle bed.

What could have gone wrong?

"It's Mrs. March," Lil explained bitterly. "She won't let Rosie stay. She's so angry, miss. I thought if I didn't wake you immediately she'd have the poor moppet bundled up and on her way to the orphanage, and it'd be too late."

Francesca pushed back the covers. "I'll talk to her, Lil. Don't worry. Go and get Rosie dressed and give her something to eat. How is she this morning?"

Lil smiled. "She's chirping away like a little sparrow, miss. You wouldn't think it were the same girl."

"We mustn't let her know what's happening. I'll deal with Mrs. March."

Lil sniffed. "I hope so, miss."

Mrs. March, in a burgundy dress with even more stiffened petticoats beneath her skirts, was waiting for her downstairs, her shoulders back and her face rigid with disapproval. "Miss Greentree," she said. "Did you invite this street urchin into Mr. Tremaine's home?"

"Her name is Rosie, Mrs. March, and she's not a street urchin."

"She certainly isn't the sort of child I am accustomed to having in my house."

"But this isn't your house, is it, Mrs. March?"

Her expression faltered, the frigid wall slipped, and for a moment Francesca saw pure rage. A moment later the housekeeper lowered her eyes, hiding her emotion, although the skin on either side of her mouth whitened.

"The master trusts me to run his house as I see fit. I am used to having my orders obeyed." She looked up, and her eyes had a shine to them that might have been spite, or triumph, as she played her final card. "Your uncle will take my side, Miss Greentree, you can be certain of that."

Francesca knew, with a hollow, sick feeling, that she was right. Uncle William, so terrified of scandal and so proud of his good name, wouldn't abide someone like Rosie in his house. Especially when it was explained to him that his niece had virtually kidnapped her from outside a child brothel. It would be yet another fault to lay at Amy's door, and Francesca knew she couldn't allow her mother to shoulder the blame for something she hadn't done, as she would to protect her daughter.

Francesca had no choice. She'd have to back down if she was to save Rosie and Amy. And that was the most important thing, wasn't it? Mrs. March could crow all she liked, as long as Rosie was safe.

"I'll have to tell him, I'm afraid," the housekeeper was saying, pleased with herself, making the most of her power. "The master will have to know. He'll insist on it."

"Mrs. March, please wait . . ." Francesca summoned up a winning smile. "There's no need to mention this to my uncle. I understand your concern completely, and I will arrange for Rosie to go elsewhere."

Mrs. March hesitated. "I don't like to keep secrets from the master."

"Yes, but on this occasion I'm sure you'd agree that it's for my uncle's own good. You know how upset he gets, Mrs. March."

Her cold eyes gleamed with malice. "I know how upset he would be with you, Miss Greentree, for bringing a guttersnipe into his house."

"Yes, you're right," Francesca said levelly, while her blood came to a boil. "But he'd be angry with you, too. My uncle will think you have failed in your duty by allowing the child into his house in the first place."

She glared. "You smuggled her in without my knowledge!"

"Yes, Mrs. March, but *the master* will see it differently. He's a very exacting person, isn't he? He'll think that you should have been aware of who was coming and going in his house at a time when it should have been locked up nice and tight."

She caught the flicker of doubt in Mrs. March's eyes. "Very well," she said icily. But as Francesca went to turn away, the housekeeper called her back. "You needn't worry yourself about finding somewhere to take the child. I'll see her to the orphanage or the workhouse."

Such offhand cruelty was almost too much for Francesca—she felt her self-righteous fury begin to bubble over and knew in a moment it would scald everything in sight—but she knew she had to bite her tongue. For Amy's sake.

"No, Mrs. March, I'll take care of Rosie. Thank you all the same."

Mrs. March looked as if she'd like to argue the point, but all she said, grudgingly, was, "Very well."

Lil, when she was told, was furious. "The workhouse!"

"Yes, Lil, but you can understand her point of view. Not about Rosie. About Uncle William. He'd be horrified if he found out about her, throw a fit, and Mrs. March would get some of the blame—and she knows it."

"You won't send her to the workhouse?" Lil whispered, glancing over to where Rosie was playing by the window.

"No," Francesca reassured her instantly, "of course not. I'll think of something . . ." She bit her lip. What *was* she going to do? Even though Francesca knew Amy would stand by her in the event of an Uncle William rant, she couldn't ask it of her. Not when things were already so tense between them. But neither was she prepared to let Rosie be taken to one of those places. Some people might do that, say it was just too hard, and wipe their hands of her, but Francesca wasn't one of them.

There must be someone who could help . . . ?

A name occurred to her, but it seemed so unlikely, so impossible that she tried to dismiss it from her mind. But it kept returning and wouldn't be dismissed. She tried to consider it calmly, even though she hardly dared to contemplate such a thing. Had she anything to lose by asking . . . apart from a promise she'd made to herself many years ago?

"There is one person," she said, trying it out aloud. "Aphrodite."

"But miss . . . !"

"Remember how you were saying, last night, that the past never really goes away? That it's always there, inside you? Well, you were right, Lil. I swore that I would never have anything to do with my mother, but now I'm going to ask for her help. I suppose it will serve me right when she laughs in my face and turns me from her door."

"Madame Aphrodite isn't bad," Lil tried to comfort her. "Courtesans are different. I can't explain it properly, miss. You should ask her."

"I don't think so." Francesca smiled a strained smile. Her head was aching. It seemed ironic that the two people she had vowed never to allow back into her life, Sebastian Thorne and Aphrodite, were now the two people she was reliant upon. And one of them in particular seemed to be occupying her sleeping mind as well as her waking thoughts.

"Miss?" Lil was waiting for instructions.

"Rosie needs to be taken care of, Lil, and there's nowhere else until Vivianna comes back. Nowhere else *safe*," she amended. She glanced over at the child and smiled. Rosie was playing with some finger puppets Lil had made for her out of scraps of cloth, and as she bent over them, giving them voices, her fair hair curling about her, she seemed like any other little girl.

"She'll be fine," Lil murmured, following the direction of her gaze. "Rosie's like us, miss. She's a survivor."

Sebastian squinted as the morning sun shone brightly into his eyes. He had been loitering across the square for an hour now, and he expected any moment to be apprehended and moved on. This was not the sort of area where he could watch a house unobserved, but there were only he and Martin, and he'd sent Martin to Mallory Street. After last night it was best not to take any chances; Sebastian might be recognized, but Martin's face was new.

Last night he'd been furious with Francesca. When he'd imagined them meeting again it certainly hadn't been in those circumstances. But there had been enjoyable moments—the challenge of losing his pursuers through the back streets and alleys of London, and the expression on Francesca's face as the cab took her away. Without realizing it, she had told him much about her feelings for him.

She was headstrong and impulsive, and even as he felt a kinship with her, she terrified him. He never knew what she was going to do next. When he finally fell into his bed early this morning, instead of sinking into oblivion, he'd found himself tossing and turning, unable to get to sleep for thinking of her. It was her fault. If he spent much more time in her company he'd be gray-haired and stooped like an old man.

His mouth twitched, and he found himself smiling. The thing was, gray or not, he knew it would be worth it.

The sound of a carriage brought his head up again, and he watched as it came to a halt in front of the Tremaine house. Sebastian straightened, instantly alert. Francesca, dressed in another of her unflattering rag-bag dresses, this time teamed with an appalling bonnet, exited via the front door. She was holding little

Rosie's hand tightly in hers, and the maid, Lil, was following closely behind. Together the three of them climbed into the carriage and were driven smartly away.

Sebastian sauntered across the street to the young crossing sweeper, whose palm he had greased earlier.

"They're off to Aphrodite's Club, sir," the boy said with a proud grin.

Sebastian nodded and paid him the second installment of the amount they had agreed on.

He was puzzled. Aphrodite had told him that she and Francesca did not get on. What had occurred to send the woman of his dreams hurrying to her courtesan mother?

She was in danger, he knew that. Whatever threat she was already under due to her birth had been increased when she stole Rosie. Mrs. Slater and Jed would be looking for her, and if they didn't know who had taken their property yet, they soon would. It was too late to stop the game. The cards had already been shuffled and dealt.

Sebastian just hoped *his* hand was the winning one.

Aphrodite dipped her pen in the ink pot and began to write. It had been a long time since she had written in her diary. She'd been busy, she'd told herself whenever she thought of doing so, but she knew that wasn't the real truth. The fact was, she'd resisted telling the end of her story because it wasn't finished yet. There was so much more to know, and until she sought the services of Mr. Thorne she'd thought she never would know.

But now she must make a start, for Francesca's sake. She'd given her other daughters the opportunity to read about their fathers and the circumstances leading up to their births. She hoped that one day Francesca, too, would wish to know her beginnings—even if she refused to have anything to do with her mother right now.

"My love?"

Aphrodite looked up with a smile. Jemmy Dobson was leaning against the door, smiling back. "How long have you been standing there?"

Dobson moved toward her with his soldier's stride. "I enjoy watching you. You're a beautiful woman."

"Ever the sweet talker, Jemmy? You do not change."

"I hope not. Not where you're concerned."

Her eyes grew dark. "Perhaps we should go upstairs. Talk about these matters in bed, *oui*?"

"Ah, if only." He sighed. "But you have a visitor, my love."

"Another one of those tedious tradesmen? Maeve can deal with him."

"It's your daughter."

Aphrodite frowned. "But . . . my daughters are away."

"But this is your other daughter. Francesca."

Aphrodite took an uneven breath. Carefully she laid down her pen and closed the red, leather-bound book. Francesca? How strange. It was as if it was meant to be. Was she finally to be given the chance to mend the rift with her youngest and most difficult daughter?

"My love? What should I do?"

"You must send her in, Jemmy."

Chapter 14

Francesca had never been to Aphrodite's Club. She'd never seen her mother in her true setting. The only times she and Aphrodite came face to face were when her mother made the journey from London to Greentree Manor. Francesca dreaded those visits. In the familiar and comfortable surroundings of the manor, the courtesan seemed out of place; far too exotic a creature. They had nothing in common. Francesca would do her duty with a few grudging words, and then escape onto the moors and stay there until suppertime. She always breathed a big sigh of relief when Aphrodite went home again.

And now it was her turn to step into Aphrodite's world, and she was beginning to appreciate how difficult a thing it was. Was this how Aphrodite had felt when she journeyed north? Did she worry over what sort of reception she would have?

I am here for Rosie, Francesca told herself. *This is nothing to do with what is between Aphrodite and myself.*

"Are you all right there, Miss Francesca?" Dobson had returned and was watching her, his gray eyes cool and assessing and, yes, sympathetic. As if he understood her turmoil. Although Francesca doubted whether he either knew or cared why she was here. What was he, after all? Just the latest in Aphrodite's long line of lovers. Although he had lasted longer than most.

"Can I see my . . . her now?"

He smiled, his eyes creasing up, and suddenly she felt there was something warm and friendly about him, and instinctively she liked him. "Of course you can. I'll take you to her. She's workin' in her office."

Startled, Francesca hurried after Dobson. "Working?" she repeated. "I thought she'd be resting," she added, when he gave her a puzzled look. "The club is open all night, is it not?"

Dobson chuckled. "Your mother does far more than stand about looking beautiful, you know, miss. This club requires a great deal of work and energy to keep it running. It's Aphrodite's Club in every sense of the word. She oversees every detail, gives the orders, and makes the decisions. She's a clever woman."

The rebuke was mildly spoken and he was still smiling, but the expression in his eyes told her he would not listen to any implied criticism of the woman he loved.

Francesca felt like a child again. Not a good start, she thought, as she passed by him and into the room. The door closed behind her with gentle finality.

Aphrodite was seated at a desk with the windows behind her. For a moment she seemed so familiar that Francesca was taken aback; it was like meeting a friend. But this was Aphrodite, and the only reason Francesca was here was that she had no other choice.

The office was small and austere, a place for working in and not for public show, like the large and mirrored salon she had glimpsed. The only touch of color and scent was a vase of white roses, overblown and dripping petals.

Francesca was surprised to see her mother like this. Whenever she imagined Aphrodite "at home," it was as the grand courtesan, indolent, smiling, naked in the arms of her many lovers. And careless of the welfare of her children.

Now, suddenly, she was confronted with a totally different picture. This woman, seated at her desk, in a plain black silk dress with no frills, had circles under her tired eyes and ink stains on her ringed fingers. She was just like every other middle-aged woman . . . well, not quite. Aphrodite would never be ordinary.

"I did not know you were in London, Francesca," Aphrodite said at last, her voice warm but not overly so. Francesca realized that the courtesan had been examining her, too.

"My moth—that is, Mrs. Jardine and I have come to stay with Mr. Tremaine. He's been . . . difficult since she remarried, and taking it out on Mrs. Russell. It's only a brief visit." *I hope.*

It was as if Aphrodite heard the unspoken caveat, because she smiled. "I know you do not like London, Francesca. You must be longing for home."

"One does what one must."

"Very true, *petit chaton.*"

Little kitten! No one was less like a sweet, furry kitten, Francesca thought, than she. But before she could respond, Aphrodite pushed back her chair and rose to her feet. She was not as tall as Francesca, and so slim as to be almost thin, but there was still a marked resemblance. As she came around the corner of the desk toward her, Francesca realized her mother was going to embrace her and felt herself go rigid with dismay. Aphrodite must have sensed it, because she changed her mind, and rested her hand briefly on her daughter's shoulder before moving on to the bell rope by the door and giving it a tug.

"You have time to drink coffee with me?"

Francesca blinked. "Eh . . . yes, thank you."

Aphrodite gestured for her to be seated in one of two chairs in a compact corner before an unlit fireplace. It had all the appearance of the kind of intimacy that struck fear into Francesca's heart. She and Aphrodite having a cozy chat? But for Rosie's sake she must do it. Francesca sat down, fussing with her skirts in a way that was totally alien to her, just to gain some time.

Ask her! Just ask her. If she says no, then so be it. You can leave

"Will you visit a modiste while you are in London?"

Aphrodite asked politely, her elbows resting on the arms of the chair, her fingers steepled under her chin, and her dark eyes fixed on Francesca.

"I expect so. Yes. Why do you ask?" she added suspiciously.

"I am not criticizing you, *petit chaton*," her mother said with a frown, "but . . ."

"But?"

"You are a beautiful woman. It is a shame you hide it."

"I am myself," Francesca retorted forcefully.

"You can be yourself without wearing clothes you found in a ragbag."

Francesca stared at her in shock. "You sound like—"

Mr. Thorne.

"Who do I sound like, *petit chaton*?"

But before Francesca could find a reply, there was a tap on the door, and a young woman with smiling eyes entered. "Mr. Dobson explained you had a visitor, Madame," she said. "I thought I'd add an extra cup." She was carrying a tray with a silver coffeepot, delicate cups, and a matching cream jug and sugar bowl upon it, and she set it down on the table by Aphrodite's elbow.

"Thank you, Maeve," Aphrodite said, returning her smile. "You do not know my youngest daughter, I think. Francesca, this is Maeve, my assistant."

"Assistant?"

"Not all of us are destined to become famous courtesans like Madame." Maeve laughed. "By the way, the little girl wants to play in the garden—with the puppy," she added to Aphrodite. "It was a gift to one of the girls from a gentleman friend. Your maid is keeping an eye on her. Is that acceptable, Miss Francesca?"

"Oh. Yes. Thank you, Maeve."

On their arrival at the club, Rosie had decided she was thirsty, and Dobson had taken her and Lil off to the kitchen.

Aphrodite gave her a curious glance but she said nothing, asked nothing. She was not going to make this easy.

"I thought Marietta was going to help you to run the club?" Francesca said when Maeve was gone.

"She is. Marietta is my heir, it is all agreed. Maeve came here to be trained as one of the demimonde, but she was not suited. Not everyone is, and the choice was always hers. So now she works elsewhere in the club." Her brows rose. "I see you are surprised, *petit chaton*. Did you think I forced my employees to have connection with men, whether they wanted to or not? Do you think I buy and sell girls like one of those brothels in Mallory Street? Who is this little girl Maeve spoke of? Why did you bring her here?"

She was upset. Her dark eyes were bright with tears.

Shocked, Francesca half rose from her seat. "No, no . . . Madame, I don't think that, not at all. I'm sorry. I am not very good at . . . at this. I am expressing myself badly because I am nervous. Forgive me."

"*I* make you nervous?"

Francesca laughed; she couldn't help it, Aphrodite

looked so outraged at the suggestion. "Yes, you do."

After a moment the courtesan smiled. "I suppose I can be formidable on occasion." Her smile wavered. "Sit down, please, and tell me why you are here. I promise not to bite you."

Francesca drew a deep breath. The moment had come. Her explanation came out stiffly. She told her mother about going with Lil to Mallory Street and what she had seen and, in a split second, what she had decided to do. "It happened so quickly," she said. "We ran and hid, and . . . and a gentleman helped us. Then I took Rosie home. At the time I didn't think what would happen afterward."

But to her amazement Aphrodite seemed to understand, cutting straight to the heart of the matter. "You want to save this girl. You want her to have a chance at a proper life."

"Yes," she replied with relief. "I do."

"Then what is stopping you?"

"Uncle William. If he finds out about her he'll blame Mama . . ." she paused, embarrassed by the slip. "I mean Mrs. Jardine, and I cannot have that, I really cannot." Her calm voice broke on the last word, surprising her.

"I never liked that man," the courtesan said stonily. "Now calm yourself, *petit chaton*. I will take her for you, just until she can be settled elsewhere."

"Thank you . . ."

"No, you must promise me something first. You must promise never to put yourself in danger again."

"That is an easy promise."

"Good. You mustn't wander the streets. There is sickness, did you not know?" when Francesca appeared surprised. "It's the cholera. No one knows how it comes and where it comes from, but it does not discriminate between the wealthy and the poor. It has no pity. At the moment it is very bad."

"I didn't realize." *Cholera.* She knew of it, and the swift death it brought. Unlike some of the other sicknesses to be found in London, it was not something confined to the slums. Cholera, as Aphrodite said, was no respecter of class or station in life.

Aphrodite sipped her coffee. "You mentioned a gentleman who helped you?"

"Yes, Mr. Thorne."

"Mr. Thorne?" Her dark brows lifted. "Mr. Sebastian Thorne?"

"Do you know him?" A dark, curling jealousy wrapped around Francesca as an image of Sebastian in the arms of one of Aphrodite's beautiful courtesans filled her mind.

"He is an investigator, no? I have heard that he is good at his work. And dangerous to those he pursues."

"Oh."

Aphrodite's smile was knowing. "You like him, *oui*? He is very handsome."

Francesca turned her face away, pretending indifference. "I hadn't noticed," she announced awkwardly.

Aphrodite considered her a moment, and then she shook her head in disgust. "*Psht!* You can lie to yourself, but do not lie to me. I see it. No"—she held up one long finger—"no more pretense between us. We are mother and daughter, however you would wish it otherwise. Drink your coffee."

Francesca did consider arguing, but Aphrodite had become so formidable that she didn't quite dare. She drank her coffee.

The conversation turned to Yorkshire, and the weather. Banal subjects to be discussing with a courtesan. It was only as Francesca was leaving that Aphrodite clasped her hand and said, "You must come back to visit your Rosie. I will expect it."

"Thank you, I will. And . . . I am grateful, Madame."

"I have always been here when you need me," Aphrodite said sincerely, her eyes bright.

Her emotion made Francesca uncomfortable, because she could not share it. But then she had always known her mother was a woman ruled by her emotions, so there was no surprise there. However, Aphrodite did surprise her in ways she'd not expected. She was intelligent and accomplished and astute—she ran her own business in a world where men predominated. She had been generous to her daughter when she need not have been.

Still, Francesca reminded herself, she must never forget that Aphrodite was a courtesan, a woman who used her body to gain favor and fortune, a woman whose passions were everything.

The sort of woman Francesca had sworn never to become.

She was grateful for her help, but it would be a relief when Rosie was settled with Vivianna.

Lil decided to stay awhile with Rosie. "She might get frightened, the little moppet," the maid said fondly. Francesca didn't think much frightened Rosie, but she agreed. So she was all alone when she boarded the empty hackney waiting outside the club.

Once she gave the driver Uncle William's address, and settled back on the worn seat, Francesca was able to let her thoughts wander. She'd asked Aphrodite a favor, and it had been granted without histrionics, emotional blackmail, or the clinging of a damaged woman. The only thing Aphrodite asked in return was something Francesca had fully intended to do anyway!

It was worrying that all these years she'd been under the impression that Aphrodite was one woman, and now Francesca had found she was another. That didn't make things right, of course. She and her mother were very different, she told herself. Very different.

But there was a doubt planted inside her—that she did not really know her mother at all.

The hackney had come to a stop.

Surprised, Francesca straightened and looked about her. Was there a holdup in the traffic? But no, they had veered off into a quieter, narrower street, and there didn't seem to be anyone about. Concern fluttered her heart.

"Driver? What is happening?"

But the driver ignored her, and now she was really concerned. Francesca reached for the door handle, intending to get out. She could find another cab, or at the very least give the driver a piece of her mind.

But before she could do either, the door was flung wide open and a man sprang into the compartment beside her.

Chapter 15

Francesca screamed.

The sound didn't end up as loud as it began. In the split second after she opened her mouth, she recognized him, and it became more of a squeak than a proper scream.

"You!" she cried, and had the bizarre sensation that once again she was trapped in a novel.

"Yes, it's me," Sebastian said. "You're not going to make that infernal squawk again, are you?" he added, his brows snapping together as he frowned.

"What did you expect me to do?" She was angry. She could feel her cheeks growing hot, and her eyes were blazing. "I thought I was about to be kidnapped! Again . . ."

She didn't really remember being kidnapped the first time—she'd been so young—but she had heard the story many times, and perhaps on some deeper level she had retained a memory of terror . . . of loss. Now she was all the more furious because of it.

And because you spent a sleepless night, worrying about him, and here he is, large as life, and without a scratch.

"I could kidnap you if you like," he said, his wicked black eyes aglow. "In fact that might be a very good idea."

Damn and blast him, he'd done it again! Her imagination shot off in an entirely new direction, with images of him and her in some safe little paradise, all alone together. This paradise seemed to bear a resemblance to a sultan's harem, and she was wearing . . . oh heavens, silken trousers! Francesca had come to the part in her fantasy where he was feeding her plump, juicy grapes, when she came back to the hackney cab and realized he was watching her, smiling, and waiting.

"Are you all right, Francesca? You seemed to go away for a moment there."

"Of course I'm all right," she retorted guiltily. "What do you think you're doing, bursting into my cab like this?"

Mr. Thorne leaned back in the seat as if this was perfectly normal behavior. "I wanted to speak to you privately."

Francesca tried to cling to her anger, but she felt it slipping away. In a moment she'd be giggling. "If you wanted to speak to me, you should have sent a note.

Or you could have called on me at my uncle's house."

"You would have torn up the note, and you would have refused to see me. Or Mrs. Jardine would have refused on your behalf. I'm not the kind of man they want sniffing around your door."

But she knew that was part of his attraction for her.

"You're in danger, and you need to understand that. I've just taught you a valuable lesson."

"A valuable lesson?" she repeated angrily.

"Anyone who wished you ill could easily pay your driver to stop his vehicle, so that he, or she, could then accost you in some deserted street. You have no maid, no friends on hand. You'd be helpless to save yourself."

Her anger was definitely draining away—he seemed so sincere. And she never seemed able to sustain it for long, not when she was with him. "Thank you," she said in a cool voice. "I'll remember to be accompanied by someone at all times, and to carry about a—a pistol with me, so that I can shoot any persons I don't like the look of. Now please get out of my way, Mr. Thorne, and allow me to continue on my journey unmolested."

He grinned as if he found her very amusing. "Not yet. I haven't said all I came to say."

She closed her eyes and held her breath. Her lips moved, counting. After a long moment she opened her eyes again. "Very well, Mr. Thorne. What?"

"Where is the girl? Rosie?"

"I've taken her to my mother to be cared for until my sister returns to London."

He groaned.

"What's wrong with that?" she asked quickly, her eyes widening anxiously.

"What's right with it?"

Her eyes narrowed again at the perceived insult. "I assure you Rosie will be perfectly safe with Aphrodite. She will come to no harm there." Her voice changed, grew ragged. "I had to do something. Mrs. March, my uncle's housekeeper, called Rosie a guttersnipe and threatened to tell my uncle. He'd make a terrible fuss, and right now the last thing we need is one of Uncle William's rages."

"Of course, we mustn't have one of William's rages."

"You're being sarcastic. You don't understand. What would you have done in my place, Mr. Thorne? Left Rosie to her fate? I couldn't do that, no matter how much it might inconvenience me."

He looked at her. There was amusement in his expression, and admiration, and desire. With his eyes as dark as night and that curve to his lips, she could have let herself look at him all day long. Despite her resolution to be indifferent to him, Francesca felt as if she was melting like ice in the sun.

"Why were you following me?" she asked, rather breathlessly.

His mouth curved up even more. "You are the cross I have to bear, Francesca."

"Nonsense. I am nothing to you, nor you to me. We are strangers who met under extraordinary circumstances. That doesn't mean we need be friends, or even indifferent acquaintances."

His expression grew skeptical. "Francesca, even a

stranger would be remiss if he didn't warn you how dangerous these people are. You stole their property. It's only a matter of time before they find the driver from your cab and get your address. They'll track you down to Wensted Square without much trouble."

The thought was frightening. She put it aside to peruse later.

"So you've appointed yourself my protector?" she demanded.

"I want to repay my debt to you," he said, and his smile was gone and he sounded strangely awkward. "I dislike being in debt," he added.

Was he lying? Was that why he sounded unsure of himself? But no, when he was lying he was much more smooth and practiced than that. He must be telling the truth. The villain was being honest.

She turned to stare out of the window. He could see the light dappled on her cheek, her skin smooth and soft, and the curve of her mouth so tempting, he had to put a firm rein on himself. His gaze slid down over her throat to the ruffle of lace on her bodice, and the curve of her breasts, and he wanted her so much he ached.

"I don't think my uncle will agree to your following me about, Mr. Thorne," she said at last, turning to face him. She looked troubled. "At the moment I have to be very careful not to upset him. He prays to the god of respectability, you know."

"But what about you, Francesca? Somehow I don't think you care much about respectability. You stride about the moors like a wild Gypsy, and go out in London in disguise to places no respectable woman would venture. What would your uncle say to that?"

Her wide, warm, kissable mouth turned up. "He would be furious," she said with delight.

He groaned aloud, and abandoning all common sense and professionalism, he kissed her.

She was still for a heartbeat, and then her lips clung to his, and she pressed against him with all the wild passion in her nature. He knew then he'd wanted this to happen ever since the night in the inn. He'd felt only half alive without her—she was in his blood.

"Let me take you somewhere," he began, breathless, half crazy with lust. His lips trailed over her throat and she arched her neck, her eyes closed, her lips swollen. He untied the hideous bonnet and tossed it out of the window and into the street.

She didn't appear to notice.

"But . . . where would we go?" she asked, wriggling closer, her arms sliding up around his neck.

"I have rooms in Half Moon Street," he said, and gave her the number. Martin could be sent off on an errand, and then they'd be alone. Be damned to everything else!

But she was shaking her head.

"I want you. You want me. Remember how it was . . . ?"

"I don't want to remember," she gasped, as he pressed his lips to the creamy skin revealed above the neckline of her dress. It wasn't enough; he wanted her naked.

"Francesca." He was kissing her mouth again. "I'm losing my mind. Feel me . . . I want you now . . ."

He laid her hand between his thighs and then wondered why he was torturing himself with her touch.

"I've been like that since the inn."

She giggled, damn and blast her! "Oh dear, that must be inconvenient," she said breathily.

"Francesca . . ."

"I'm sorry." She drew her hand away and moved back into her seat, away from him.

"You're a free spirit, Francesca. Don't let them tame you. Let me set you free of your cage." He sounded like a madman, but he didn't care. She wasn't swayed.

"No!" She was shaking her head, her eyes were wide and dark and frightened, and all humor was gone from her face. "Don't you see?" she said, and her voice sounded raw and painful. "That's what frightens me the most. Sebastian, I can't afford to be a free spirit. I can't afford to leave my . . . my cage, as you call it. It isn't safe for me."

He didn't understand. All he wanted to do was touch her again, run his fingertips over her soft skin, and then kiss her until she forgot about everything but being with him. Why couldn't it be that simple? Why did they have to think about the future?

"Go. Please."

"Francesca," he tried one more time, and he sounded as raw as she.

"No, Sebastian." She wanted to deny the night in the inn had ever existed. He was confused by her.

One moment she didn't seem to care a hoot about Victorian respectability, and the next she was pushing him away as if she was frightened of him. Of herself.

There was something here he wasn't seeing properly, and perhaps if he discovered what it was, she would be his again.

Reluctantly, Sebastian climbed down from the hackney. "Drive on," he told the driver curtly, ignoring the man's smirk. The vehicle began to move off, one of the iron-framed wheels rumbling over Francesca's bonnet, still lying on the road.

Sebastian left it there.

"This is your mess, you clean it up."

He felt distaste sour in his mouth. Angela Slater was like a parasite, like something that, once fastened into his flesh, could never be gotten rid of. In a weak moment, a moment of desperation, he'd used her to escape a tricky problem, and he'd regretted that weakness bitterly ever since.

Would he go to his grave with this creature and her cohorts?

She smiled, and despite the changes in her, it was the same sly and wicked smile, and no doubt the same sharp intelligence behind it. She'd read his mind, and it gave him an uncomfortable shiver to know it.

"No, no, my fine gentleman," she crooned, "you are in this up to your neck."

"The girl means nothing to you. You have plenty more. Forget her."

"But I can't. I have a reputation to maintain. No one steals from me, especially not one of them chits I kidnapped for you all those years ago. That's who did it. Miss Francesca Greentree. And she's taken the child to her mother for safekeeping. Now isn't *that* a fine joke?"

"Angela—"

"I know the truth of what happened, and why. Oh yes, I know why. I can tell, and I have lots of friends. And I have the letter. Don't think of turning your back on me, sir."

The cursed letter! What he'd like to do was take her skinny throat in his hands and squeeze. He'd never been a violent man, but she had driven him to it. But, pleasurable though it might be, killing her would do him no good. There were others to take her place, and no doubt they would see that her death was avenged. Besides, he'd never get the letter if she was dead.

"I'm not turning my back," he said, as if he'd never thought of it. "I have as much to lose as you."

"So will you see to Miss Francesca, or do you want me to do it?"

The evil in her was a palpable thing—fascinating.

"It may come to that, but not yet."

If necessary he would be ruthless and deal with Francesca Greentree, but first there was someone else to tackle. Someone even more dangerous than Francesca—someone who knew the whole truth and suspected the rest. All these years he had watched her and waited to see when she would make her move, but she'd stayed silent. Until now.

"She's hired Thorne to try and flush me out," he said bitterly.

"Has she now?" Her voice was even more slurred than the last time he'd visited, something that had become increasingly noticeable with the advance of her illness. "After all this time."

"She knows what'll happen to her now. She must know. And yet still she did it. To be honest, I never thought she would. She had her suspicions but no proof."

Mrs. Slater chuckled. "You sound almost as if you admire her for it. She knew what would happen if she took this step, so she's only got herself to blame. Brave of her, yes, but reckless." Her watery eyes grew bright with mockery. "Are you still in love with her? I remember you were, once."

He didn't answer. Denial would only encourage her. And anyway, there was a time when he'd been extremely fond of Aphrodite. More than fond, he admitted reluctantly. She'd filled his thoughts and his heart—she'd been an obsession that had nearly killed him.

Now he was planning to kill her.

It seemed like revenge, but he decided it was justice.

Chapter 16

Sebastian strode along briskly, barely registering his surroundings. His heart was still rattling in his chest, the blood pounding through his body. Francesca tended to do that to him.

Dobson let him into the club with a surprised frown. "Madame Aphrodite is tired, Mr. Thorne. Do you have to see her now?"

"I'm sorry. It's important."

Dobson hesitated and then gave a resigned nod. "You won't keep her long?"

"Barely any time at all, Mr. Dobson."

Once he was shown into her presence, Aphrodite seemed pleased to see him, but then she was a good actress. "Mr. Thorne, again!" She must have seen something in his face, and her smile wavered. "What has happened?"

Sebastian explained about Rosie and where she had come from.

"Then . . . this girl belongs to *her*?" She was obviously shocked; her hand trembled as she rested it against the chair back.

"Yes. And Mrs. Slater will want her back."

"But why can't she be arrested for such a thing? And the kidnapping all those years ago . . . Mr. Thorne, if you know where she is, then we must . . . we must . . ."

"I don't know where she is, not yet. And if, when I do, I take her to the police, that means we probably won't be able to find her master. She'll keep her mouth shut in the hope he'll help her out of her difficulty— which he probably will. Madame, you do still want to find the name of the man who arranged to kidnap your daughters?"

Aphrodite nodded.

"Then can you send Rosie somewhere else? Just to be on the safe side? I'm sure you don't want Mrs. Slater knocking at your door."

"My daughter has asked me to care for Rosie. She has asked *me*, Mr. Thorne. I will not break my promise to her, no matter what it costs me. And as for Mrs. Slater . . . if she comes to my door I will see her in hell."

"Madame . . ."

Her gaze was firm and direct, and any arguments he had dried up unspoken. Aphrodite might have been slow to take action, but now she would not be swayed from her course, even if it meant she was heading into disaster.

It was Sebastian's job to avert that disaster.

"You are protecting my daughter?" Aphrodite's urgent question interrupted his thoughts.

"Yes, Madame, I am."

"I am glad you were with her when she saved Rosie. It was a wonderful thing she did, but she must not be allowed to risk herself again."

"I told her not to, but . . ." He shrugged. "Your daughter is headstrong, Madame."

Aphrodite smiled. "She followed her heart. That isn't bad, that is good. She should do it more often, instead of playing the part of Miss Respectability."

He laughed. "I wish she would," he said. If her heart led her into his arms and his bed, then he'd be very happy.

Perhaps something of his thoughts showed on his face, or perhaps Aphrodite was especially intuitive, because she reached out and pressed her fingertip to his chest. "Are you sure it's not *your* heart we're discussing, Mr. Thorne? My daughter is a beautiful young woman. It would be a shame if she lived her life alone because she was afraid to love."

He smiled, but his eyes were bleak. "I have no heart, Madame. I cut it out years ago."

"Then I pity you," she said quietly. "Because without love, Mr. Thorne, we may as well be dead."

Francesca awoke to the sounds of London. She'd been having a wonderful dream. Sebastian Thorne had climbed up the wall outside her window and in through the dusty panes. She had felt his hands on her, sure and strong, as his body moved with hers. Now she felt flushed and warm, tingling in places she hadn't known could tingle.

She missed him, and that frightened her. There was a yearning within her to be in his company, to seek him out, to go to his rooms in Half Moon Street. Aphrodite would have done such a thing; she would have abandoned everything for love, and ended up with nothing. And that was why Francesca couldn't.

With a groan, she sat up in the dawn light. She needed to escape this place as soon as possible, and return to the moors where she was safe. *He* was here in London. And although Francesca kept telling herself that she would continue to resist him with all her might, she knew that when she was with him it wasn't that simple. She didn't trust him . . . she didn't trust herself.

Perhaps if she'd married some safe, dull gentleman she wouldn't have this problem. However tempted she might be by Sebastian, her marriage vows would have stopped her from throwing caution to the winds. Why hadn't she wed? But Francesca knew why. She hadn't been able to bear resigning herself to a loveless marriage. It would be worse than remaining a spinster and never knowing love at all, but she'd been prepared to do so . . . until she met Sebastian.

Now she was so confused, she didn't know what to do. Either way she was going to be hurt.

Ask Aphrodite. She'll understand. She'll know the answer.

The voice in her head shocked her. She didn't doubt that her mother would understand, but as to knowing the answer . . . Aphrodite hadn't been able to organize her own life; how could she help her daughter?

Washed and dressed, Francesca went downstairs to breakfast. Yesterday they had visited Trafalgar Square and taken tea with an old acquaintance of her mother's. Amy was already busily planning this day's activities, filling up every moment so that she couldn't miss her husband.

She looked up at Francesca with a smile. "Francesca, there you are! Today we are taking Helen shopping with us."

"Mama, please, I really don't need a new wardrobe."

Amy raised an eyebrow. "I was thinking of myself, my dear. You wouldn't deny me the pleasure of your company, surely?"

Francesca wouldn't, of course, but she strongly suspected it was one of Amy's ploys to "smarten her up."

"Mrs. Jardine. Miss Francesca. Good morning." Mrs. March appeared in the doorway to the breakfast room, her face as impassive as ever. Her glance flicked to Francesca, and she gave the faintest of smiles. Since Rosie's departure, and her own victory, she seemed to have grown in confidence.

"Good morning, Mrs. March," Amy replied sweetly. "We will be going out this morning and may not be back until this evening. We have a great deal to do. Will you tell my brother?"

"In fact, Mr. Tremaine asked me to inform you that he will be at his club this evening."

"Oh, I see."

"Mr. Tremaine is a very busy man."

"I'm sure there will be plenty of other occasions when my brother and I can chat."

Mrs. March looked as if she doubted it, but she didn't comment and left the room as regally as a ship in full sail.

"William seems to be making himself scarce," Amy said, reaching for more toast. "Anyone would think he didn't want to repair our relationship."

"He'll come around, Mama."

"I hope so. I mean to win this war between us, Francesca."

"Speaking of wars . . . I have the distinct impression that Mrs. March is fighting one with us for possession of Uncle William. Is he such a prize, Mama?"

"She may be concerned about her position in the household, my dear, that's all. Being a servant can be tenuous, and I imagine she has seen many others come and go. My brother is an exacting man with a fiery temper."

"I shouldn't think she'd have to worry about him bringing a wife home just now, not if his behavior the other night, when you mentioned it, is anything to go by. He's a confirmed bachelor. Surely that is every housekeeper's dream?"

Amy sighed. "Francesca, William is quite a catch. And he's had his fair share of amours," she added, and laughed when she saw the expression on her daughter's face. "You're surprised! But it is so; in fact, William considered himself quite the ladies' man when he was younger."

"Please, Mama, stop. The thought of Uncle William breaking hearts is making me feel quite ill."

"I don't know why, you silly child." She paused and grew thoughtful. "Though now I come to think of it, Thomas was the real heartbreaker, not William. The ladies always fell for Thomas. It wasn't his fault—he just seemed to draw them like flies to jam—but it was another reason for William to dislike his elder brother. How I wish . . ."

Amy was growing maudlin. Francesca decided it was time to cheer her up. "Hurry up, Mama! We are going shopping, remember? Finish your tea and toast."

Amy's eyes lit up, and she cast a speaking glance over her daughter's dowdy ensemble. "So we are."

"I know of a new modiste," Helen informed them when they arrived in Bloomsbury to collect her. "She's quite the rage."

Francesca was relieved to discover that Toby was out, visiting a dentist. He'd been suffering with a troublesome tooth but had refused to have it seen to until he found a modern-thinking dentist, one who used ether to reduce the pain. Toby was never one to suffer if he could help it.

"I thought only Her Majesty uses ether, when she—"

"Why, anyone can use it," Helen broke in, "not just women in childbirth." She sat back in the carriage, fussing with her gloves. "Have you seen the latest fashions, Amy? I have a copy of the *Ladies' Gazette of Fashion* you must look through. There is a style that would have looked splendid on me when I was a young girl." Poor Helen looked momentarily woebegone, before shaking off the past. "I am too long in the tooth for that now, of course, but what I meant to say was that I am quite certain it will suit Francesca very well."

Francesca's heart sank down to her boots. She could just imagine herself in the sort of frilly, frothy, girlish outfits Helen would favor; all ribbons and flounces. "Under no circumstances," she whispered to Amy, as Helen rambled on about an assembly she'd once attended at Almack's and what she'd worn.

"Now, my dear," Amy murmured in reply, "we all have to make sacrifices. Poor Helen needs cheering up and it's our job to do it, even if it means buying an entire new wardrobe of pretty dresses."

Regent Street, with its plate-glass windows, was the premier shopping street in London, but there was also Burlington Arcade, with small dressmakers' shops and specialty shops. There was so much to see that despite herself, Francesca was tingling with excitement, but most of the time she was kept too busy listening to Amy and Helen chatter and trying to prevent them from getting lost among the splendors of fashion.

She wasn't sure when she first noticed the man. He was leaning against the wall in one of the smaller arcades, and he had sandy hair and was wearing a brown jacket. Tall and gangly, he had the air of someone with time on his hands. There was nothing special about him, nothing that should have drawn her attention, except that when their eyes met, he immediately turned his back and pretended to peer into a window full of confectionary.

The next moment Helen was diving into a glove-maker's, giggling like a girl, and when Francesca glanced around again for the man he was gone. For some reason she wasn't relieved, and she began to take more notice of her surroundings.

Several shops later, she thought she saw him again on the other side of the street, but it was only his back in the brown jacket. *You're being ridiculous*, she told herself. *He's probably waiting for his wife and spending his time ogling other women. You're making something of nothing, and all because Sebastian frightened you with his tales of dangerous people.*

Just then Helen fell into raptures yet again, this time over some millinery in the window of Swan and Edgar, calling for their opinion on one of the new straw bonnets with the rounded shape and horizontal crown. Suddenly Francesca was weary of the expedition. She quite liked the bonnets, but what was the use in giving her opinion, when neither Helen nor Amy listened to it anyway? She strolled farther down the street and stopped in front of a haberdasher's.

A bolt of rose red satin seemed to jump out at her.

Francesca gave a groan of sheer feminine pleasure.

"Oh, how pretty!" Amy was at her side.

"Yes." She glanced back toward the milliner's. "Is Aunt Helen finished swooning over those bonnets?"

"Not quite. That color would suit you very well, you know," Amy announced, tucking her hand into Francesca's arm and leading her inside.

"Mama . . ." she protested, but her voice was weak from exhaustion and a sudden desire to own the rose silk. She could imagine the expression on Sebastian's face, when he . . . *if* he saw her in a dress made up from it.

"The pale blue crepe, too," Amy was directing an assistant who had coming hurrying to serve them. "And I think . . . yes, lace for an overskirt, and ribbons, and . . ."

It was pointless protesting. Amy was like a railway train, sweeping away all in her path. In no time Francesca found herself being bustled onto the premises of a supercilious-looking modiste, and Amy and Helen were engaged in a series of discussions on style and cut, and the short sleeves as opposed to those with a fall of lace to the elbow.

"She's not *petit*," the modiste announced, sharp eyes taking in every detail of Francesca's figure.

Francesca opened her mouth to argue—*My mother calls me* petit chaton—and then realizing what she was going to say, closed it again.

"With such a striking figure, she needs to make something of herself. Her height, her waist and bosom and hips, are all to be put on show. No frills and clusters of ribbons. No fussy little prints. She would look ridiculous. Colors that complement her dark hair and eyes, and that flawless creamy skin. Necklines to show to best advantage her excellent bosom. Stiffened petticoats to hold out her skirts and accentuate her tiny waist."

Francesca wanted to squirm, but at the same time she knew that the modiste was right. This was a woman of good sense, even if she did lack tact. Why pretend she was petite like Helen and Marietta? She was a statuesque woman, like Vivianna; one who would always stand out in a crowd. It was the truth and she should make the most of it.

"She will need gloves, bonnets, stockings, drawers, chemises, stays, petticoats, boots, shoes and evening slippers." Helen began listing them off on her fingers, her eyes shining with excitement. "Oh dear, I haven't had this much fun in ages!"

At that moment any last protests Francesca might have voiced died on her lips. How could she be churlish when Amy and Helen were having such a marvelous time? And what harm could it do? She might—she realized with a tremble of excitement—even enjoy herself. It would be a change to wear clothes that enhanced her best features, rather than hiding them. Mrs. Hall, the seamstress in the village, seemed to have only two dress sizes—big and bigger.

By the time they were finished, Francesca was dizzy from looking at so many patterns and standing still, or turning around, while she was poked and prodded, draped and pinned. Altogether she was to have six new dresses, and a rose red satin ball gown. Francesca, who had never had a ball gown, wasn't quite certain what she was going to do with one now, but she had an uncomfortable feeling that Amy and Helen did.

She'd forgotten about the loose-limbed man with the sandy hair, but as they were leaving the modiste's establishment, she saw him again. This time he was standing by a drinking fountain, and he was looking directly at her. There was no possible doubt about it.

Fear crept over her with spidery fingers.

Once again he looked away, pretending to be interested in a smart pair of horses pulling a barouche. But Francesca wasn't deceived. All Sebastian's warnings came back to her in a rush. She hadn't listened to him, not really. She hadn't believed him. Oh, why hadn't she believed him?

She turned, looking about her, and saw that there were plenty of shoppers in the street. It was three o'clock in the afternoon and everyone was going about his tasks in an ordinary manner. She was safe; no one could hurt her in such a public place. Who had ever heard of a woman being kidnapped in Regent Street during the most fashionable hour for shopping?

The realization calmed her.

"I think that will do for today," Amy was saying. "Unless you've changed your mind about those other silk stockings, Helen?"

"No, I think I will leave them, Amy. Toby is certain to make a fuss if I buy more than *one* pair."

"If Toby can find the money for a dentist who uses ether, then you can certainly have more than one pair of stockings!" Amy retorted sharply.

"Amy, he's not as bad as you think."

"He is, Helen." Amy must have been tired, to have said such a thing. Usually she displayed more tact.

Helen chewed her lip, giving her sister a guilty glance. "I know he's not perfect," she said tentatively, "but I haven't always been the perfect wife, either."

"Nonsense," Amy retorted, still with less than her

usual discretion. "You are far too good for him, Helen. He is a fortunate man to have you."

Helen's eyes widened and, to Francesca's horror, filled with tears. "You don't understand. I've been a very bad wife to Toby. I don't know how he puts up with me."

"Helen?" Amy gasped, as shocked as Francesca. "What do you mean?"

Helen had a hectic flush in her cheeks. "It was years ago," she murmured, fanning herself with her hand, "and I promised I would never speak of it, so I'm afraid I cannot."

"Promised Toby?" Amy asked, bewildered. "What are you talking about?"

"Toby and William," Helen said, and then shook her head and closed her lips firmly, as if she had said too much.

"You really are infuriating, Helen." Amy sighed. "And no matter what you say, I shall never believe you have done anything bad."

But Helen didn't answer her, and the journey back to the Russell house in Queen's Square seemed an anticlimax after the excitement of the day.

"I wonder what on earth Helen believes she did that was so terrible she must never speak of it," Amy mused later, when they were alone in the carriage. "I thought running off with Toby was the worst mistake she could have made."

"If Uncle William knows and has sworn her to silence, then it must be scandalous."

"Yes," Amy murmured. She rested her hand over her eyes, as if it was suddenly all too much for her.

Francesca reached to touch her arm. "You have a headache, Mama. Why don't you go up and take a rest before supper? I'm sure Mrs. March won't mind holding back the meal."

Amy spread her fingers and gave her a droll look.

Francesca laughed, and at that moment she happened to glance out of the window. The carriage had become snarled in a traffic jam between a cart and an omnibus. No wonder so many people preferred to walk, she was thinking; it was far quicker. And then he was there, the man with the sandy hair. He was standing on the corner opposite them, and he was staring at their carriage.

There could be no mistake this time. He was following her, watching her. *Pursuing her.* Francesca knew this was too important and too dangerous for her to take matters into her own hands. Besides, what would she do? She needed help from someone who was familiar with the dangerous and turbulent world she seemed to have entered. Someone who fit in perfectly.

She needed Sebastian.

Chapter 17

As soon as Amy had gone upstairs to rest, Francesca went in search of Lil.

"How is Rosie?"

"She's havin' a lovely time," Lil said with a smile. "Madame's girls are all spoilin' her rotten." Her expression turned anxious. "You don't think that her aunt can take her back, do you? After what she did, trying to sell her?"

"Has Rosie asked for her?"

"No, not once."

"Then I don't think we should worry about it. The aunt obviously is not a suitable person to care for a child. Rosie is better off with us." She paused before she went on. "Lil, have you seen anyone around the club who is acting suspiciously?"

Lil smiled. "Miss, you are talking about Aphrodite's Club. To my mind there're a lot of suspicious gentlemen around that place. Is there anyone in particular . . . ?"

"No, it was just a thought. Never mind."

But Francesca was more worried than she let on to Lil. Sebastian's warnings and now the sandy-haired stranger were playing on her mind, and she felt guilty and concerned that she'd endangered those closest to her by her actions, well-intentioned as they were. What if these people had discovered where Rosie was hidden? What if they decided to take her back? Kidnap her?

Dobson! Francesca remembered with relief. It would be difficult for them to get past Dobson. But her relief faded; Dobson was only one man. There was no time to waste.

"I'm going to see Mr. Thorne in Half Moon Street."

Lil's face was a picture. "Miss!"

"I have to. It's urgent, Lil. I'm worried . . . about Rosie."

Lil considered that, but she wasn't mollified. "And I suppose you think you're going on your own?"

"Lil, I am perfectly capable of—"

"I'm coming with you, miss. I'm not making the same mistake with you that I made with your sisters."

Francesca sighed, irritated and amused at the same

time. "Lil, I am twenty-five years old and far too old to require a chaperone."

"No respectable man will want you if your honor is besmirched," Lil said knowledgeably.

"Good heavens! Do I care?" She rolled her eyes.

"That's what Miss Vivianna and Miss Marietta said," Lil said darkly. "And they did care, eventually. I'm waiting to see what happens when their children grow up. You can be sure they won't want them up to the games they played!" Lil was enjoying herself. "Oh yes, those little ones will lead them a merry dance, you mark my words."

Francesca decided it wasn't worth arguing with her when she was in this moralizing mood. "I'll go and change into my new dress and we can set off."

Lil narrowed her eyes. "What new dress?"

"The modiste was able to fit one she already had made up. It only needed a few tucks here and there."

"And why are you wearing this new dress to Mr. Thorne's rooms?"

"Lil, even I know that men are much more likely to agree to a woman's wishes if she's looking her best. And Mr. Thorne is a man, after all."

"He's a villain, miss."

Francesca smiled. "Yes, he is, isn't he?"

Lil shot her a despairing look and muttered, "Just like the other two."

They walked to Half Moon Street. It was only a short distance, and after the ride home in the carriage, Francesca felt she'd had enough of the noise and dust of London's streets. Perhaps it was being able to walk freely, or perhaps it was the new dress, but Francesca was feeling very pleased with the world and everyone in it.

Which was strange, when there was danger all around her.

But she'd decided that a little danger was actually stimulating to the heart and brain. And, in a purely feminine way, she enjoyed the swish of her turquoise moiré dress and her five petticoats. Certainly the few gentlemen who passed them noticed her, all of them tipping their hats. One of them ogled her in a startling manner, until Lil gave him a glare and sent him on his way.

Perhaps I am turning into a Londoner, with nothing in my head but the latest fashions? But it was more to do with herself than London. She'd changed. And she had the feeling that was to do with Mr. Thorne.

"You look very happy, miss," Lil said, suspicious, as they reached the building containing Mr. Thorne's rooms.

"Do I, Lil?"

"You be careful, Miss Francesca," her maid warned her.

But Francesca wasn't listening. She had already begun to climb the stairs to the front door.

Sebastian had spent a wasted afternoon watching one of Mrs. Slater's other houses. After another conversation with Dipper, he'd made his way to Hackney. Dipper believed Mrs. Slater lived here, in a sober-looking house with curtained windows, although she was rarely seen. Her neighbors knew her as Mrs. Brown.

If she was here, Sebastian didn't see her. She might well have gone into hiding, warned that he was seeking her. By the spy who had given him away in the first place. He had yet to discover the identity of that person, but he had his suspicions. That was the reason he'd set Pretty Polly on the trail.

Dipper was as proud as punch. "Yer'll see, guv'ner, she'll find yer snitch for yer."

Sebastian was just preparing to go out again, to see how Pretty Polly was managing, and then to hunt up another acquaintance who owed him a favor, when there was a knock on the door.

Sebastian frowned.

Martin, his manservant, had yet to return from his own assignment, and Sebastian kept only one servant. He rented these rooms, and they were large and comfortable, but most important of all, they were private. He rarely gave out his address because he didn't like visitors. He didn't trust many people enough to tell them where he lived.

The knock came again, this time more vigorously, as if whoever was out there was determined to be let in. He put his eye to the hole he'd had drilled through the wood for the purpose of inspecting his callers. It gave him a clear view of his visitor.

Sebastian's mouth twitched upward.

Miss Francesca Greentree, looking extremely attractive in a dress the color of a tropical sea, with her dark hair swept up under a fetching straw bonnet. If he wasn't very greatly mistaken, she had been touched by the hand of a London modiste. Had she come to dazzle him with her new finery?

Well, he was dazzled.

He opened the door.

Her bright eyes widened. Those beautiful lips parted in a half smile, as if she were mocking him, or herself, or both of them. "Mr. Thorne," she said in her melodious voice. "I find I need your help after all."

He bowed and stepped back to allowed her entry. Lil, her maid, trailed after her. At least she'd the sense to bring a chaperone. After the kiss in the hackney cab, Sebastian didn't trust himself alone with her, but he relished the challenge.

"Come in and sit down, Miss Greentree. Tell me what's troubling you."

She was examining her surroundings. The sitting room was furnished with some of his favorite pieces, and she paused a moment in front of the Gainsborough, admiring his grandmother.

"What a beautiful woman."

"Yes."

"She looks like you," she said, narrowing her eyes at him.

"Oh?"

He could see her watching him, considering whether it was polite to ask more questions. She changed her mind, perching herself on a straight-backed chair and folding her hands neatly in her lap.

"Someone is following me."

His gaze sharpened. "When did this happen?"

"We went shopping in Regent Street today . . ."

He smiled, letting his gaze run over her just enough to annoy her. "I noticed."

She flushed and a crease appeared between her brows, but she didn't drop her gaze from his. "He was also in the street on our way home. He was watching me. I'm not mistaken and it couldn't be a coincidence."

"Did he threaten you? Do you think he meant you any harm?"

"I don't know. That's why I am here, Mr. Thorne. You seemed to believe I was in danger, and you're the expert."

"Ah, now I'm an expert."

She shifted uncomfortably. "I never disputed that, Mr. Thorne. I'm sure you're very good at what you do."

He leaned forward, keeping his eyes on hers. "Oh, I am. Very good."

Fascinating. She seemed unable to look away from him. She'd done that before. He wondered what she was thinking, and whether they were the same hot, dark imaginings that he had when he gazed into her eyes. Despite what she'd said last time, nothing had changed. They were meant for each other.

The tap on the door startled them, and she blinked as the spell was broken, and then turned as the key rattled in the lock.

"Well, that was a complete and utter waste of time," Martin declared loudly, as he erupted into the room, all long legs and arms. And then he froze, mouth and eyes wide, like a dying fish.

Lil gave a little scream, and Francesca rose to her feet.

Martin swallowed, his prominent Adam's apple bobbing up and down. "Excuse me, ladies. I didn't realize you had company, sir."

"Martin, I have a feeling you are already known to these ladies, but I'll introduce you anyway. Miss Greentree and Lil, this is my manservant and partner in business, Martin O'Donnelly."

Francesca turned accusing eyes on him. "This is the man I saw!"

"Martin has been following you when I am otherwise engaged, Miss Greentree. You must understand, I can't be everywhere at once. I am a busy man."

Her gaze narrowed.

"I trust Martin completely. You are safe in his hands."

He could see she was burning to give him a good rollicking, and he took pity on her. "Martin," he said, "take Lil for a little walk. Please."

At once Lil began to protest, but after a quick look at his master, Martin took her arm firmly in his and led her toward the door. "Come on now, Lil, we're servants and we have to do as we're told. Anyway, it's a beautiful day, so why not enjoy it?"

The door closed, and their steps, and Lil's protests, faded.

"Now," Sebastian said, "Francesca. Is there something you want to say to me . . . ?"

She was standing over him, gloved fingers clenched, her body so taut she looked like she might burst with the effort of holding in her anger. He knew that, if he was a gentleman, he would stand, too. But he wasn't, so he didn't.

"You should have told me about him! I was terrified!"

Sebastian leaned back. "Terrified? Francesca, I don't believe you know what terrified is."

"Terrified for my family," she qualified, her voice trembling with the effort to subdue her emotions. "I've brought danger upon them. It's up to me to protect them. That's why I came here today—for their sake, not mine."

She was magnificent. He watched her struggle with her temper and decided at that moment that he wanted to see her lose it. He wanted to see her fly her cage. "Very noble," Sebastian murmured, and smiled a mocking smile.

He saw the lightning flash of fury in her eyes, and then, like the storm they had been caught in the first time they met, the emotion poured out of her. "You wouldn't know what noble was," she burst out. "You are a man who cares for nothing but the money he makes from his unfortunate and desperate clients. How else could you afford this?" She waved her arm wildly at his room and what was in it.

"You're quite right. I'm everything you say I am. But you need me, Francesca."

"I could hire a man off the street," she retorted, her face flushed. "I don't need you!"

He stood up, so abruptly that she stepped back with a gasp. "But you do. You need me. You want me, Francesca."

"No," she groaned. "No, no, no!"

He smiled. "We're alone, there's no one here to see or hear. Tell me why you really came. Or better still . . . show me."

She opened her mouth, closed it, and then launched herself at him. She was warm and soft and all woman, and he groaned as her mouth searched for his, bumping his nose with her chin until she got it right. His eyes watered. Her bonnet was in the way, and he removed it. She clutched at his shoulders, and then his hair, pulling him closer. Fire ran through his veins like a lit fuse, and he felt himself grow instantly hard.

She was like a tigress in his arms, unrestrained, almost savage. Was this the proper Miss Greentree? No, it was Francesca, full of twenty-five years of passion, and now it was bursting to get out. Sebastian had no intention of bringing her to her senses. This was his chance to take what he wanted.

"Come into the bedchamber," he said, walking backward, half leading her, half carrying her.

The bedchamber was even more private than the sitting room. A magical place of color and light, it was his sanctuary against this world he had chosen as his own.

She was still clinging to him, her mouth hot and moist against his throat as she planted kisses wherever she could. "Let me," he whispered, his hands delving for the buttons on her dress.

"It opens at the back," she gasped.

He spun her around and dealt with the fastenings, planting kisses on her nape, then down her spine as each inch of skin was revealed. She trembled and shook as if she were ill, as if she had a fever. Her gown sagged, slipping down her arms, and he helped it, releasing her wrists and hands from the cloth. He ran his hands around her, reaching to cup her breasts above her stays, and she groaned, leaning back against him, her head resting on his shoulder, her throat arched.

Her mouth was close enough for him to turn his head slightly and take it with his. She covered his hands with her own, pressing his palms against her flesh. He could feel the hard nubs of her nipples.

"My stays," she breathed, her chest heaving. "I feel light-headed."

"That's me," he teased, but began hastily to release her from the lacing. He tossed the garment onto the floor, and turning her in his arms, admired her naked breasts. "Oh yes," he whispered, and bent his head so that he drew the nipples of first one breast and then the other into his mouth.

She was sensitive and she enjoyed it. Her fingers dug into his shoulders, before she decided that it was time for him to remove his clothing.

"This doesn't mean anything," she told him breathlessly, wrenching at his coat.

"You're right. Not a thing."

"It's a physical reaction. Any animal can experience it."

"Lust, pure and simple."

The bed was a four-poster with draperies drifting

about it and a bright quilt. She pushed him down onto it and flung herself on top of him. Her mouth brushed his. She was still clothed from the waist down in her petticoats, and they formed a frothy barrier between him and what he wanted. He ran his hands up under them, cupping her bottom through her drawers.

She straddled him. He found the opening in her drawers, delving into the heat of her. She gasped and wriggled against him, her hair falling in thick, loose curls about her. "Beautiful," he whispered. He stroked her slowly, caressing her toward completion. Francesca cried out, her body clenching, carried away with her pleasure in such a natural and unembarrassed way that he was charmed.

Here was truly a woman whose passions ruled her—if she would allow them to.

He kissed her, murmuring reassurance as he tenderly rolled her over. Her body was pliant and warm, her eyes half closed and sleepy as she gazed up at him, her hair a cloud about her. "Sebastian," she whispered, with a catch in her voice. "Oh, Sebastian."

He smiled, gently raising her skirts, and fitting himself between her thighs. He watched her face as he entered, pressing deep into her hot, slippery body. It was better than last time, and he had to fight to keep control of the urge to plunder her like the raiders of old.

She didn't help, clutching him with her thighs and her arms, gasping and crying out. In the end the pleasure snuck up on him, like the storm in which they'd first met, leaving them both shuddering and exhausted.

Her eyes were wide open, gazing up at the canopy. She turned her head to inspect the furnishings and the wall hangings. "This is a beautiful room," she murmured. "It's like a robber baron's cave."

"I promise you, nothing here is stolen," he said, but in a way that made her wonder differently. He reached out to smooth her cheek with the backs of his fingers. "I'm glad you showed me why you came to see me, Francesca."

She bit his knuckle, her eyes sparkling. "You are wicked, Sebastian, and you make me wicked, too."

"Not wicked. I allow you to be free to be yourself."

Her expression sobered and she sat up, her hair covering her shoulders and breasts. "It was true, you know. I am worried about my family. I have placed them in danger, and now it's up to me to make them safe."

"I'm already watching over you, Francesca . . ."

"I don't want you to. At least not without payment. I want to hire you. I want to *pay* you."

"No," he said, and reached up to pull her down into his arms again. "This is payment enough."

Francesca was caught in a web and Sebastian was the spider. Why hadn't she resisted him? And that in itself was a laugh. *Resist!* She had done everything she could to have connection with him, behaved in a manner that was completely unlike her usual respectable self.

She shouldn't have come here. Why didn't she send Lil? Or better still, a note?

But she knew that it was easy to tell herself what she should and shouldn't have done, now that she was sated, and the boiling, writhing emotions that Sebastian stirred within her had calmed to a millpond. Of course it wouldn't last. Already she could feel little ripples forming beneath the surface.

Francesca began to dress, accepting his help without a word.

"Will you come again?" he asked her levelly, when she was clothed in everything but her straw bonnet.

Francesca laughed weakly. "I don't know; I wish I did. I don't seem to know what I'm doing from one moment to the next."

"My love," he murmured, and tucked her wild hair behind her ear.

She looked up at him, as if unable to do otherwise, and tears filled her eyes. "I knew you were a danger to me from the moment I first met you," she said. "I tried to drive you away, but you refused to listen. I only stayed with you at the inn because you promised you were leaving. I didn't expect to see you again."

"You saved my life, Francesca. I don't want you to go away. I want to make love to you forever."

"I can't allow that," she said in a brittle voice. "You don't know what you're asking."

"Damn and blast it, every second day then!"

She pulled away. "I blame Aphrodite for this," she said bitterly.

He seemed taken aback. "Why?"

Dramatically, Francesca paused at the door. "Because I am her daughter," she said.

Chapter 18

"**M**iss Francesca," Lil began, her eyes suspicious. She'd been waiting downstairs with Martin.

"Don't, Lil."

But Lil couldn't be stopped, and she followed Francesca out into the street. It was later than she had thought, the long summer evening beginning to fade. "You be careful, that's all I want to say," Lil said.

"Be careful?" Francesca repeated, feeling slightly hysterical. "I thought I was being careful, Lil, but somehow it went wrong."

"Well, sometimes things happen. Men have a way of making them happen," she added darkly.

"As much as it would make me feel better, Lil, I

can't allow Mr. Thorne to take all the blame for his actions. It was my fault, too."

Lil shrugged. "Have it your own way. Mar— Mr. O'Donnelly says that Mr. Thorne isn't what he seems, but I don't believe a word either of them says. Peas in a pod, those two."

Francesca frowned. "What did you and Martin get up to, Lil? Perhaps it's you who should be careful."

"Nothing, miss. We walked around about and he bought me an ice. Very nice it was. But I'm not fooled by him. He's Irish, isn't he, and he's kissed the Blarney Stone." But there was a little smile playing at her mouth, the sort of smile Francesca hadn't seen on Lil in a very long time.

Mrs. March waylaid Francesca in the hall to tell her Mrs. Jardine had retired with a headache. "Will you be dining as usual?" Her cold gaze was taking note of the rumpled skirt and the untidy hair beneath the bonnet.

Self-consciously Francesca cleared her throat. Mrs. March could not possibly know what she'd been up to, but at that moment it seemed as if she did.

"Mr. Tremaine is dining at his club," the housekeeper added with a hint of impatience.

"Oh yes, of course. No, Mrs. March, I'll have something in my room. I am tired and I'll retire early."

"Very well."

Wearily, Francesca made her way to her room, but decided to check on Amy first. Her mother was pale but her headache was fading. She asked if Francesca could get her some sweet tea, because the beverage often helped.

"Of course." She reached out to ring for a servant, but Amy stopped her.

"Please, my dear, would you mind terribly going down to the kitchen to fetch it? The cook is a kindly sort of woman, and Mrs. March made such a fuss the last time I rang. The girls, she said, had enough to do with all the extra work I was causing."

Francesca was furious. The woman was insufferable! "She'd better not say anything to me," she declared, but for Amy's sake, she went back down the stairs to fetch the tea herself.

The cook was as kind as Amy said, and Francesca was soon on her way back with the tea and some sweet biscuits to tempt Amy's appetite. She was thinking of Sebastian. She admitted to being surprised by the unexpected luxury of his rooms in Half Moon Street—the carpets and hangings in deep rich colors. And the portrait that hung over the fireplace of the eighteenth-century woman in the white wig, with dark eyes so very like Sebastian's.

He must be her grandson or great-grandson, she realized, but the painting had been that of a gentlewoman, perhaps even a great lady. Was Sebastian the product of a liaison between an heir and a maid? Or had his branch of the family fallen low for one reason or another? Whatever the truth, the portrait meant something to him.

Francesca realized she had paused in the hall, beside a grandfather clock. As she made to move on, she heard voices farther along the corridor. One of the voices belonged to Mrs. March. Curiously, she made her way closer to the sounds, which she now realized were coming from the best sitting room. The door to the room was ajar, just enough to enable her to see the backs of Mrs. March and a dark-haired woman. There was something familiar about the second woman—her voice or the look of her—but even as Francesca struggled to recall where she'd seen her before, Mrs. March turned and spied her.

She was startled. "Miss Francesca!"

Francesca forced an innocent smile. "I was fetching tea for Mrs. Jardine. I went myself so as not to be a nuisance to the servants. I know how busy they are."

Mrs. March's nostrils flared. She gave a quick glance over her shoulder and then moved to fill the doorway, almost as if she meant to prevent Francesca from seeing the other woman. Anyway she, whoever she was, had moved toward the far corner and was lost in the shadows.

"Nevertheless, you should have rung for a servant," Mrs. March said coolly.

Francesca was sorely tempted, but she managed to control her tongue. "I must remember to do so next time. You have a visitor, Mrs. March?"

"Yes."

Francesca waited a beat, but Mrs. March was silent. "Good night, Miss Greentree," she said firmly, and she closed the door in Francesca's face.

"Miss Greentree has hired us to watch over her family," Sebastian said as Martin put his clothes away.

"That will be interesting," Martin replied with a comical look. "Does that mean we're working for

Miss Greentree or Madame Aphrodite? Or are we working for them both?"

"We're working for Aphrodite," Sebastian said, with a frown. "Miss Greentree only thinks we're working for her."

"Ah, I see." Martin grew thoughtful.

Sebastian wondered whether he did. Keeping Francesca safe was his main objective. It filled his head; it kept him awake at night. Today, when he'd held her in his arms, he'd felt the wildness in her, that primitive emotion he had known was there the first time he saw her. She kept it leashed but he had set it free, and she admitted that she couldn't think straight around him.

What would happen when Mrs. Slater was caught and her secrets were out in the open? Would Francesca still come to him? Or would she accuse him of duplicity and return to her lonely life on the moors?

Since she'd saved him from the mire, he couldn't remember what his life was like without her. The thought of being without her again unnerved him as it never had before, as if he'd shed the person he'd been for the past eight years, and become another. He'd begun to remember events, moments from his boyhood. He'd begun to remember Barbara, his sister.

It was Barbara who'd caused him to turn his back on all he'd known and become someone else. He'd been punishing himself. Was it possible to forgive himself after all, something he would never have believed when the tragedy happened? Would Barbara have forgiven him already, if she'd still been alive?

"Sir?"

He looked up, startled. "Sorry, Martin, I was miles away."

"Are you going out again tonight, sir?"

"Yes, Martin, I am. And so are you."

Martin sighed. "I thought I might be."

Helen arrived early the next morning, and she and Amy were closeted in the breakfast room. By the time Francesca came down—after another restless night— they were flushed and bright-eyed over breakfast, and obviously up to something.

"Please, I beg you, no more shopping," Francesca groaned. "As much as I love my new wardrobe, I don't think I would survive the experience."

Amy laughed. "No, my dear. But your Aunt Helen has had another wonderful idea, haven't you, Helen?"

Helen leaned forward excitedly. "Francesca, your mother and I wanted to do something to bring this old house to life again. It has been so long since your Uncle William held any sort of entertainment here . . ."

"I think the last truly memorable gathering was your coming-out ball, Helen." Amy gave her daughter a pleading glance.

"Yes." Helen sighed, and for a moment she fell silent, remembering.

"You must have looked a picture," Francesca said gently.

Helen smiled but shook her head. "This isn't about my coming-out ball. This is about you, Francesca. We want to throw a ball in your honor."

Francesca looked from Helen's excited face to Amy's hopeful one. "Oh no, I . . . I'm too old to come out!"

"I know that." Helen laughed. "It's not a coming-out ball, not as such. It's an—an introductory ball. To introduce you to London society!"

"*Oh please* . . ." Francesca groaned.

Amy poured her some tea and handed her the cup. "My dear, I know this isn't strictly what you prefer, all this fuss, but I'm asking you for my sake, for Helen's, for Mr. Jardine's, for Uncle William's! It seems such a perfect way to bring us all together. And Tremaine House can return to life again, and become the wonderful place it was when we were young."

Their eyes shone, their faces glowed.

Francesca sipped her tea, refusing to be won over so easily. They watched her without blinking, trying to guess what she was going to say. After a moment Helen grew impatient and began to speak, but Amy touched her arm and hushed her. Eventually Francesca set down her cup.

"I'll agree. But," she added loudly, when they tried to talk over her, "only if Uncle William does. After all, we can't hold a ball in his house if he refuses, can we?"

Helen clapped her hands together. "He will agree, I know he will!"

Amy appeared more uncertain.

Francesca tried not to feel relieved. She couldn't imagine Uncle William agreeing to a ball, especially one in her honor. Although it was a shame to disappoint the two older women, Francesca did not think she could survive it. A ball meant being thrust into London society, and then what next? A list of suitable beaus? No, Francesca didn't want to be remade in someone else's image. She was herself, for better or worse.

But her relief was short-lived.

"A ball!" William repeated, when he arrived at breakfast and Amy determinedly broached the subject. He didn't sound enthused.

"We used to have them, remember?" Amy said wryly. "The last time the house was full of guests was for Helen's coming out. How long ago was that, brother?"

Francesca watched them with interest, waiting for the shouting to begin. But to her amazement and horror, Uncle William grew maudlin.

"Helen was an angel that night."

"Thank you, William." Helen flushed with pleasure. "I did think I looked very well. The gown was—"

"You could have made a great match, you know. There were several very important gentlemen interested. But no, you had to go and spoil it all by running off with that half-wit Toby!"

"Francesca is not about to run off with anyone, William," Amy said quickly, to avert Helen's tears and William's bad temper. "But you never know, she may make just as good a marriage as her sisters." She gave Francesca a sharp glance, stifling any protests.

"Do you think so?" William gave Francesca a doubtful look. "She is pretty, I grant you, or would be if she would only leave off those frightful Yorkshire bags and wear something smart. Her manners . . . well, she can be opinionated, but all of your girls are, Amy. At least there is no scandal attached to her name. Yet!"

"I think Francesca could shine almost as brightly as Marietta," Amy said slyly.

"Max Valland will be a duke one day," William followed on with her train of thought. "But an earl would be acceptable. Is that what you mean, an earl?" His eyebrows rose. "Well, I suppose anything is possible. What do you say to that, girl? Do you have an earl hidden up your sleeve somewhere?"

As always, Francesca had the impression he disliked her, but she gave him a wan smile.

"Do you really think she could do the family proud?" William asked Amy, as if he didn't hold much hope.

"Yes, I do."

"Francesca is a very beautiful woman, just like her mother," Helen added, trying to be helpful.

There was a silence. William gave one of his most savage frowns. "The less we say about *that*, the better."

Helen's lip wobbled.

"And she has her portion of the Greentree fortune for her dowry," Amy hurried to move matters on to something William found more palatable. "She is not penniless, William, and she has connections. *You* are her uncle . . ." She let the sentence drift, watching him.

William nodded. "Yes, I see what you mean. She can't help but be touched by my own respectability. You're a good girl, niece?"

"Uncle, I am—"

"Francesca is a very proper young lady."

"Well, then."

Francesca tried her best to appear "proper" beneath his steely gaze, and she must have done a reasonable job of it, because he looked almost benevolently upon her.

"Very well, then. I will speak to Mrs. March about it. Thank me, girl!" to Francesca. "You are about to have more money and time lavished on you than you no doubt deserve."

"Uncle William, I have no wish to—"

"Thank your uncle, my dear." Amy's eyes could be just as steely as her brother's.

Francesca knew when she was beaten. "Thank you very much. Now, if you will excuse me. The excitement . . ." She closed the door and stood a moment, feeling sick in the pit of her stomach. A ball meant people she barely knew assessing her looks and her prospects and her secrets. And all the time Uncle William would be watching her, waiting for her to make a mistake. Waiting for the *real* Francesca to escape her bonds and scandalize London.

She shivered.

And what about Sebastian? If Uncle William knew about him, he would have an apoplexy. Two apoplexies. But was it likely he'd find out? Sebastian was not someone who would ever be invited to the ball. He belonged in the shadows, and that was where he must stay.

Francesca realized then that she'd miss him. It would have been very pleasant indeed to waltz in Sebastian's strong arms. She would have enjoyed seeing the expression in his eyes when he saw her in her new ball gown. *He* wouldn't mind if she scandalized London. In fact, she realized with surprise, he probably wouldn't care what she did as long as she was being herself. Sebastian didn't approve when she played at being the sort of young woman Uncle William wanted her to be.

He wanted to set her free.

Francesca couldn't decide whether that was a good thing.

Chapter 19

❧❧❧❧

"You see that man over there?"

Lil peered across the square, following the direction of Martin's pointing finger. The house was in darkness, but there was a gas lamp nearby and she could just see a shadow, moving.

"I think so. What of him?"

Martin laughed softly, as if her abrasive manner amused him. "He's off to visit his mistress. We'll follow him as far as her house and then our job is done."

"What do you mean?"

"Mr. Thorne has been engaged by the lady's husband. The fellow has doubts about the heir she is carrying."

Lil snorted. "He thinks he's been cuckolded? Does he really need Mr. Thorne to tell him that? Why doesn't he just ask her himself?"

"Ah, these society marriages, Lil. I don't think they talk to each other at all, except at the breakfast table, and then it's only 'Pass the toast, beloved,' and, 'More jam, sweetness.'"

Lil snorted again. "What do they expect when they marry for money or position or because their father tells them to!"

Martin turned to look at her with interest. "Why do you think they should marry then?"

"Well, for love, of course!"

As soon as the words were out she bit her lip, hard. Why had she said that? And to him of all people! He'd think she was angling to marry *him*.

"You're a romantic little thing, aren't you, Lil," he said, with that soft Irish lilt that made her heart skip a beat.

"I'm a widow," she retorted. "There's nothing romantic about that."

"Oh, are you now? Is that what the black is for? I thought you'd given up color for the sake of your soul."

She gave him a look.

"I'm sorry. Sometimes my jokes fall very flat. Did you love your husband, Lil?"

"He was a good man."

Martin pondered this a moment. "A man can be good without being lovable."

Lil wished he'd stop. "Aren't you meant to be following your gentleman."

"Oh God," Martin muttered, and tugged her arm, hurrying her along the side of the square. "Where is he? Can you see him?"

"I think . . . over there."

"Thank the Lord for that!"

Lil, who kept her private feelings very much to herself, giggled at his emotional display.

Martin's teeth flashed white. "You may well laugh, Miss Lil, but you don't know what Mr. Thorne can be like. I've only just recovered from my last beating."

Lil stopped, wide-eyed with shock. "He *beats* you! Martin, you must leave him at once."

Martin put his hands on her shoulders. "It was a joke. Of course he doesn't beat me. But he can look very fierce."

Lil pulled away and strode off ahead of him. She was upset with him for teasing her and forcing her to show the sort of feeling she usually kept hidden.

"I'm flattered you care," he called softly, loping after her to catch up.

"I'd care for any dumb creature who was mistreated," she said primly.

"Oh there, that's put me in me place."

Lil glanced at him and couldn't help but laugh at his mournful expression. He grinned back, and suddenly Lil had the most peculiar sensation, as if she was falling.

"Lil?" Martin was holding on to her arm, steadying her, and this time his concern was genuine.

"I . . . I came over all dizzy," she said. "Sorry. I'm all right now."

"Do you want me to take you home?"

Lil took a shaky breath. Strangely, she didn't want to go. She wanted to stay here with him, but she couldn't tell him that, so she forced herself to smile. "And get you another of Mr. Thorne's beatings for not doing your job? Course not."

Martin smiled back. "You're an angel, Lil."

Her heart skipped again. An angel? She was far from that, but she wasn't about to tell him so. She hadn't told Mr. Keith, her ballooning beau, and she hadn't told Jacob, and she wasn't going to tell Martin.

No matter how much she wanted to.

Francesca escaped from Helen and Amy, who were already plotting visits from the modiste and various others, and set off for Aphrodite's Club. She had promised to visit Rosie, and although Lil said the child was well and happy, Francesca wanted to see for herself.

Dobson led her upstairs to a small sitting room, where Rosie was giggling as she played with the puppy. She ran to take Francesca's hand, pulling her across to meet the fat, roly-poly creature.

"I've called him Jem," she announced, with a glance at Dobson and another giggle.

"She tells me he looks like me," Dobson explained, with a smile.

Francesca glanced from the puppy to the man and shook her head. "I can't see it."

"It's his nose, see?" Rosie placed her fingertip gently on the puppy's pink nose. "They're both crooked."

"You will visit your mother?" Dobson said, when

they had duly admired the puppy and Rosie's new dress, and left her to be spoiled by Henri, the cook, who was making a cake especially in her honor.

"Yes, of course. If she isn't too busy."

"She is busy, but she will be hurt if you avoid her because of that," he said. He looked as if he was going to say something more, but then he changed his mind, instead leading her in silence to Aphrodite's little office.

Francesca was shocked.

Aphrodite looked ill. Her face had always been pale, but now it was white, with touches of hectic red on her cheekbones, and her eyes looked so bright as to be feverish. But she lit up with smiles when she saw her daughter.

"*Petit chaton*, but what a lovely surprise! No one told me you had come."

"I was admiring Rosie's puppy."

"She is a sweetheart," the courtesan said. "Did she tell you what she is calling him?"

"Jem, after Dobson."

"She says they are alike." Aphrodite laughed. "He pretends to be insulted, but he is really quite touched. He would have made a good father."

Her words seemed to surprise her as much as Francesca, and she was silent for a moment, fiddling with the large diamond ring on one of her fingers.

"Madame . . ." Feeling awkward, as if she was intruding on something very private, Francesca sat down in the straight-backed chair in front of the desk. "As dear as Rosie is, I wish now I had not brought her to you."

Aphrodite's fingers grew still, and Francesca noticed that as usual they were ink-stained. The lines on her face seemed more pronounced. "Why do you say this? She is happy, is she not? Has she said otherwise?"

She'd said the wrong thing again. What was it about her mother that always seemed to bring out such gaucheness in her? "No, I did not mean . . . it is not that I think she is *unhappy*."

"Oh? What is it then?"

"It has been explained to me, Madame, that by bringing her to you I have put you in danger. I am very sorry."

Aphrodite relaxed, and her voice gentled. "I knew what I was doing when I agreed to your request, Francesca. Yes, these are dangerous people. Evil people. But I refuse to be intimidated by them. If no one stood up to evil, who would be left? Tell me, who told you that you had placed me in danger?"

"Mr. Thorne." She tried not to show any emotion as she said it, but Aphrodite was an expert in reading such signs.

"I see," she said, a little smile quirking her lips. "Mr. Thorne seems to be everywhere lately, does he not?"

"I've asked him to protect us, Madame."

Aphrodite's eyes widened. "Have you? That is very interesting. What did he say?"

"He said he would do it for nothing, but I insisted I would pay him."

"He said he would work for nothing? How odd. Why do you think he would say that, *petit chaton*?"

"Because he does not like debts, and I saved his

life in Yorkshire. On the—the moors, in a st-storm."
To her horror her voice wobbled.

Aphrodite's gaze sharpened.

"I'm sorry, Madame. I'm all right now. Pay no attention to me."

"You have nothing to be sorry for. Have you allowed yourself to fall in love with Mr. Thorne? I do not think it is a very good idea to love a man who leads such a dangerous life. If you must fall in love, Francesca, then do it with someone who will live to be an old man."

Francesca gave a shaky laugh, and then couldn't seem to stop. Horrified, she covered her mouth with her hand. The respectable Miss Greentree was coming apart. "Madame, I am so sorry," she began again.

"*Psht!* Why are you sorry? You are hurting, and no doubt you have had to pretend there is nothing wrong, so as not to worry dear Amy and her horrid brother. Am I right? But you are here now. You can say anything you wish to me. Tell me your secrets, *petit chaton.* I am listening, and I will help you if I can."

"I don't know what to do," she whispered. She bowed her head and squeezed her eyes shut, wishing the floor would open up.

She heard Aphrodite stand up and come around the desk, and then her arm came around Francesca's shoulders and squeezed tightly. "You will talk to me, *petit chaton*, and then we will decide what to do together."

"I feel ridiculous," she murmured. "You are the last person I should be talking to."

"But that is exactly why it should be me you talk to! It will go no further and it will not matter to you, will it, what I think? Because you do not love me as you do Amy."

Startled, Francesca looked into her face.

Aphrodite was staring back at her with a knowing expression in her eyes. "I know this, Francesca. You cannot help what you feel, and it will make it easier for you to tell me things you would prefer others not to know."

"Madame, I—"

"No, do not fib. You will not hurt my feelings, I promise you. Tell me what it is that troubles you over Mr. Thorne. You never know, I might be able to help," she added, with the sort of smile that suggested she had helped many others before.

Again Francesca opened her mouth to protest but the words died on her lips. Aphrodite had spoken the truth, and what was wrong with being truthful? Far better that their relationship should be based upon honesty than any false hopes. She nodded.

Aphrodite removed her arm, but she did not move away.

Francesca took a deep breath and plunged in. "I have always sworn never to become involved, passionately involved, with a man. I don't want to be like you, Madame. I don't want to be the plaything of a man, of men. But now I find myself drawn to Sebastian in a way that is almost impossible to resist. I think about him all the time. I dream about him. When I am with him I feel as if I want nothing more. If I did what I long to do, and gave myself to him wholeheartedly, I believe I could be . . . happy. But for how long? A feeling like this cannot last—it is too intense. But if I turn away from him, I ask myself whether I will regret it all my life."

Aphrodite's silk skirts swished as she moved about the room. "It is a dilemma," she said quietly. "But maybe this is not a grand passion?"

"This is my first passion, so I have no experience as to whether or not it is a grand passion."

"I see. It is intense, though, *oui*? Sometimes passion such as you describe wears itself out. It cannot be sustained, and soon it dies and goes cold."

"But now I have tasted this passion, won't I wish for more?"

"You mean you will seek it out with other men?" Aphrodite said dryly. "You do not need a man's love to make you whole, Francesca, but your body may crave a man's touch. You may take lovers for that reason, but if you are a woman who loves one man, then you will find such experiences a degradation of your spirit."

She returned to her chair and sat down, steepling her fingers under her chin. "A courtesan makes her living from the men who love her, admire her, need her to be their companion. I did love the fathers of my children, and at that time I was searching to re-create a greater love. A love that I had lost long before. But then I found it again, and now I know that without that great love—that grand passion—my life would be empty."

"I don't want to be like you."

Aphrodite sighed. "Loving is not a weakness, and

it need not make you unhappy. You and Mr. Thorne may finish your *affaire* without scars. You may find you are the better for having known him and loved him. You do love him, don't you? You are a passionate woman. If you try to stifle that passion, then you will grow sour and bitter and lonely. As much as you might want to, you cannot change what . . . who you are."

Abruptly Francesca stood up. "I must go."

"I have not helped you," her mother said unhappily.

"Yes, you have. I think you have." She reached the door and then paused. "Thank you, Madame," she said, and closed the door behind her.

Dobson was hanging around the front of the club, as if he was waiting for her. "How did you find your mother, Miss Francesca?"

"She was a little tired, perhaps."

"I've asked her to take a holiday from the club, but she won't. I'm worried about her."

Francesca drew on her gloves. "I'm sure she'll be fine. I can't tell her when to take a holiday, Dobson. She wouldn't listen to me."

"She might," he said quietly.

"I very much doubt it." Dobson obviously loved Aphrodite very much. Francesca wondered whether the feeling was returned just as strongly. Her mother had said that she had found the great love of her life, but did she mean Dobson or someone else, someone who was now gone?

"You will visit again soon?" Dobson asked her, following her down the steps to the street.

"Yes." Francesca smiled and held out her hand. After a pause, he took it. "Good-bye, Dobson, and thank you for your kindness to Rosie."

His surprise vanished in a broad smile. "She's a sweetheart," he said.

He would have made a good father.

Francesca left him standing there and began to walk. She felt confused and emotional. Should she do as the courtesan said and allow this grand passion to run its course? Should she risk her heart and her future on a man? Should she place herself in the most vulnerable of positions and say, "Here I am, take me, make love to me, and then discard me"?

But the truth was that Sebastian made her heart beat faster and her throat tighten with longing. There were times when he seemed to understand her better than she understood herself. *Surely that means something?* she told herself, as she reached the corner.

That was when she heard the step behind her. She knew who it was—she didn't need to glance back—and knowing that she could recognize him from his step made her want to push him away. For her own self-preservation.

"Stop following me," she said.

"You asked me to follow you," Sebastian replied in his deep voice.

"I asked you to look after my family."

"Damn and blast it, Francesca, what do you think you're doing? Are you going to stroll all the way back to Wensted Square? Alone?"

"No."

He'd come up beside her and was frowning at her, but she wouldn't look at him.

"Then what are you doing?" His voice dropped, became a caress.

She felt her body respond, melting, aching.

"I'm going to stroll all the way to Half Moon Street," she said. "Will you come with me?"

Francesca knew she was burning her bridges. She was taking Aphrodite's advice, something she once would never have imagined possible. Heart beating fast, she turned to face him.

He was staring into her eyes, reading them, reading what she was saying without words. And then he smiled and reached to take her arm. His fingers smoothed the cloth as if it were her skin. "It would be my pleasure," he said.

Chapter 20

"**F**rancesca ..." he began, as the door to his rooms closed behind them.

"Don't speak," she murmured, and touched her fingertip against his lips. "I don't want you to ask me questions or make promises. I just want to be here, with you."

He cupped her face, drawing her against him, and her arms slid so naturally about his neck. Was this the sort of passion she would remember all her life? Or would Sebastian be forgotten in the dozens to follow?

Francesca couldn't imagine forgetting him, or anyone else replacing him. And yet her family history foretold that was what would happen.

His mouth brushed against hers, teasing, and she felt the heat and languor of desire begin to possess her. The kiss deepened and she closed her eyes. The clean male scent of him filled her nostrils, the woven cloth of his coat abraded her fingers, and the hard muscles of his body moved against her soft curves. She was drowning in his presence, and she didn't care.

He dropped to his knees before her.

Francesca swayed, taken aback. He was gazing up at her, a wicked glint in his eyes and a far more wicked smile on his mouth. "I want to do something else."

She rested her hands on his shoulders, and bent down to kiss his mouth. "Will I like it?" she murmured.

He didn't reply, but his smile broadened.

Sebastian placed his hands oh-so-carefully on her thighs and began to gather her skirt and petticoats up. Francesca felt her excitement growing as he drew out the moment, his hands sliding under the last petticoat and finding the cotton of her drawers, and the silk ties. With one tug the undergarment fell to her ankles, and she rested her hand on his shoulder as he helped her step out of it.

His fingers were warm, knowing, as he stroked her inner thighs. She wriggled, and he knew that she wanted him to touch her *there* but he resisted, caressing all around, before delving into the slippery folds and making her whimper with need. And then, to her amazement, he began to use his tongue.

Shock soon gave way to pleasure. What he was

doing was wicked, beyond anything she'd imagined, but it felt wonderful. She began to quiver as the unstoppable feelings of ecstasy came upon her, and then she was gasping and sobbing out his name, her legs so weak they could barely hold her upright.

She was unaware of him standing up, of him lifting her and carrying her toward the bedchamber. The sunlight glinted through the curtains, highlighting the jeweled colors of rugs and draperies. He laid her on top of his bed as if she were precious treasure.

"Does everyone feel like this, at least once in their lives?" she whispered, looking up at him through her lashes.

His teeth flashed white as he grinned. "How do you feel?"

"Ethereal."

"Hmm. We'll have to bring you back to earth then, my angel."

He began to kiss her, deep kisses that made her toes curl, his body heavy on hers. The tight bodice of her dress restricted her, confined her, and her breasts were aching, longing for his touch. When he began to unfasten the back of her dress she almost wept with relief, and then he was caressing her, his mouth hot and open against her soft flesh, and the pleasure was so great that she almost reached her peak then and there.

His hands were beneath her petticoats, and she felt them on her thighs as he lifted himself over her and slid inside her.

The sunlight through the window caught in his hair, on his naked chest and shoulders—when had he undressed; she didn't remember it. Suddenly he was more than a man. She couldn't look away from him. It was as if he had cast a spell on her, and with each thrust of his body into hers, that spell bound her tighter.

"Darling," he groaned. "My darling girl."

Intense pleasure spiraled through her, making her cry out more loudly than she meant to, but she couldn't help it. She felt him deep, deep inside, as if he wanted to lose himself in her as much as she wanted to lose herself in him. And then he was shouting her name, spilling himself inside her, his face pressed to her shoulder.

He was heavy, and hot, but she didn't tell him to move. Francesca realized, with surprise, that she felt quite tender. She wanted to cuddle him close and kiss him. She reached for the truant lock of hair that had fallen over his face, tucking it back where it belonged. He opened one eye and looked at her, and the wicked gleam was full of carnal thoughts.

"Francesca," he rumbled, "you are the woman of my dreams."

"Am I?"

"Oh yes, there's no doubt about it."

"Even though my nose isn't quite straight?"

He shifted slightly, releasing her from his weight, and kissed the tip of her nose very gently. "I wouldn't have a straight nose for any amount of gold. This is the nose for me."

She giggled. She felt light-headed.

Downstairs, the street door slammed shut.

Sebastian's eyes widened in shock, and then he was swearing, leaping off the bed and dragging on his clothing. "Martin," he said breathlessly. "Damn and blast it, he's back . . ."

With shaking fingers, Francesca began to try to make herself presentable. Watching Sebastian hopping around the room attempting to pull on his stockings made her giggle again, and she was still helpless with laughter when he rolled her over and began to refasten her dress. He stood her up and allowed her skirts and petticoats to drop back into place.

"Your hair," he said, running his fingers through the heavy weight of it.

"I'll have to pile it up under my bonnet. Unfortunately"—she narrowed her eyes at him— "my best bonnet was run over by a cab."

He grinned. "Should happen more often. I like this one better."

They were out in the other room now, Francesca busy with her hair. Sebastian glanced down and swore, and suddenly grabbed something up into his hands, just as the key rattled in the lock.

He turned his back, moving to the bookcase in the corner, and Francesca saw him stuff a cotton garment into a gap behind the books, and realized with a frisson of delighted horror that he was hiding her drawers.

She choked. He turned and frowned at her, and she flopped down into a chair, folding her shaking hands tightly together and composing herself as best she could.

By the time Martin entered the room, they were both perfectly respectable. The manservant's eyes narrowed suspiciously, but Francesca assured herself there was nothing to see. She might be a little flushed, a little disarranged, but that could have been the walk to Half Moon Street.

"Miss Greentree," he said, with a glance at his master. "I didn't know you were expecting a visitor, sir. I would have delayed my return."

"That is perfectly all right, Martin. We're finished now." Sebastian put down his glass and reached for Francesca's hand. "Come, Miss Greentree, it is time you went home."

Outside, the breeze cooled her cheeks, but she still felt wonderfully replete. The contented feeling made up for the knowledge that what they had done was very shocking indeed. Then why did she still feel like giggling?

"Why do you fear being Aphrodite's daughter?" he asked suddenly, harping back to a previous comment she had made.

Some of her glow began to fade. She didn't feel like laughing anymore. "I am afraid I will become like her."

"What do you mean? She is a beautiful, desirable woman who has worked to make her business a success."

"She has had her heart broken many times, and men have used her for their own ends."

"I would have thought she used them."

"She abandoned us."

"You were kidnapped."

"If she wasn't off pursuing some man, it wouldn't have happened."

"Francesca . . ."

"No." She pulled away from him, tears sparkling in her eyes. "You've spoiled it now," she whispered, and turned and fled up the stairs to her uncle's house.

Sebastian stood and watched the door close behind her.

So that was what was wrong. She believed she was Aphrodite's daughter in more ways than one, and to give free rein to her emotions, to her desires, would be to invite disaster. So she bound those emotions inside her, keeping them in tight check, restraining them as a prisoner was restrained in a cell.

It was time someone unlocked the door and showed Francesca Greentree that she was no ordinary woman, and as such she must live her life to the full. There might be tears, there might be hurt, but there would be happiness, too. And yes, there would be desire.

And who better to teach her that than Sebastian?

Aphrodite's death was taking far longer than he'd hoped. But he had to be careful. He didn't want any suspicion attached to it, and he certainly didn't want doctors and magistrates crawling all over the place, pointing the finger of suspicion. The whore couldn't last much longer.

But there was another problem looming. The little spy he had planted in Aphrodite's Club wasn't happy. She hadn't said so, but Angela knew, and had reminded her where her true loyalties lay. He might have to do something about the spy. But he'd allow the dust to settle on Aphrodite's coffin first.

He was a patient man, not by nature but because he'd learned that wishes were usually granted if you waited long enough. Obstacles were removed, or died, and if they didn't . . . Well, there was always murder.

First Aphrodite, then the spy, and then Francesca.

After twenty-five years he'd finally be free of the dark cloud that had hung over him. He'd finally be able to enjoy himself without fearing discovery.

It was a heady thought.

Francesca could barely keep still as each new dress was draped around her, discussed as if she wasn't even present, and then removed. Helen was in raptures over the ball gown, chattering away, all her unhappiness completely forgotten. Amy caught her daughter's eye as if to say, *Take heart, your suffering isn't for nothing.*

Toby arrived as they were sitting down to afternoon tea, and greedily piled his plate with slices of cake and little sandwiches. "Ah, here she is, the belle of the ball," he said, with heavy-handed flattery.

"You're very kind, Uncle Toby."

"Kindness has nothing to do with it, niece. You're looking as gorgeous as ever. A goddess! Are you hoping to catch yourself a husband? An earl, I hear!"

"No, a chimney sweep will do."

For a moment Toby thought she was serious, and then he laughed good-naturedly. That was the trouble with Toby, Francesca decided; he could always take a joke, and therefore one could not hate him as fully as he deserved.

"I think your uncle William is expecting something better than 'trade,' if he's forking out all this blunt. Not known for his kindness and generosity, is he? Not without getting something in return."

"Aunt Helen is doing a marvelous job helping to arrange everything," Francesca said hurriedly. "I can't thank her enough."

"It's almost like having a daughter of my own," Helen gushed, and then her eyes swiveled abruptly to Toby and away again. "If I had one, of course, which I haven't. A daughter, I mean."

"But Francesca is the next best thing," Toby said gruffly. "Come on, my love, time to go. Cook says we have roast beef and gravy, and you know how I love roast beef and gravy."

"Of course, Toby." Flustered, Helen rose swiftly to her feet, and Toby bustled her out.

Francesca collapsed into a chair. "I wish Helen did have a daughter; then she could be the belle of the ball and not me."

But Amy didn't answer, lost in her own thoughts.

* * *

"My love."

Aphrodite looked up at him, her love, her Jemmy, and sighed. "I don't feel like getting up this evening. I'm sorry, Jemmy. Can you manage without me? Perhaps, if I sleep for a while, I will be myself again."

"I'm going to find you another doctor."

"I'm just tired, dearest." She'd been ill, unable to keep down any of the treats he had found to tempt her appetite. Now all she wanted was sleep, deep and restoring, but she forced herself to ask the questions he would be expecting her to ask.

"Henri will be able to manage supper, but he will not deal with any of the suppliers. Maeve must speak to the butcher about that ham last week, and the strawberries we bought were rotten before they reached us."

"My love, forget the strawberries. Rest."

"I will, in a moment. How is the new girl? I wasn't sure whether I liked her or not, but she is very clever with her tongue. The guests are always asking for her."

Dobson sighed and shook his head. "She is booked up with clients until next week," he said.

Aphrodite nodded, her eyes closing. "Good," she breathed. She felt his hand on her hair, stroking the wild curls back from her forehead, and then she was drifting, down a long tunnel. She was traveling back into the past, and the years flew by. Soon she was young again, a woman at the peak of her powers. She had two daughters, but that did not lessen her attractiveness to men. If anything her maturity made her more so.

I met him at the salon of one of the most modern hostesses, where there is a mingling of the demimonde and the aristocrats of London society. I am restless, looking for change, and I have found it.

T. is tall, dark, and handsome, but more importantly to me, he is kind. I fall in love with his kindness. And Jemmy is gone, so what does it matter who I live my life with? I don't want to be alone.

T. isn't married and he doesn't seem to want to be. He is a gentleman who enjoys adventure, like a little boy who has never grown up. I am an adventure to him. He has never had a famous courtesan, and my world is new to him, and at first he is a most attentive lover.

We are having a child. T. is very excited. He will be an affectionate father, but I see now that the child and I will not be enough for him.

The world is too big and life too short for him to settle himself down here with us.

I know he cannot be satisfied any longer, and I understand. After all, I cannot give him all of myself, either. A big part of my heart will always belong to Jemmy.

"My love?"

Aphrodite blinked, trying to focus.

"Mr. Thorne is here, Aphrodite. I think you should see him."

He didn't wait for her to answer, and when she opened her eyes again, Sebastian Thorne's handsome face and lively black gaze were before her.

"Madame, I am sorry you are unwell."

Aphrodite managed a smile. "I will be better soon."

Her eyes sharpened, and suddenly she seemed more lucid. "I know your secret, Mr. Thorne."

He looked politely puzzled, but she recognized his anxiety.

"Francesca," she prompted him slyly.

"Francesca?" Confusion now, and relief.

Aphrodite smiled. "You desire her, and she you. It is a pity your social position makes it impossible for you to accompany her to all of the places you wish to. How can such a man as you, Mr. Thorne, walk beside Francesca in anything other than secret? If you were a gentleman to her lady, you could keep her safe more easily. And you do want to keep her safe, don't you?"

He didn't like what she'd said. He didn't like what she was seeing in his face. "Francesca wouldn't accept me at her side, Madame," he told her gruffly. "It wouldn't matter whether I was a gentleman or not."

"Sometimes what a woman says and what she feels are two different things. But you will never know, will you, because you're not a gentleman. Such a pity. I think you are good for my daughter, Sebastian. You're not afraid to let her be herself."

"You know, don't you?" he said quietly. He was watching her closely. "You know who I am?"

She closed her eyes. "I know it is a shame you cannot face the truth. How can Francesca be true to herself if you are not?"

"Francesca has a will of her own, Madame, and I cannot sway it."

Her eyes opened, fever bright. "But there are ways

of bending her to your will, Mr. Thorne. My daughter is very like her father. She is not at all proper, oh no, no matter what she believes. She wants adventure. To experience life through adventure. The more risky . . . the more risqué, the better." She smiled. "You can help her to do that. You can show her how to be true to herself."

He sighed. "Can I?"

"*Oui.* You can make her very happy."

Sebastian smiled. He had the sort of smile women swooned for. She beckoned him closer to the bed.

"Tell me, Mr. Thorne, have you ever made love to a woman at a ball?"

Sebastian closed the door softly behind him. Aphrodite was asleep. He was rattled, he admitted it. Give him a thief or a murderer, and put them in a dark alley, and he was right at home. But Aphrodite had crept under his guard. She knew who he was, what he was. She knew about Francesca.

Thinking over what she'd said, he wondered if he would have the courage to do it. He was Mr. Thorne, the man no one wanted to admit to hiring, the man from the shadows. How, he thought bleakly, could he attend a London society ball?

"There you are."

Surprised, he looked up. She was standing with her hands on her hips. "I thought you were supposed to be a cultured courtesan," he said, amused, and glad of a respite from his own uneasy musings. "You look more like a disgruntled fishwife."

"I am." In a moment she'd changed from fishwife

to seductress, fluttering her eyelashes at him. "I like this place," she said. "Plenty of food and nice soft beds. And they only let the better toffs in. Some gent slapped one of the girls the other day, and now he's barred from 'ere altogether."

"You mean you'd leave Dipper?" he mocked.

She grinned. "Nah. Dipper's special."

"So, Polly, tell me . . . what have you found out for me?"

She gave a wriggle, preparing to tell her story. He crossed his arms and prepared to listen, not expecting very much. But, after she had finished her tale, Sebastian was no longer in the mood to be amused.

"We need to find Dobson, and then you're going to tell him exactly what you've just told me."

"He'll be in the salon. Now Madame's ill, he's doing his best to keep things running as she'd like them. He's a good man, Jemmy Dobson, and he loves her truly."

Dobson, when they found him, was looking both harassed and worried. He was a man whose whole world had just turned upside down. At first he was loath to leave the salon, but Sebastian persuaded him that it was extremely important he hear what Sebastian had to say, and ushered him into Aphrodite's office.

The room was still scented with roses and her perfume.

"What is it then?" Dobson demanded, running a hand over his jaw. He looked as if he hadn't slept for days. "I ain't got long, so tell me quick as you can."

"First I need you to speak to someone." Sebastian went to the door and beckoned Polly in.

Dobson's eyes narrowed. "What's this then? Louisa? Shouldn't you be in the salon?"

"Her name is Polly, and she works for me. I'm sorry to be underhanded, Dobson, but when I spoke to Aphrodite about the possibility of there being a spy in her club, she wouldn't believe me. Polly has been keeping an eye on things and listening for any useful information. I want you to hear what she has to say."

Dobson looked as if he'd rather not, but he nodded brusquely. Polly began to tell her story, and as she went on, his face grew whiter and more strained. By the time she'd finished he was shattered.

"Poison," he said, and swallowed, pulling himself together. "What sort of poison?"

"We're going to have to ask the poisoner that."

"Aye," he said grimly, "I intend to." When he looked back at Sebastian there were tears in his eyes. "I only hope it ain't too late. If she dies . . . I might as well be dead, too."

"She's a strong woman. A fighter."

"She's worn down to nothing over this business with Mrs. Slater and that bastard who kidnapped her daughters." His eyes widened. "Does that mean *he* planned this, too?"

"I'll find out." Sebastian hesitated. "Do you want me to fetch Francesca?"

"Yes. She'll like that. It'll comfort her to see her daughter. Francesca's the one she worries about the most." His eyes gleamed as he looked up, tears mingling with rage. "What are we going to do about . . . ?"

"Say nothing just yet. Give me time to plan. Then we'll close the trap."

Chapter 21

Lil's elfin face was so serious. As soon as Francesca saw her standing at the door, she knew there was something very wrong.

"Miss, I have bad news. Your mother . . . Madame Aphrodite, she is very unwell."

Francesca heard herself say, "Unwell?" but she didn't believe it. Was her mother playing at illness to bring her running? But no, that was the way of an emotionally unstable woman—the woman she used to think of as Aphrodite. Not the real Aphrodite, the woman with the ink-stained fingers and tired eyes. "What do you mean, unwell?"

"They're saying she has the cholera, miss, and they're blaming Rosie for it, saying she brought it into the house. But it's not true. Rosie's not sick. There's nothing wrong with her."

Francesca tried to comprehend what Lil was saying, but it wouldn't seem to sink in. She felt numb.

"She's very bad, miss," Lil went on gently. "You need to come."

"Do you mean she's dying . . . ?" Her voice rose on the last word, incredulous, disbelieving. Aphrodite couldn't die! She was indestructible. And besides, there was so much more to be said between them . . .

"Miss?" Lil had taken her arm, and Francesca understood that the maid was seriously alarmed by her behavior. She must pull herself together. She must be strong.

"I'm all right, Lil. Just let me get my cloak and we will go. We will take Uncle William's carriage. Ask for it to be sent around to the door."

Lil, who seemed to be glad to have something to do, hurried off to carry out her orders. Francesca stood a moment in her room, aware that she needed to fetch her cloak and gloves, but strangely unable to move. Some of Lil's words echoed in her mind. *Cholera. Rosie.* If that were true, then Francesca knew she was to blame for this. She had taken Rosie to her mother and asked her to hide her. She had brought danger into Aphrodite's life in the form of Mallory Street, and now this.

I will never forgive myself.

Halfway down the stairs Francesca heard Mrs. March, her voice raised. When she reached the hall she found the housekeeper and Lil toe to toe, glaring at each other.

"Miss wants the carriage. Now."

"The carriage is not hers to order. This is Mr. Tremaine's house."

"Are you sure it's not yours?" Lil sneered. "You treat it like it was. You're not the lady of the house here. You're nothing but a servant, just like the rest of us."

Mrs. March lifted a hand, and for one awful moment Francesca thought she meant to slap Lil across the face. Shocked, Francesca cried out, and both women's heads swiveled around. Lil looked relieved to see her, but Mrs. March's eyes glittered wildly.

"Mrs. March." Francesca spoke clearly and calmly as she came forward, reaching out to take Lil's arm and draw her closer. "I want the carriage brought around to the door. My mother is very unwell and I need to go to her, urgently."

"Your *mother*?" Mrs. March repeated, face full of disbelief. "As far as I know, miss, your mother is upstairs, tucked up in her bed. I think you are up to something. Some mischief or other. Another guttersnipe to rescue, perhaps?"

Francesca didn't believe for a moment that the housekeeper believed what she was saying. This was another of her ways of showing them she was the mistress of this house, in her own mind anyway. But Francesca was in no mood, and had no time, to talk her around to a more amenable frame of mind.

"Mrs. March, you are making yourself look ridiculous. Do as I ask. Immediately."

Mrs. March's eyes gleamed with malice. She was enjoying this, and was not about to give up the game without a fight. "I will not do as you ask! You have overstepped your authority, Miss Francesca. I'm going to fetch Mr. Tremaine; he needs to know about this. He'll soon put a stop to your—"

"Mrs. March, my uncle is asleep. I insist that you—"

"No, I'm not."

The voice was Uncle William's, and it was coming from behind them. Her heart jumping, Francesca turned toward him. Were there any more shocks to be had this evening? Her uncle was standing at the library door, a glass of brandy in one hand and a book in the other. His austerely handsome face was lined with weariness, but his gaze was as steely as ever.

"What is going on, Francesca? You are shouting. Mrs. March? I demand an explanation."

The housekeeper drew a breath, preparing to lay her grievances before him, but Francesca was too quick for her.

"Aphrodite is ill, Uncle," she said in a quiet and reasonable voice. "I need to go to her at once. I asked for the carriage to be brought around but Mrs. March refuses to allow it."

"She's planning some mischief, that's what it is," Mrs. March insisted, a hint of a whine in her voice. "I don't trust her, sir."

"It isn't your place to make those decisions," Francesca reminded her. As she expected, Mrs. March flew into a rage.

"My place is to see that you don't take advantage

of your uncle! Who knows what she's up to now, sir. You don't know what—"

William hadn't taken his eyes from Francesca. "Order the carriage around," he said abruptly, cutting through his housekeeper's complaints.

Mrs. March's mouth opened and closed.

"Do it," he said, sharply.

There was no arguing with that tone, and she turned away with an angry rustle of silk skirts, her shoes tapping, her feelings clear for all to see. Mrs. March didn't like losing, she wasn't used to it, and Francesca had a feeling she was the sort who would take pleasure from plotting her revenge.

"Thank you, Uncle William," she said. Perhaps he wasn't so bad after all, she thought. Perhaps she could even grow to like him.

"I never liked the bitch." His voice was emotionless. "But she is your mother."

Francesca took a step toward him, wondering if she had misheard, but he'd already turned and walked back into the library and closed the door. Such cruelty, such heartlessness, at a time when most people would expect some tact and kindness. But this was Uncle William, and all he cared about was the gossip Aphrodite and her daughters had attached to his family. He would probably be glad if she died, she thought bitterly. It would be one less scandal for him to worry about.

"Miss Francesca, the carriage will be here in a moment."

She'd forgotten about Lil. "We'll go and wait outside," she said, forcing away the tears and lifting her chin. "I need to breathe fresh air."

"Yes, miss, so do I."

"Oh . . . I forgot. I should tell Mama . . . Mrs. Jardine."

"I can ask one of the servants to wake her if it becomes necessary, miss."

"Yes. Thank you, Lil."

Outside, the square was quiet, apart from the occasional passerby. Francesca looked in the direction of Half Moon Street, and wondered what Sebastian was doing. Was he out wandering the streets and the rookeries, hunting for people who were running from their misdeeds? Or was he asleep in that magical room, like a sultan in his palace? She wanted him beside her. She felt suddenly bereft without him. But such thoughts were romantic dreams—she and Sebastian could never have that normal sort of relationship. They could never be other than brief, if passionate, lovers.

"Miss?"

Lil was there, and so was the carriage, creaking its way across the cobbles toward them. Francesca gathered her cloak about her and stepped down the stairs to meet it, and prepared herself for the worst.

Aphrodite was dreaming. Restless, feverish dreams of her famous past.

He's dead. T. is dead. I am finding it difficult to believe such a man can be dead. My T. was so alive. My daughter, my Francesca, will be the poorer for not knowing him. I look into her smiling baby face and see T., and I weep.

The sadness makes me vulnerable. I turn to the other one. For a time I trust him, I believe in him. But he isn't a good man.

He is not a kind man.

"My love? My dearest love?"

She blinked and opened her eyes. For a moment she saw *him*, the man she blamed for her life's tragedy, but then it changed and became the face she loved above all others. What was his name? Oh, why couldn't she remember his name?

But he seemed to sense her frustration.

"It's only Jemmy," he murmured, stroking the damp hair from her brow. "And you have a visitor, dearest one."

Another face came into focus, and just for a moment she thought she was dreaming again, and that this was herself, made young—Aphrodite, at the height of her powers and her beauty. And then Francesca said, "Mother?"

Of course. It was Francesca, her youngest daughter. Her most troublesome daughter. The one she worried about the most.

"*Petit chaton,*" Aphrodite whispered, "I am sorry you must see me like this. I am not at my best. I have been unwell. But I will get better, you will see. Soon I will be myself again."

Tears filled Francesca's eyes, and her mouth trembled. "I'm so sorry," she said shakily. "This is all my fault."

Aphrodite frowned. "Nonsense!" she said, as

strongly as she could manage. "It is not your fault. It is not anybody's fault. I was sick once for a year, but I forced myself to get better." Francesca's face shimmered, changed. "You look like your father," she whispered, and smiled. "He was a wonderful man, *petit chaton*. You know, you are very like him."

"Who was my father?" Francesca gasped. "Please, tell me who he was?"

"He died," she whispered. "I'm sorry you never knew him."

A grief Francesca had never expected to feel filled her heart.

"But he had plans for you. Grand plans. He wrote and told me. The letter was stolen . . . long ago."

"What was my father's name?"

"Tommy," she said, and smiled. Aphrodite's eyes closed, but she reached out her other hand, and Dobson closed his fingers over it. "The letter." She was struggling to get the words out. "We must . . . the letter . . ." But she had slipped back into her feverish sleep.

"Will she get better?" Francesca sounded stark as Jemmy walked with her to the bedchamber door. Despite his own pain, his gaze was compassionate for her. Such kindness from a man she hardly knew, while her own uncle treated her with contempt! She felt as if her heart would break.

"I won't lie to you," he said. "She's not strong in her body. But there's no one else I know with a stronger will. She'll fight."

"This is my fault."

"No, it ain't," he retorted.

"But Rosie! I sent Rosie to her."

"She made you a promise that she'd care for Rosie, so she did. It meant a lot to her that you'd asked."

Francesca stared up at him, a lump in her throat.

"It weren't Rosie who made her sick. This ain't the cholera. Believe me," he said with certainty, "I've seen it and I know. This is something else."

"My sisters . . . ?"

"I've already sent a message."

Her mother was dying. It was true. He wouldn't have sent for Vivianna and Marietta otherwise. The acknowledgment was suddenly too much for her, and Francesca began to sob.

A step behind her, and someone turned her around. Arms enclosed her, amazingly strong and comforting. And familiar. With a gasp, Francesca lifted her ravaged face.

Sebastian?

He looked into her eyes, his own full of compassion. Her lips trembled. "Poor darling," he murmured. "You have enough to bear, but there is more, Francesca, and I can't spare you. You must be strong for me, for your mother."

She pulled away and wiped her cheeks impatiently. "What do you mean? What are you doing here?"

"Francesca." Jemmy Dobson looked weary beyond words. "Mr. Thorne is here to help. Your mother's sickness . . . someone is poisoning her."

She felt as if the floor were moving under her feet.

Sebastian gave her a little shake. "I haven't time to explain. We need your help, Francesca, if we're to get this person to admit what they've done, and tell us what they are using. Your mother's life may depend upon it. Do you understand me?"

"I understand you," she said, "but I am finding it difficult to believe you."

"Believe me."

His eyes were dark and deadly serious.

Francesca nodded her head jerkily. "What do you want me to do?" she whispered.

"Wait in the sitting room, and when a certain person comes to join you, engage them in conversation. Be natural. We'll do the rest."

Francesca gave a little laugh and covered her mouth. She had just been told that her mother was being poisoned, and now they wanted her to sit and wait for a poisoner to appear, and engage them in conversation. Be natural?

Sebastian turned her away from Dobson, cupping her face in his hands. He was warm and alive, and somehow the feel of him, the sight of him, fed her strength. "Darling girl," he murmured and, bending, kissed her lips, once, and then again. "Do this. Be brave and strong and it will all be over. I will explain afterward, I promise. But you must trust me now. Do you trust me, Francesca?"

"I trust you," she said, and she did.

He smiled, but it was a serious smile. "Dobson will show you downstairs. I'll be about, though."

She nodded and tried not to cling to him as he stepped away. But she turned her head back on the landing, for a last, comforting glimpse of him. He was watching her, and there was an expression on his face she had never seen before. Deep emotion and determination, and sadness, too.

"I'm sorry," she said shakily to Dobson. "This must be awful for you. You . . . you love her very much, don't you?"

He smiled into her eyes. "Course I do. And Aphrodite knows how much I love her, so I've got nothing to prove. It's you who 'as to make your peace with your mother, Francesca, not me. Now, it's time." He squeezed her hand, and Francesca followed him into the sitting room.

Chapter 22

She'd imagined the room as dark and empty, but it wasn't. Lamps and candles were blazing, and a fire was burning merrily in the hearth. In fact, now she came to look about her, the whole club was full of light, and she could hear music and voices coming from the direction of the salon.

"Is the club open tonight?" she said in disbelief.

"Aphrodite insisted on it," Dobson replied, "and we do as she tells us. It matters to her that things go on as normal. The club is part of her, and I think if it were to close, then she would lose hope. Now, make yourself comfortable."

He closed the door so quickly that she suspected he didn't want her to ask any more questions, or change her mind. Francesca stood for a moment, feeling at a loss, and then she went to the sofa and sat down. The room had an expectant feel, as though at any moment Aphrodite might walk in. Her presence was everywhere, in the elegance of the furnishings, in the Egyptian chair with its sphinx armrests, in the miniatures of her three daughters. Francesca remembered when her mother had asked to have them painted, and how she had railed against her own particular sitting, saying it was a waste of her time.

She shut her eyes, trying not to cry again. She was being self-indulgent. She needed to be strong, like her mother. Aphrodite was one of the strongest women she knew, and she'd only just realized it. Francesca prayed her new appreciation had not come too late.

The tap on the door startled her so much that she came to her feet. Was this the one? Was this the poisoner? But with relief she saw that it was only Maeve. The pretty Irishwoman looked somber, and she was carrying a tray.

"I'm sorry to trouble you, Miss Francesca. Mr. Dobson sent me. I have some coffee, nice and hot and strong. I thought you might be needing it to keep your spirits up."

The smell of the coffee was delicious, and suddenly Francesca couldn't wait to sample the reviving brew. "Thank you, Maeve."

"This is a very sad time for all of us here at the club," Maeve said, pouring the coffee into a cup and handing it across to her. Francesca noticed then that she had two cups.

"Please, if you have time, do sit with me and have a cup yourself. I don't want to be alone." She needed a moment to gather her thoughts, to come to terms with what Sebastian had told her.

Maeve smiled. "Thank you, miss. Mr. Dobson did suggest I stay with you awhile, but I didn't want to intrude."

"You're not intruding, Maeve, I'm glad of your company. My mother is sleeping, and I don't really know what I'm still doing here, but . . . I don't want to go home." She wondered if Maeve knew about the poisoner, but thought it best not to mention it.

Maeve sat down on the sofa beside her, and gave Francesca a tentative glance. "If Madame leaves us, then what will happen to her club? She's the heart and soul of this place. There's no one can take her place. It'll be like an empty shell without her. I really don't know what we will do." She looked down at the coffee in her hands, and then changed her mind and put the cup back on the tray.

"Dobson says she's the strongest person he knows," Francesca said, willing herself to believe it. Her sisters had told her that the club had been Maeve's home for many years. If she lost Madame and her home, what would she do? Where would she go? "That won't happen, you know," Francesca spoke to herself as much as Maeve. "I mean, whatever happens, the club will stay. My sister, Marietta, will take it over."

Maeve said nothing. She looked as if she might burst into tears, and she turned her face away so that Francesca could not see her grief.

In that moment there was something familiar about her, something that niggled at Francesca's memory, and it had nothing to do with Aphrodite's Club. Francesca searched her mind, trying to remember what it was, but the urgency faded as the silence stretched out.

"She's been so kind to me," Maeve whispered. "I pray she'd understand if she knew why I did . . ." But she shook her head and didn't go on with whatever she'd been about to say. "Never mind," she said instead. "I'm rambling. Please forgive me. Do you want more coffee? I think Henri has some of his special little cakes in the kitchen pantry. He locks them away but I can always find them."

"No, I couldn't eat anything. Maeve—"

"Maeve?" The door had opened without them noticing, and a woman Francesca had never seen before stood there watching them. She was short and plump, and when she smiled she had dimples either side of her mouth. "I'm sorry. Didn't mean to interrupt." But that didn't stop her from coming right inside the room and closing the door behind her.

Francesca felt a chill run down her back. Was this the poisoner, the one she'd been waiting for?

"What do you want, Louisa?" Maeve said it so sharply that Francesca was taken aback. She had never heard Maeve speak in such an unfriendly manner.

"What do I want?" the woman said with a smirk. "I wanted to ask you a question. Yesterday Mr. Dobson was asking me about any medicine that Madame might 'ave had from the apothecary. I couldn't remember fetching her any. And then I remembered about that little packet you had delivered at the door that time. Was that from the apothecary, Maeve?"

There was a strangely ominous silence. Francesca looked from one to the other of them, confused, but with a growing sense of foreboding.

"What little packet?" Maeve asked levelly. "You've made a mistake, Louisa."

"No, I saw it right enough. It was the boy from the apothecary, and he gave you a little packet, and you paid him for it."

"I . . ." Suddenly she smiled, more like the Maeve Francesca knew. "Ah yes, I remember now. They were drops, for my head. I get the headache something fierce."

"Then why were you putting them into Madame's coffee?"

Maeve stared, her smile slipping away. "What are you saying? How dare you . . . ?"

But Louisa wasn't about to be stopped. "Madame always gets you to make her coffee, because you do it just the way she likes it. No one else but Maeve can make Madame's coffee!" she added, with a dimpled smile at Francesca that contained more than a hint of malice. "It's a bit of a joke with us, you see."

"You probably saw me with the sugar," Maeve said flatly.

"Oh no," Louisa exclaimed, "it weren't no sugar. It were those drops from the apothecary that the boy delivered. Did Madame have a headache then? Maybe that was it?" Her accent was quickly slipping in the direction of the East End of London.

Maeve's gaze narrowed, and her face looked pinched. "You're wrong, or lying. I didn't put anything in Madame's coffee. I don't know why you're saying these things." She stood up, moving toward Louisa.

Francesca had been listening with surprise and concern, but as Maeve walked away from her, suddenly she remembered what had been niggling at her a little while before.

"Maeve," she burst out, "do you know Mrs. March?"

Maeve spun around, her eyes wide and frightened. "Why do you say that?" she cried in a brittle voice. "What has that to do with anything?"

"Because I saw you talking to her at the house in Wensted Square. I've only just realized it."

"It wasn't me," Maeve wailed. "I didn't do it."

And then she seemed to break, folding in on herself, with her arms wrapped about her waist and her face screwing up like a child's. Suddenly she opened her mouth and let out a shrill scream.

Francesca was too shocked to move, but Louisa was smiling with satisfaction as Maeve screamed again. The door opened abruptly, and Dobson and Sebastian came inside.

Maeve was still screaming. Dobson pushed past Louisa and caught her, shaking her and then pulling her against him when she refused to stop. The Irishwoman's eyes were blank, as though her mind had gone beyond what she could bear. But at least, when he held her against his chest, she stopped her terrible cries.

The door was open into the vestibule, and Francesca could see others gathering to see what the fuss was about, before Sebastian closed it firmly in their faces.

"She's the poisoner!" Louisa said, all but jumping up and down. She looked as excited as a child at a birthday party.

"Polly, go out there and tell everyone to go back to work," Sebastian said impatiently, moving her toward the door with a hand around her plump arm. "And say nothing about what's happened, do you hear me?"

He seemed very much at home, Francesca thought, almost as if he'd been here many times before. And then she realized what name he had called Louisa.

"Polly?"

"That's me." Louisa curtsied an acknowledgment with a glint in her eyes.

"Out," Sebastian said. She gave an exaggerated sigh and vanished outside.

"Is that Pretty Polly?" She took a step, felt her knees buckling, and hastily sat down.

"I'm sorry," Sebastian said. He looked sorry, too, but she wasn't sure what he was sorry about: Polly being here with him, or the lies he had told her? Either way, Sebastian could wait, she thought, her gaze sliding to Maeve. There were more important matters to deal with.

"Was it really Maeve?" she asked Dobson. "Did she really poison my mother's coffee?"

"That's what we need to find out," Sebastian answered for him. He came over to where Maeve was huddled in Dobson's arms, her face hidden against his red coat. "What did you give her, Maeve?" he said almost gently. "What was it? Help us."

Maeve's breathing grew louder. "They made me," she said in a muffled voice. "My life has never been my own, not since I was nine years old. I was sold to *her* and she's owned me ever since." She shook violently, clinging to Dobson. "That's why I was put to work here. So I could watch Madame, and then tell *her* what I heard and saw."

"Who do you mean by 'her,' Maeve?"

Maeve gave a bitter laugh. "You already know," she whispered. "It was her paid the apothecary's boy to bring me the medicine, who told me what to do. I was to give her small doses, she said. To make it look natural."

"Maeve, what did you give Aphrodite?" Dobson asked her, the urgency plain in his gruff voice. "What you've done is very wrong, but you can help us now. You can make up for it. Please, tell us."

But Maeve heaved a deep sigh. "It'll be too late anyway," she said painfully. "You won't believe me, but I tried to make it last as long as I could. I tried to keep her alive as long as I dared. But *she* knew, she always knows, and she sent me a message to say I was to get it over and done with."

"Goddamn it, tell me!"

"Arsenic. I gave her arsenic."

Dobson went still, shock wiping his face blank, and then he was gone, the door slamming hard behind him. Francesca could hear him shouting for someone to go and fetch the doctor at once, and to tell him that Madame had been poisoned with arsenic.

Without Dobson to support her, Maeve stumbled and fell against a chair, clutching at the back of it to keep herself upright.

"Who told you to do this?" Francesca stared up at her, wanting only a name so that she could find this woman and punish her for the tragedy she'd caused. "Tell me her name."

"Don't you know?" Maeve replied bitterly. "Didn't he tell you?" with a nod at Sebastian.

"Was it Mrs. March?" she asked, but that didn't seem right, and she could tell from Maeve's expression that the housekeeper wasn't the one.

"Mrs. March?" Sebastian repeated, puzzled.

"My uncle's housekeeper in Wensted Square. I saw Maeve speaking to Mrs. March," she went on. "They were together in one of the rooms, and it was obvious Mrs. March didn't want me to see who it was she was with. I didn't realize it was Maeve then, not really, but now I know it was she."

"Why did you go to see Mrs. March?" he said, moving closer to Maeve, his voice threatening. "Was she owned by Mrs. Slater, too?"

Francesca felt the room begin to spin around her. *Mrs. Slater.* Oh dear God, was that what it was about?

Maeve made a choking noise, half laugh and half

sob. "You'll have to ask Mrs. March that, Mr. Thorne. I've said enough to get myself hanged and I'm not saying any more."

"I need to know."

"Why do you need to know?" Maeve shouted. "For Madame's sake? Or for her?" pointing at Francesca.

His brows drew together.

"This is all your fault," she wailed to Sebastian. "If you hadn't come nosin' around then I wouldn't have had to . . . to . . ." Her voice failed her. She slid down onto the floor, and her sobbing was the only sound in the room.

"We need to pay Mrs. March a visit."

Francesca saw that he was watching her. He'd lied to her, kept things from her, made her believe they were having an adventure when all the time he'd been twisting the truth. She thought she knew him, but now she realized she didn't know him at all.

"You want me to explain," he went on, "and I will. I'll talk on the way to Wensted Square. Will you come with me?"

"I feel as if I'm dreaming," she managed.

"I'm sorry, it isn't a dream. Mrs. Slater is alive and as dangerous as ever."

"When I think of her I think of a childhood monster. An ogress with long teeth and sharp claws. She isn't human. She isn't real." She shuddered, then glanced at Maeve as she continued to weep. "What about . . . ?"

Sebastian went to open the door. "Polly!" he shouted. In a moment Pretty Polly was there, smiling expectantly. "Take Maeve somewhere safe and watch her. If she escapes it'll be on your head."

Polly hauled Maeve to her feet, not ungently, and led her away.

"She said arsenic," Francesca whispered, when they were alone again.

"Yes."

"She poisoned my mother, and yet she was sitting here with me and saying how much she loved her. How kind my mother had been to her." Francesca was appalled by such duplicity.

"Some people can justify anything. I've been in the shadows for so long that there isn't much that shocks me. I'm more surprised when I find something good. Perhaps that's why I want you, Francesca. I think if I bury myself in you, then some of your goodness will rub off on me." He smiled and held out his hand. "Come on," he said gently.

She looked at it for a moment, and then she deliberately folded her arms tightly and walked past him with her head held high.

With a sigh, Sebastian followed after her.

Chapter 23

"You lied to me." It was the first thing she said as they sat in the dark and musty interior of the cab, bowling through the never sleeping streets of London. "You told me to trust you, and all the time you were lying."

"Yes. I'm sorry, but I had no choice. I was specifically asked not to tell you what I was doing in Yorkshire, and I had to abide by that person's wishes."

"By 'that person' you mean my mother. She hired you, didn't she?" Francesca's voice was accusatory.

"Yes, she did."

Francesca fell silent. A sudden shower of rain swept across the street in front of them, driving many of the pedestrians into shelter.

"Let me explain," he said, when it was clear she wasn't going to ask him to. "Your mother wanted to find Mrs. Slater and her associates. She wanted you and your sisters to be safe; she was also tired of being afraid. I think she even knew that she was being watched. She was certainly aware that she was in danger. When she hired me, she accepted that the danger to her would increase, but she was willing to take that risk, Francesca. She wanted justice. She is a courageous woman."

"I see." Francesca cleared her throat. "So when you were in Yorkshire it was because you were looking for Mrs. Slater?"

"Yes. I met Hal, and he told me he knew someone who was a friend of hers. I believed him. But it was a trap, and I nearly died. If it hadn't been for you . . ."

"Then you went after Hal again?"

"And this time it was Jed who tried to kill us both. But Hal told me enough for me to be able to find one of Mrs. Slater's houses in Mallory Street. The very same one from which you saved Rosie. That's why I was so concerned for your safety, Francesca."

"I see that now." She watched a hackney go rushing by, the driver standing up in his coat of many capes. "Why are we going to see Mrs. March? How can she be involved in all of this?"

"I don't know."

"She hates me," Francesca added thoughtfully. "From the first moment we met, I've felt as if she resents me for being here. I thought it was because she's in love with my uncle, or with what he stands for."

"We'll find out the truth," he promised her.

"Why did Dobson want me to sit with Maeve? Why did you send Polly in while I was there?"

"That was my idea," he apologized. "I thought you could draw Maeve out, make her comfortable, perhaps even make her feel guilty. You being there was almost like Aphrodite being there, reminding her of what she'd done."

Francesca nodded. "Sebastian, did you know your father?"

The change in subject was surprising, but he answered her anyway. "Yes, I did."

"Aphrodite told me tonight that my father is dead. So I will never get to meet him or know what he was like. I didn't think I wanted to, I told myself I didn't want to, but now that the choice has been taken away from me . . . She said he wrote a letter about me and all the things he was planning for me. His name was Tommy."

He took her in his arms, but she sat there stiff and unyielding.

"You and I were a mistake. By following my heart I've only made everything worse. I have to stop it."

"Francesca, my darling girl . . ."

"No." She pushed him away.

They said nothing more until the cab reached Wensted Square and drew up outside the Tremaine house. Sebastian helped her down, asking the driver to wait, and then went to sound the knocker.

There was a delay before anyone answered, and when the door was finally opened the servant looked half asleep. "Fetch Mrs. March," Sebastian said, before Francesca could speak.

The girl looked uneasy. "She's in bed, sir. She don't like to be woken once she's in bed."

"Fetch her anyway. And fetch Mr. Tremaine while you're at it."

She looked surprised, but Francesca nodded for her to do as she was told, and she hurried away. Francesca led him into a masculine-looking library, where the shelves were full of leather-bound books, and there was a large portrait hanging over the mantel. It seemed to capture her attention, because she went to look up at it.

"I'd forgotten this was here," she said. "It's my uncle and his brother when they were boys."

Sebastian cast a glance over it. They were both dark-haired, both pale-eyed, but whereas one of them was smiling and open-faced, the other was solemn and serious.

Just then there were footsteps behind them, and a chilly voice said, "What is the meaning of this?"

Mrs. March in her night attire and a shawl was thin and tall, with a haughty expression. And Francesca was right, he thought, as he watched the woman's gaze fix on her. The housekeeper did resent her.

"I want to ask you some questions, Mrs. March," Sebastian said in a level voice, and was glad when her eyes moved on to him and away from Francesca.

"And you are?" she said imperiously.

"My name is Sebastian Thorne."

Recognition flickered in her eyes before she could stop it, and something else besides. Was it fear? Plenty of people were afraid of him, and often for no other reason than that they'd heard of him and what he did.

Or was it anger? Was Mrs. March simply angry with him and Francesca for waking her up in the middle of the night?

"I'll go and get Mr. Tremaine," she said, half turning to leave.

"He's already been called," Francesca told her. "He should be down any moment."

"Besides," Sebastian said smoothly, "you may prefer to answer my questions in private."

She hesitated, and he could see a sharp mind at work. "Very well." She shrugged. "What is it you want to ask me, Mr. Thorne?"

She thought she was superior to him. She believed she could outwit him. He could read it in her eyes, in the way she held herself. He'd met people like her before.

"Madame Aphrodite has been poisoned with arsenic," he said baldly, hoping to shock her into some sort of admission.

But she was ready for him. "Oh? Well, a woman in her profession must make a great many enemies. Jealous wives, disappointed lovers. What can one expect? I hope you don't think I can help you capture the culprit?"

"No, Mrs. March, you misunderstand. We already have the poisoner in our custody."

She was rattled, and she grew wary. "Then I suppose it is an ex-lover or a disgruntled client?"

"No, it is a protégée of Aphrodite's called Maeve."

Mrs. March said nothing, waiting, but her eyes were watchful.

Sebastian might have waited, too, played her along

a little longer, but Francesca wasn't used to the game. She was too impatient for the truth.

"I know you know who Maeve is, Mrs. March," she said, angry and upset. "I saw her here. With you. Why are you pretending not to know her? What was she doing in this house? You must tell us immediately!"

"I don't have to tell you anything," Mrs. March retorted, leaning forward so that her face was very close to Francesca's. She seemed to tremble with malevolence. "What are you but a whore's daughter? A bastard!"

Francesca stared back at her, and Sebastian could see she was shocked.

But her lack of response only made Mrs. March more volatile. Her voice went on and on, and she didn't seem able to stop. "Why are you given such privileges? Why do we have to do as you say? 'Yes, miss,' 'no, miss.' It's not as if you're any better than the rest of us. Why should you have money to spend on new clothes and pretty things? It isn't fair!"

"You have overstepped the mark," Francesca whispered, pale and trembling with emotion.

"Oh dear, have I?" she mocked. "But it's the truth, isn't it? Your mother is a high-class whore and your father—" but as if realizing at last that she really had gone too far, Mrs. March closed her mouth.

But it was too late. "What do you know of my father?" Francesca demanded.

"Nothing. I know nothing about him."

She was lying. Sebastian smelled it, and her fear. Her hatred of Francesca had led her to say far too much, and now she was frightened.

"Is it true, Mrs. March," he said, "that you're one of Mrs. Slater's girls?"

A tremor seemed to run through her, under her skin.

Francesca was too shocked to notice. "Mrs. Slater! How could you be associated with that dreadful woman? How could anyone?"

"What dreadful woman is this?" asked a male voice.

Mrs. March gave a faint cry of relief and turned, almost stumbling in her eagerness to reach his side. "Mr. Tremaine, sir," she babbled. "I'm so glad you're here." And she cast a look back over her shoulder toward Sebastian, a look that told him that she was saved and now everything would be all right.

Chapter 24

"**U**ncle William."

Francesca didn't move, watching him warily. After their earlier clash in the doorway to this very room, she was not eager to welcome his arrival on the scene. Certainly not as eager as Mrs. March.

"Mr. Tremaine," Mrs. March said with all the delight of a school tattletale, "this man is trying to make out I have done something wrong. Tell him to leave. I won't be questioned in this way, I won't!"

"Hush, Mrs. March," William said with a frown. "I can't say I'm particularly happy at being woken at this hour. What is this all about? Francesca?"

"Why are you asking her?" Mrs. March burst out.

William looked at her. She seemed to recollect herself, falling silent.

"Uncle William," Francesca said, "this is Mr. Thorne."

William gave Sebastian the full force of his disapproving stare. "Oh? And who is Mr. Thorne? What are you doing here at this time of night with my niece? Explain yourself, sir!"

If Uncle William thought to intimidate Sebastian as he did others, then he was mistaken. Francesca watched with enjoyment as Sebastian smiled and answered confidently. "Oh, I intend to, Mr. Tremaine. I have been hired by Madame Aphrodite to find the woman who kidnapped her daughters."

William gave a grunt of amusement. "Have you now? Bit late for that, isn't it?" His gaze strayed to Mrs. March and back again. "What are you doing here? Shouldn't you be out looking?"

Mrs. March gave a dutiful laugh, but her heart wasn't really in it.

"I'm here because I think it possible that Mrs. March can help us in our search."

William looked surprised. "My housekeeper is connected to Mrs. Slater? I hardly think—"

"There has been a spy in Aphrodite's Club, informing Mrs. Slater of what goes on there. I suppose Mrs. Slater was always aware that one day Aphrodite would begin to search, and she wanted to be sure she knew in advance. We have captured that spy, Mr. Tremaine."

"Well, then, if you have her, what do you want here?"

"Because the spy—Maeve—has been seen visiting Mrs. March. Now, you'd have to agree that it would make sense for Mrs. Slater to have a spy in your household as well as the club, in case there was any news about your sister and her family that needed to be passed on."

William flared up. "What you are saying is preposterous! Mrs. March is a honest and diligent woman. I have no doubt as to her loyalty to me and my family."

Mrs. March glowed. "Thank you, sir," she murmured.

"Then tell us why Maeve was here?" Francesca cried. "If it means nothing, if this is all a mistake, tell us!"

"I didn't know her name," Mrs. March retorted. "She came and told me she had a message from my mother and I let her in, but it was a lie. She didn't know my mother. So I sent her on her way and never saw her again."

Was it possible? The woman's chin was up in a belligerent manner and her eyes were flickering from one face to another, waiting to see if she was believed.

"You see?" William said quietly. "There was a reasonable explanation. Now, can we be left in peace to—"

"I don't believe you," Sebastian broke in.

Mrs. March's mouth opened, then closed again. She shot William a pleading look.

"Mrs. March?" Sebastian said quietly. "The truth, if you please."

"Tell him," William instructed her. "What are you waiting for?"

"If you don't tell me, then I will have to call in the police to ask the questions," Sebastian went on.

William's nostrils flared, as if he'd smelled something bad. "The police?"

"It will probably be necessary to have the police here anyway," Sebastian went on, sensing weakness.

Mrs. March must also have seen something in her employer's eyes because she gave a little moan.

"Tell them," he said coldly. "I'll do my best for you, Mrs. March, but I will not have the police at my door, pawing through my belongings."

"No," she gasped.

"It will be better for everyone if you are open about your dealings with this woman," William said. "Certainly it will be better for you." He nodded at Sebastian and turned and left the room, removing himself from any further connection with an unpleasant and possibly scandalous situation.

Left behind, abandoned, Mrs. March had given up. "Stupid old cow," she whispered, rage and despair making her face ugly. "I knew she'd bring me down, the stupid old cow."

"Who would bring you down?" Sebastian asked.

Mrs. March glared at him and shook her head.

"Tell me," he demanded, in a voice every bit as steely as William's, and far more dangerous.

"Who do you think I mean? Mrs. Slater. *My mother.*" She laughed aloud at the shock she'd caused.

"How's that for a family, eh, Miss Francesca? Tops yours by a mile, don't it!"

"Dear God," Francesca breathed, appalled.

"I'm her daughter all right," Mrs. March said, and there was a hint of twisted pride in her voice now. "The only child she had from her own body. There were plenty of others, but they weren't hers. She always promised me a better life than she had. She promised me wealth and a grand house and a man to look after me."

"And you blame her for not getting any of it?"

"Of course I do! This is her fault, all of it. Why didn't she smother the three of you when she had the chance?"

Francesca didn't remember being left in the library, but Sebastian must have taken Mrs. March out, because when he returned he was alone. He took her hands in his, rubbing her gloved fingers, trying to warm them. She let him; she didn't have the energy to pull away.

There was too much to think about, too much to try and fit together, and hanging over everything like a black shroud was her concern for Aphrodite's condition.

She might already be dead.

"Damn and blast it, Francesca," Sebastian said softly, "are you listening to me?"

She looked up and realized that she hadn't heard a word.

He sighed and bent his head, kissing the top of

hers. "What do you want to do now? I can take you back to the club."

Yes. She opened her mouth to voice it, and then she thought better of it. "Where are you going?"

"You can't come with me. It's too dangerous."

"You're going to see her, aren't you? Mrs. March told you where she is? Mrs. Slater." He didn't have to answer her, she knew it. "I want to come."

"Francesca . . ."

"I want to come. I have the right to see the woman who stole me and caused my mother such grief. You can't stop me, Sebastian."

He could stop her, of course he could, but would he?

"Please," she murmured. "I will go in Aphrodite's stead. For her."

After a moment he reached out to take her hand. "I'm taking some constables from the Metropolitan Police with us. This is a dangerous game we're playing, Francesca, and Mrs. Slater is a dangerous woman."

"I understand that. I'm not afraid."

"Very well," Sebastian said gruffly. "But don't say I didn't warn you."

"Who's that? What do you want with a sick old woman?"

The slurred voice was even more slurred than usual. She was drunk, thought Jed in disgust.

"It's me. We have to get you out o' here."

She stared at him blearily from her chair by the fire, and he stepped closer, into the flickering light.

"Jed," she muttered, mouth slack. "What do you want, Jed? Come to take me money, have you? Well, you won't find it. I've hidden it well."

"The bobbies are comin', cousin. T'girl you had at the club has told 'em, and they're on their way. We need to go."

"You're lying," she insisted, shrugging off his hands as he tried to lift her. "You want me money, you do. I know you Jed Holmes. That's all you've ever wanted. You're not the man your father is. You'll never be half the man Hal is."

The words sparked a rage in him. All the times he'd refused to listen to Hal and returned back here, to be with her. All the loyalty he'd given to her, and now she was telling him she preferred Hal? Hal, who had gone into hiding like the rat he was!

"God rot you then," he growled. "You can stay here and get took. I'm off. And I won't be back, neither."

She gave a raucous laugh.

He strode through the house, pulling out drawers, throwing aside anything that might be used to hide money. He wanted his share. What was wrong with that? She owed it to him.

He didn't hear the front door open. He was too busy rifling through a bureau, bills and receipts raining down around him. There was an iron box at the back of a drawer, and he drew it out with a smile. It was heavy. There were probably jewels in here, or sovereigns. Aye, gold sovereigns. Cousin Angela liked her gold.

"Hello, Jed."

The voice was familiar, but for a moment he couldn't place it, and then he remembered. Sebastian Thorne. He turned, hoisting the heavy box to his shoulder, ready to throw it, but Thorne wasn't alone. Behind him stood several police constables in their blue jackets.

He lowered the box.

"I should've left without it," he said bitterly. He nodded his head toward the other end of the house. "The cow's in there. Take her with my good wishes."

Francesca stepped quietly into the cozy sitting room. The house itself had been a surprise, sedate and respectable-looking, and nicely furnished. The house of someone who obeyed the law and worked hard. Except that Mrs. Slater's work was of the cruelest and wickedest kind, and she had never obeyed a law in her life.

The woman now slumped in the chair in front of the fire was the woman who had taken three sisters away from their home and their mother. She had caused great pain and suffering. She was a monster.

Francesca came closer, so that she could see her face.

She was asleep, and from the gin fumes wafting from her, she was also drunk. Her mouth was ajar, her face slack, and her gray hair untidy. Then, with a snort, she woke up. She opened her eyes, and her face went blank with surprise.

"Aphrodite?" she whispered. "Is that you? Or are you a ghost?"

Her heart was pounding, her mouth was dry, but Francesca found the courage to speak. "I am Francesca, Aphrodite's daughter."

The woman's breathing was so loud, Francesca wondered if she had even heard her. "He'll finish you, you know that," she rambled. "He won't never rest until he's rid himself of you."

"Who? Who will never rest?"

But she gave a shudder, her entire body jolting and shaking, and then she went slack. Her eyes flickered, the whites showing. A line of spittle ran from the corner of her mouth.

Frozen, Francesca stood staring down at her.

"Francesca?" It was Sebastian, grim-faced from his encounter with Jed. He glanced at her, as if satisfying himself she was all right, and then turned to the slumped figure in the chair. She watched as he bent over her, examining her for signs of life.

"She's had some sort of fit," he said. "Jed said she was unwell."

"I keep telling myself that she's Mrs. Slater, the monster who's ruled my life since I was a baby, but she doesn't seem like a monster."

"Don't you believe it. This woman has caused endless suffering and misery. The world is better off without her."

"I want her punished. She will be punished, won't she?"

"If she lives long enough, then she will go up before a judge."

"Good." Francesca sighed, suddenly weary beyond speaking.

"You're free of her now, Francesca," he said gently. "She can't frighten you anymore."

"Then why do I still feel as if I'm in danger?" she wailed.

"Because you are. Whoever it was who gave Mrs. Slater her orders, who gave Maeve her orders, is still out there. Aphrodite knows who he is, but she won't speak. She wants me to find proof."

"Why won't she speak?"

"He must be a powerful man. Without proof she will never get anyone to believe her. He will destroy her, and maybe he will destroy you and your sisters, too."

She shivered, and when he put his arms around her, she didn't resist.

I'll stay here for a moment, she told herself, *just a moment. It can't hurt to allow myself a moment. I don't trust him anymore, how can I? Soon I will break with him forever, but just now I want . . . I need to be held by him.*

Chapter 25

It was the following day, and Aphrodite was dreaming again. She was shifting through her memories like someone shuffling a pack of cards. She had reached the point where Francesca's father had died and she was alone. There was the other one, of course, and at first she'd thought he might be enough. But it wasn't long before she realized he wasn't the man she thought him.

He wants to possess me. I see it now. He doesn't love me, not like T. did. He has no love in him, no joy. When T. laughed, I knew he was filled with the wonder of life. When this one laughs it is a mean sound, a small sound, and there is no wonder.

London keeps me busy. The club takes much of my

time, and I love it. I think perhaps it is the club that is my lover now.

Something dreadful has happened.

I cannot write, and yet I cannot not write.

My children are gone . . . my babies! Someone came in the night and took them away from me. I think I will go mad if I do not find them. I must find them. Why has this happened? I don't understand why they have been taken. Who in this world could be so cruel?

I will find them. If it takes all of my life, I will find them.

But she hadn't found them. He'd helped her, the lover she'd scorned, and she'd been grateful for his generosity. She'd trusted him. He'd sent out letters and hired men to search. Sometimes she thought he had mobilized the entire country for her darlings.

Or at least that was what she had believed at the time. Now she wondered if he'd even lifted one finger.

But despite all the efforts to find them, her children were gone, and as the days, the weeks, the months slipped by, she knew it. Her health failed and she grew weaker. For a whole year she was ill, and her friends wondered if she would recover. But she was strong; she had to be.

Today I returned to life. I rose from my bed and dressed in black mourning—I vow I will always wear mourning from now on—and I made my way to the club. I have come back to life, but there will always be a part of me missing. How can it be otherwise? I have lost my children.

And as the years slip by, I begin to think I know who was behind the taking of them.

She woke with a start. Francesca was sitting beside her, holding her hand. She realized with a flash of insight that although her daughters had been returned to her almost ten years ago, it was only now that that reunion was complete. Now that the wayward heart of her youngest daughter had been restored to her.

"Francesca," she murmured, and smiled.

"How are you feeling, Mother?"

"A little better, I think." She grimaced. "The doctor has done unspeakable things to me, *petit chaton*."

Francesca couldn't help but smile. "If it makes you better, and cleans the poison from your body, then it was worth it, surely?"

But Aphrodite had fallen asleep again.

Francesca heard Dobson come forward, and his warm hand rested gently upon her shoulder. "She is sleeping," he said. "We are very fortunate that Maeve administered such small doses."

"Fortunate," Francesca breathed, and shook her head over the word. "Where is Maeve now?"

"Locked up in a police cell, where she belongs, but I think she'll always be in a hell of her own making." Sebastian was there, too, on the other side of the bed. He was watching her face, trying to read her thoughts. "She loved Aphrodite, and to harm her has caused her great grief."

"I can't understand why she didn't stand up to Mrs. Slater and say no. She could 'ave come to us," Dobson said.

"I think she was so used to obeying orders that it

didn't occur to her that it was possible for her to do other than what she was told," Sebastian said.

"Did you speak to her, that woman?" Dobson asked, and he didn't have to name her; the savage tone of voice was enough.

"Mrs. Slater appears to have had some sort of seizure. From what I can make out she's been ill for years, and getting worse. She can't talk at all for now. And Jed refuses to."

"So we'll never know the truth? Why she did it, and who else was involved?"

"Who else was involved? Do you mean the man who gave the orders?" Francesca asked.

Sebastian answered her. "Aphrodite always believed there was someone else, someone who paid Mrs. Slater to kidnap you and your sisters. She would not tell me who he was. She wanted a witness or some kind of proof first. She wanted me to name him."

"One of her lovers," Francesca murmured, and then bit her lip, casting Dobson an apologetic glance. "I'm sorry. I was thinking aloud. To do such a terrible thing, the man most have hated her very much, and love can turn to hate."

"Perhaps," Dobson agreed, "but I think it was more than that. The man must have had something to gain from it. Money, that's what drives most folk."

"You think he was going to force Aphrodite and our fathers to pay money for our return? And then it went wrong. Yes, that makes sense."

Dobson said nothing.

"I haven't given up yet," Sebastian said.

"At least my sisters and I are out of danger," Francesca went on as if he hadn't spoken. "You won't have to follow me about anymore, Mr. Thorne."

His brows slashed down over his eyes. She felt as if he were drilling holes into her. "You could still be in danger."

"I don't need your protection," she said flatly. "I am returning to Yorkshire as soon as my mother is well again, and I will never come back."

"You're running away," he said in a flat, angry voice.

Her eyes flashed, and for a moment he hoped she would flare up into temper, but she quashed the emotion and put on her proper face. "No, I'm going home where I belong."

"*Non, non, petit chaton,*" a voice whispered from the bed. Aphrodite was awake again, her dark eyes brighter than before. "You have forgotten. There is to be a ball in your honor. Amy sent me a little note. You are to be introduced to London society, is that not so?"

"I can't possibly—" she began.

"But you can. You must. I insist upon it." She turned her head and found Dobson. "Jemmy," she murmured, "you must act for me in this. Mr. Thorne needs his instructions."

He looked into her eyes, and then he nodded abruptly.

"That is good," she whispered. "All is well."

Outside the room there were voices, and then quiet footsteps mounting the stairs. The door opened, and Sebastian stepped aside as a short, plump woman with fair hair peeped in. Francesca stood up with a gasp, and came around the bed and into her arms. Neither of them said anything, Francesca's head resting on Marietta's. It was only after she released her that she realized that Marietta was with child again, as round as a pumpkin.

"How is she?" Marietta asked anxiously, looking over to the bed where their mother lay.

"Sleeping, I think. She drifts in and out."

"Is it true? That Maeve . . . ?"

Francesca knew that Maeve and Marietta had always been close; it must be a terrible shock to her sister. Francesca squeezed her hand. "It's true."

Marietta moved toward the bed, and Francesca left her alone with Aphrodite. She felt Sebastian following close behind her, out onto the gallery. His fingers clasped her elbow, and his voice in her ear was angry.

"You're not serious about not needing me?" he said. "Damn and blast it, Francesca, you're still in danger!"

"Not in Yorkshire. You've made certain of that."

He looked as if there was a great deal more he wanted to say, but she didn't want to hear it.

"You're going to climb back in the cage and close the door," he said bitterly. "You don't know what you're missing out on, Francesca."

She gave a shaky laugh. "Oh, but I do. That's the trouble. Still, with most of England between us, I hope to forget. Eventually."

"Francesca?" It was Marietta calling her, and without another glance at him, she returned to the bedchamber and closed the door.

Sebastian stood in the gallery and wondered what he was going to do. He felt as if his job wasn't completed, and yet perhaps Francesca was right and she was no longer in danger. Perhaps he would have to learn to live without her.

"Mr. Thorne?"

Dobson was watching him. "I 'ave something to tell you. A name."

Sebastian frowned, and then he realized what it was Dobson was going to tell him. "You know?"

"Of course I know. I've always known. And when I tell you, you'll understand why Aphrodite is so worried about Francesca." He moved closer and spoke it softly. "So you see now the difficulties?"

"Yes, I do see," Sebastian murmured. "I see it all. Then her father is . . . ?"

"Yes."

"Damn and blast it." He sighed, and shook his head. "It's not over, then, is it? I need to protect her even more vigilantly than before."

Dobson nodded. "He feels threatened and he'll strike out. Francesca's a threat to him now. She can take everything he's clung to all these years. He'll try and stop her before she learns the truth."

Sebastian didn't reply, and, satisfied, Dobson left him there.

Sebastian didn't know what to think. The name brought everything in focus, he understood so much now, but it also increased his anxiety where Francesca was concerned tenfold. The man in question was a gentleman, someone who could pass through society without anyone giving him a second glance.

It didn't matter if she was in Yorkshire or London, Francesca was going to be exposed to him—she was exposed to him already. How could Sebastian look out for her? How could he be where she was, taking care of her? He was Mr. Thorne, and Mr. Thorne would be told in no uncertain terms that he was not welcome in the places where Miss Francesca Greentree could go with impunity.

But then again what if he was no longer Mr. Thorne?

Aphrodite had suggested as much. *How can such a man as you, Mr. Thorne, walk beside Francesca in anything other than secret? If you were a gentleman to her lady, you could keep her safe more easily. And you do want to keep her safe, don't you?*

His hands tightened their grip on the ebony railing that circled the gallery. He'd promised himself he'd never go back, but Francesca needed him. He had to save her.

Whatever the cost to himself.

Chapter 26

"So she really can't speak?" Lil asked, wide-eyed.

Martin nodded. "She really can't, and she's not playacting, either. She can't tell Mr. Thorne who was giving her orders, and now he's pulling out his hair with worry, because he thinks whoever it is will come after Miss Francesca next, and she's refused to let him near her."

Martin often told her things no one else knew, things he probably shouldn't have. But Lil liked it. She didn't let him know that, though; men were best kept in the dark when it came to what women were thinking.

"Good job, too." She sniffed. "Miss Francesca's too good for the likes of him."

Martin laughed. "As if that has anything to do with it, Lil. They're mad for each other, can't you see that?"

"No, I can't, and I don't believe you."

"Well, you take note of the way they look at each other next time you see them together. You'll believe me then."

Lil sniffed. "There are more important things than lust, Martin. When a lady marries, she marries for breeding and blood, and she wants a man who'll look after her and give her all the things she's used to."

"What about if someone who isn't a lady marries?" Martin asked. "Does she go for breeding, too? Or can she marry for love?"

"It depends," Lil said primly.

"On what?"

"On the someone."

He chuckled. "Now I find that strangely encouraging," he murmured. Lil felt a pang in her heart. She'd promised herself to have nothing more to do with men. There was too much heartache involved, and she had too many secrets. Martin would want to know all about her, too; they all did. He'd pick and pry until he'd winkled the past out of her, and then he'd turn up his nose and walk away.

She couldn't bear that. She'd rather stop it right now, as she had with Mr. Keith. And as for Jacob, he hadn't cared enough about her past to ask. All he'd wanted was someone to cook and clean his clothes and roll about with in bed. He thought Lil was a good choice because she was a lady's maid, a step up from a village girl.

But Lil knew that it would be different with Martin. He was articulate and intelligent, and he made her laugh. She could see them together; she could see them happy together.

And that was what frightened her.

"I'll be going back to Yorkshire soon," she said. "Miss Francesca will want me to go with her."

"That's a pity." Martin shook his head. "What if I asked you to stay with me? You could help me look after Mr. Thorne."

"I don't think so. What would Mr. Thorne want with a lady's maid?"

Martin smiled. "I have a feeling Mr. Thorne is thinking of getting married, Lil."

"Married?" she was astonished.

"Yes. I found a pair of lady's drawers stuffed into the bookcase the other day."

Lil's eyes grew even wider.

"You think about it, Lil. It would be comfortable, you and me together in London. I reckon we'd make the perfect couple. Professionally speaking, that is."

She couldn't help but smile. Professionally speaking! Who did he think he was fooling? But it was tempting. Surprisingly tempting, when she remembered what she would be leaving behind.

"I'll think on it, Martin."

He nodded, as if he was satisfied with that, but she noticed that he was smiling, too.

There they were, both of them grinning as if they'd

won the lottery and neither of them brave enough to admit it.

"Where is Mr. Thorne now?" Lil asked. "Miss Francesca said he's gone away. Can't say she was looking very happy about it."

"He's gone home," Martin said. "But he'll be back. You wait and see."

The house had hardly changed. Ramshackle, he used to call it, but only because so many generations of his family had built their own bits and pieces onto the original Tudor manor. Worthorne Manor.

It was evening when he arrived, and he tethered his horse halfway down the driveway so he could walk to the front door. He wanted to take his time and allow the feeling of magic to creep over him. It was so beautiful, with the gold of evening reflected in the Tudor bricks and the small glass windows, while the lush gardens overflowed with flowers. The scent of roses drifted over him, and he thought about Barbara.

As a child she'd run through these gardens, more often than not with Sebastian chasing her. As twins, they did most things together until they were five, and then it changed. Sebastian went to school and Barbara stayed home.

She was a beautiful child, and she grew into a beautiful woman. It was Sebastian who brought Leon home to Worthorne with him. They'd met in London and become friends. Barbara and Leon fell in love.

He still remembered when his sister came to him, smiling, hopeful, to tell him that Leon wished to marry her. He'd been overjoyed. His friend and his sister to marry; it was surely meant to be. And then she said:

"He can be a little jealous."

He was surprised. Leon, jealous? Impossible. He laughed and smoothed the cuffs of his brand-new coat. "You must stop flirting, Barbara, then he will not feel jealous."

She smiled, but there was doubt in her eyes.

He ignored it. The wedding was arranged and his sister was suffering from nerves, he told himself, nothing more. Everything was perfect. The truth was, everything wasn't perfect. He was twenty-two years old, self-centered, and unfamiliar with the shades of light and dark to be found in the world. He couldn't conceive of a man who wanted to harm women, who enjoyed harming them. He preferred to believe his sister was suffering from prewedding nerves.

The wedding was held in the village church, with all their friends and family around them. Sebastian gave her away, as her brother and the head of the family. Their parents had died ten years before, and Sebastian had come young to the title. Barbara and Leon were to live in London part of the year, and for the rest of it they were to reside in Northumberland, on Leon's estate.

Sebastian did not see her for four months, and when he saw her again she had changed. She was no longer his sunny-tempered, sweet sister. She didn't smile as often, and she was wan and somehow timid. Leon went on to London to visit his friends, and she stayed with Sebastian at Worthorne. By the end of her visit she was more like her old self, and he told himself that it was the cold, bleak estate in Northumberland that was the trouble, that she should ask Leon to stay in London, or better still, at Worthorne.

"I will ask," she said somberly, as if it was something she didn't relish. He laughed, because the Leon he knew could be persuaded to change his mind very easily. "Anything for a friend" was his motto.

Sebastian saw Barbara only twice more.

Once was in London, at Leon's house. She was quiet, she moved stiffly, and when he asked her if she was all right, she looked to Leon before she answered. Sebastian thought it strange, but when she would not talk to him, he shrugged. There were things to do, and he was a wealthy young aristocrat on the town.

The next time he saw her she was lying on her bed, laid out in her favorite dress, with flowers twisted through her hair, her dead, still face as beautiful as ever. Her murderer, Leon, had taken his own life in remorse, or so they said. Sebastian thought it more likely that, having murdered Barbara, he was not brave enough to face the consequences. His family had carried him back to Northumberland, to his estate, for burial, but Sebastian refused to let Barbara go with him. She had been shackled to her murderer in life, she would not lie beside him in death. At least, he told himself, he could give her that.

He wept. He berated himself for his blindness and

his stupidity. Now that she was dead, he saw things so much more clearly, and understood what they had meant. Leon had hit her, hurt her, made her life a living hell. And he, her twin brother, had neither known nor cared. There was nothing he could do or say that would make it better.

That was when he decided to go away and turn his back on the man he'd been—the selfish and foolish boy—and become someone else. He must make recompense by helping others. That was when Mr. Thorne was born.

"Sebastian?"

He lifted his head. He realized he'd been standing in the middle of the driveway, staring at the front of the house. The sun was nearly gone and the air had a balmy, calm feeling, as it did sometimes just before night fell. A moth blundered into his face.

"Sebastian, is that you?"

There was a man standing at the bottom of the steps leading to the front doors. Sebastian knew him at once, even though it had been eight years since he last saw him.

"Yes, Marcus, it is me."

Marcus laughed. A joyful sound. "You've come home!" he cried. "Here you are at last. Come in, come in. Everything is ready for you. Everything is waiting."

Touched beyond speaking, Sebastian followed his younger brother into Worthorne Manor, and into his past.

* * *

"You're only glad I'm back because you want to join the army," Sebastian said, later, when he had eaten and drunk a bottle of wine, and was ensconced in his favorite chair. The summer evening was warm, too warm for a fire, and they had opened the long windows to let in the scents of the garden.

"You know me too well," Marcus admitted, sighing.

"I thought you might have grown to like being squire of Worthorne. I don't want to take your place if you are content to keep it."

Marcus chuckled. "No, brother, it doesn't suit me at all. I will relish the freedom of the army. You know I've always wanted to travel. You can stay here at Worthorne and raise your heirs, and I'll go off and have all the fun."

Sebastian smiled at his naïveté.

"You've changed," his brother said abruptly. "You've grown gloomy."

"I have a lot on my mind."

"A woman, do you mean?"

Sebastian tried to frown, but wasn't very successful.

"What is she like? Come on, brother, tell me. You can't imagine how damned boring it's been here for the last eight years."

Sebastian tried to imagine Francesca's face and form, and found it all too easy. "Dark hair, curling and thick, the sort of hair you can take in your hands and drown in. A pretty face. Very pretty. A tip-tilted nose. Brown eyes with long lashes, with a gleam in them, when she's not pretending she's Miss Proper.

Lips that were just made for kissing. The top of her head comes to my chin, and she feels lovely and soft in my arms."

"And character, brother? Or is that less important than her kissable lips?"

"She says what she thinks, and she argues with me, and she's not at all intimidated when I swear. She makes me laugh, too. She makes me happy. In fact, she's a woman to spend a lifetime with. If she'll have me."

Marcus laughed, thinking he was joking. "Why wouldn't she have you!"

"Because she doesn't trust me not to hurt her, and who can blame her for that?"

Quietly Marcus got up and opened another bottle of the excellent wine. He poured his brother a glass and handed it to him. "Drown your sorrows," he suggested.

Sebastian stared at him in mock disbelief. "Is that the best you can do, brother? Is that your considered advice? Drown your sorrows?"

Marcus shrugged. "I never was one for affairs of the heart, Seb. After Barbara . . . I don't give advice."

Sebastian sighed. "No," he agreed, "it's difficult to recover from something like that. I didn't think I would, but somehow . . . Francesca has healed me, or rather she's made me want to heal myself. I want to be the sort of man she can love."

"Grand sentiments, brother," Marcus replied, raising his glass. "Here's to new beginnings!"

Somberly Sebastian raised his own glass. "To new beginnings."

* * *

Three days later, Sebastian stood in a drawing room in Belgravia, feeling as if he were treading on eggshells. He was dressed in the clothes his brother had lent him, but although they fit well and were fashionable, he didn't feel comfortable. It would take a while, he supposed, to throw off Mr. Thorne.

The door opened and an attractive, elderly woman entered. She met his eyes, and he saw her own widen. "Sebastian?" she gasped. "It can't be!"

"Yes, it is Sebastian," he said, and grinned.

"But where have you been?"

"I've been away, Ma'am, but I'm back now. I want to ask a favor of you."

"Oh do you now? Well, it depends what the favor is."

"My brother tells me you're having a ball here in a week's time. I want you to send out some more invitations."

Lady Annear's elegant eyebrows lifted. "I may be your godmother, but that doesn't mean I have to do as you tell me." She paused. "I will send your invitations out if you promise to dance with my granddaughters. All seven of 'em!"

"Very well. I promise."

She smiled. "It must be serious. Come, sit down and tell me all about it."

Chapter 27

Marietta sat down and put her feet up. "You have no idea how much my back is aching," she said cheerily.

"Poor Marietta," Aphrodite murmured. "You should complain to Max, however, not us. It is he who caused this problem."

Marietta wagged a finger at her. "You are very wicked, Mother. I will do no such thing. He might stop."

"Marietta, show some decorum," Francesca said, more for Amy's benefit than because she really expected her sister to obey. But Amy was busy with the morning mail.

Aphrodite had been invited to visit now she was

so much better. But Jemmy Dobson still insisted she wasn't well enough to make an appearance in the salon at the club, or to work in her office. She was to rest and regain her strength, and put on some flesh.

"He complains if I do not finish my potatoes," she said with a grimace. "I do not like potatoes!"

"Like them or not, you are looking a great deal better," Francesca assured her, smiling.

Aphrodite smiled back. "Yes, but I told you I would not die. I am strong, *petit chaton*. Too strong for that horrible woman."

Marietta wriggled her aching feet. "I always liked Maeve," she said sadly. "I still can't believe she could do such a thing."

"I did not mean Maeve," Aphrodite said somberly. "I think I could forgive her. But the other one, Mrs. Slater, no, I will never forgive her."

"She still hasn't said a word," Francesca announced the latest news. "Lil says she just sits and stares at the wall. And Jed hardly ever speaks, either, and when he does, it's to blame her for everything. Leading him astray, he says. As for Mrs. March . . ."

"Shhh!" Amy glanced over at the door, just in case William might suddenly arrive and overhear them. "My brother is still very upset about all of that. He was very fond of Mrs. March, or at least he was fond of her efficiency. She ran the house like clockwork, he tells me."

"Never mind that she was a horrible woman who thought it would have been better if her mother had smothered us all." Francesca shuddered. "I'm glad she's in jail."

"I've been interviewing new housekeepers for him, and I think I've found someone suitable," Amy went on. "I've warned him not to glare at her, at least not until she's grown used to his ways. His bark is worse than his bite."

Francesca and Marietta exchanged a glance.

Amy took up another letter and opened the crisp paper. "Oh," she said, and her face lit up. "It's an invitation! *Lady Annear requests the presence of Mr. Tremaine, Mrs. Jardine, and Miss Francesca Greentree at her granddaughter's first ball . . . *" She dropped the paper in her lap. "It's only two days away! Francesca can't possibly be ready."

"Yes, she can," Marietta said, her eyes closing. "Remember, Francesca has a ball gown completed. She can wear that, and have another one made up for our own ball. Plenty of time."

Francesca was appalled. "I can't go about ordering ball gowns to be made up like . . . like confetti! If we must go to Lady Annear's ball, then I will wear the same one to both. No one will notice."

"Or you could get Mrs. Hall to make one for you," Marietta suggested, with a grin. "I wonder what sort of ball gown she'd make? Brown sacking, probably."

"Please, Marietta, don't encourage her." Aphrodite shuddered.

"No, don't," Amy agreed, thoughtful. "But your other idea is a good one. Francesca can wear the rose satin gown to Lady Annear's ball, and have the modiste make up a new gown for our ball. You'd better go to her immediately . . . after I reply to this invitation, of course."

Francesca had come to peer over Amy's shoulder. "Why would Lady Annear invite us to her ball?" she asked, puzzled. "Do you know her, Mama?"

Amy wrinkled her brow. "It's odd, but I can't recall ever meeting her. Perhaps she knows William. He is invited, too. Well, whatever the reason for the invitation, we can't ignore it. She is an influential woman in London society."

"Never mind, *petit chaton*," Aphrodite murmured, when Francesca sat down beside her, "you will look very pretty, and there will be many men asking you to dance. I feel so sorry for you."

Francesca smiled. "I must seem churlish. I don't mean to be."

"You miss your handsome Mr. Thorne."

Francesca knew she could argue and deny it, but this was Aphrodite and there wasn't much point.

The truth was, she did miss him. Everything seemed gray and dull, like a winter's day, now he was gone. Life held no excitement for her, no adventure. She knew that if she really did marry and spend her time in London attending functions and being respectable, she would probably do something wild and ruin herself completely.

She had become aware the other day, as she was walking in the gardens, of a sudden urge to take off her shoes and run barefoot across the grass. Not exactly the thoughts of a proper young lady.

Which made her wonder if Sebastian was right, and she wasn't proper at all.

Lady Annear's house in Belgravia was brilliantly lit. Unlike William Tremaine, she was not too old-fashioned to connect her house to the gas supply. As their carriage drew up, there seemed to be a large number of other carriages, and soon they were politely jostling with the other guests, awaiting their turn to be admitted.

"You look beautiful, my dear," Amy whispered, squeezing her hand.

Francesca thought she looked very well, too, even though she knew it was vain to think it. But her mirror had told her it was true. The rose red satin was very flattering against her dark hair and eyes, and her creamy skin seemed to glow. The expert cut of the garment accentuated her narrow waist and the swell of her bosom. With sleeves so small as to be almost nonexistent, her arms and shoulders appeared almost naked, and the overskirt was very plain, without any adornment. She wore matching slippers on her feet, and some of Aphrodite's diamonds gleamed around her throat.

The woman Amy had employed to dress their hair had teased and twisted her dark curls into neat ringlets, and placed a wreath of flowers upon her crown.

She decided that she looked like someone she had always wanted to be. It gave her confidence. Perhaps Aphrodite was right; perhaps she would enjoy herself after all. Was it possible that she could be the

woman on the moors, wild and free, and also someone sophisticated enough to glide through London
society? Look at her sisters, they managed it!

"Miss Greentree? You are new to London, I think?"
Lady Annear's curious eyes slid over her.

"I admit to preferring the country, my lady."

She had made a faux pas already. So much for
gliding through society. Lady Annear's well-bred
face had gone blank. "How very odd."

"My daughter will soon grow used to town ways,"
Amy put in quickly. "London has so much to offer."

"Indeed. Especially when the girl is pretty and
has a large dowry." Lady Annear's voice was droll.
"What do you think, Mr. Tremaine? Your niece is
quite a catch, is she not?"

William gave her his frosty smile. "Indeed."

"Rumor has it, sir, that you are looking for an earl?"

William frowned. "I cannot imagine how such a
rumor began."

"Can't you? Speaking of earls . . . here is someone
you know." Lady Annear beckoned toward an approaching gentleman, a gentleman who looked very
familiar. "It is the Earl of Worthorne. My lord, I believe you have met Miss Francesca Greentree?"

The room was spinning.

She heard a gasp from Amy and a muffled curse
from Uncle William, but they were no longer important. All she could see and hear was Sebastian, Mr.
Thorne, in the guise of an aristocratic gentleman—an
earl, no less! Immaculate black evening wear, a crisply
starched white shirt and necktie, his dark, wind-blown
hair tamed and brushed, and his handsome villain's

face closely shaved. His wicked black eyes fixed on hers with an apologetic smile that quickly changed to a bright spark of desire as they slid slowly over her new ball gown and the creamy skin it exposed.

Carnal thoughts filled her head. She struggled to lock them away, forcing her attention back to the conversation. But he knew. She saw it in his smile.

"The Earl of Worthorne has been away," Lady Annear was proceeding smoothly, as if completely unaware of the ripples of shock her words had caused.

"Away?" Amy said faintly.

"I have missed him." Lady Annear smiled. "I am his godmother, you see, and I take an interest in him. When he lets me."

Was that true? Or was Her Ladyship in on whatever clever game Sebastian was playing? It didn't matter, Francesca thought with despair; her evening had just been completely ruined.

She wasn't looking at him. After that first, startled glance, she'd turned her eyes away and pretended he wasn't there. He could see the flush on her cheek, the rise and fall of her bosom, the flutter of her long lashes.

He needed to speak to her alone. He had to explain. And the only way he was going to achieve that was to remove her from the chaperonage of her mother and uncle.

"Do you dance, Miss Greentree?"

"No."

He laughed at her impolite answer. Mrs. Jardine was scandalized. "Francesca!" she hissed.

"Then, please, allow me to teach you? You will have to learn, eventually." He tucked her hand into his arm, holding it there. Apart from struggling in a most ungenteel manner, she had no choice but to allow him to lead her away.

In the other room, the orchestra was playing a waltz.

"You are as stiff as a marble statue," he murmured, "although not nearly as cold. I think, if I stroked you, you would grow more responsive."

He felt her tremble.

"What are you doing here?" she hissed. "You're impersonating this Earl of Worthorne. Have you no shame?"

"Damn and blast it, Francesca, I'm not impersonating the Earl of Worthorne. I *am* the Earl of Worthorne."

She narrowed her eyes at him, but at least she was finally looking. "I don't believe you," she stated baldly.

"I really am the Earl of Worthorne," he repeated. "If you want to accuse me of impersonating someone, then it would be Mr. Thorne. When I put the earl away, I took part of the name for my new identity. Worthorne . . . Thorne, do you see. But I was always the earl, underneath, and now I am back again."

She looked miserable.

"You're not pleased? My godmother heard rumors that your uncle was looking for an earl for you to marry."

"My uncle is not me," she whispered furiously. "I

will never marry! I told you so. How dare you accuse me of being so mercenary and shallow as to hunt an earl, simply to please my uncle! If I had wished to marry an earl, I would have come down to London years ago."

"Hush," he said, squeezing his fingers around her elbow. "I know you better than that. I'm sorry. I was teasing."

Her mouth trembled, and he wanted to kiss it. He wanted to lose himself in her sweetness.

He led her around the edge of the ballroom, and through the open glass doors at the other end. Suddenly they were outside in the garden, with the lights and the noise behind them.

"I thought you were going to dance with me," she said, surprised and wary, her steps slowing. "We shouldn't be out here alone."

"I'm concerned I might act in a manner not entirely earl-like," he said wryly.

He thought she smiled, but she turned her face away before he could be sure. "You have lied to me. Again."

"The earl was a naïve and spoiled brat, and Mr. Thorne made him grow up. You wouldn't have liked me eight years ago."

"Who says I like you now?" she said airily.

He stroked her bare arm. "I think you do, Francesca."

"Why did you hide your true identity from me?" she asked hastily, her voice low. "Why did you need to become Mr. Thorne in the first place? I don't understand."

He was quiet for so long that she wondered if he was ever going to tell her the truth. But after all he was simply gathering his thoughts. "I had a sister once; her name was Barbara. She was more than a sister; she was my twin."

His voice went on, weaving the story. It was a sad story, and her eyes filled with tears, but it helped her to understand him and why he had lived the last eight years the way he had. She knew very well how the tragedies in one's past could mold one's character.

"I decided that I couldn't live with myself, not as the man I was. I turned my back on all that—left it to my brother—and became someone else. I wanted to hunt down men like Barbara's husband. I wanted to do for others what I should have done for her."

She glanced at him sideways. "So you were always a hero? And here I was thinking of you as a villain committing dastardly deeds. I feel quite let down, Lord Worthorne."

He bowed gracefully. "My apologies. What can I do to mend matters?"

She gave him another glance, but this one was flirtatious. "Do you realize that we're outside, alone together, without a chaperone?"

"Now that would concern me if I were still Mr. Thorne, but as I'm now an earl, I think your reputation will be safe."

She felt like laughing, but she supposed that would only encourage him.

"You're very beautiful tonight, Francesca," he said quietly. "I wish we were alone. Completely alone."

She glanced about her. "I can't see anyone."

Had she really said that? She must have, for the next moment he was pulling her into his arms and kissing her as if he wanted to gobble her up.

It had been too long since the last time they were together in his rooms. Wrapped in his arms, she was drowning in the feel of him, the scent of him, the taste of him. He had introduced her to the world of sensuality, and now she never wanted to leave it.

"Am I to call you my lord now whenever I want something from you?" she asked huskily.

"Yes. 'Kiss me, my lord,' 'Caress me, my lord,' 'My lord, place your engine of delight within my—' "

"You are outrageous!" She laughed, tilting her head to look at him. She was flirting, urging him on, and she couldn't seem to help it. She felt wild and out of control. She felt *alive*.

"The portrait in my rooms in Half Moon Street was of my grandmother," he said, tracing the shape of her mouth with his finger.

"Oh?" It seemed an odd topic of conversation in the circumstances. She turned her face, rubbing her cheek against his knuckles.

"She was a wild one, so I've been told. She led my grandfather a merry dance, but she lived a life to remember. A full life. And never regretted a minute of it."

"Is that what you plan to do?" She kissed the side of his jaw, running her tongue over his smoothly shaven skin.

He shuddered and held her closer, his breath warm as it stirred her ringlets. "I am pointing out to you how important it is to live your life to the full, Francesca."

"And you think I haven't, *my lord*?"

"I think you're afraid to, *Miss Greentree*."

He thought she was afraid! Francesca felt an insane urge to show him just how unafraid she could be. He was throwing down a dare, and she had never been able to resist a dare.

There was a fountain playing through the shrubs and trees, its waters bubbling and splashing. As they drew closer, she could see that the fountain itself was nicely encircled by closely clipped hedges, while a couple of seats made it a pleasant place to sit and reflect. There was even a gate that led into the area.

No one else was about, and the lanterns that illuminated other areas of the garden had not been strung here. Perfect, Francesca thought as she strolled toward it, Sebastian following.

She heard him click the gate shut, and reached up to try to unfasten the back of her gown, but it was too difficult. Frustrated, she presented her back to him, giving him a helpless glance over her shoulder. "Will you undress me?"

"Damn and blast it, Francesca, what a question," he groaned, running his hands over her bare shoulders and down her arms. He kissed her nape, his lips trailing over her sensitive skin, making her shiver. "Francesca, if someone—"

"There's no one here, Sebastian. You said I was afraid of living, and I want to show you I'm not."

"You don't need to undress to do that," he retorted, his mouth against her bare skin. He turned her about, hot gaze traveling over the opulent swell of her breasts. He ran his fingertip along the edge of her gown, dipping into her cleavage. "We can live as much as you like without stripping ourselves naked to the elements."

"Coward," she whispered.

His eyes gleamed as he swooped to her mouth, his lips hovering just above it. "There will come a time when you will regret saying that," he growled, "but not tonight, my Francesca."

He rested his hands on her narrow waist. With a glance behind him at the rustic bench, he promptly sat down. She stood before him, with her hands on his shoulders and her eyes shining. "What now?" she said. He reached down and began to draw up her skirts, as he'd done the last time, and slipped his hands beneath them.

She could feel his warm palms sliding up over her stockings, pausing at the garters just above her knees, and then closing on the bare flesh of her thighs. His eyes widened in amazement, and she almost laughed aloud. "You are not wearing drawers," he said, and swallowed.

"I know. Shocking, is it not? I wondered what it would feel like." She bent down and ran her fingers over the hard ridge of his cock. "May I inspect your 'engine of delight,' my lord?"

He caught his breath, but he didn't stop her. She could see him watching her, his eyes dark beneath his half-lowered lids.

Her fingers found the fastenings and began to undo each button. She felt powerful and sensual, and suddenly it occurred to her that this was what it was like to be a courtesan, giving a man pleasure, and herself as well. But she also knew this was different, because the man she was touching was Sebastian, and it was more than pleasure she was giving him.

I love him.

He had taken her hands in his and was urging her forward. Francesca stepped closer, bemused, dizzy with need, and her skirts frothed over his black evening trousers. He lifted her, helping her to arrange herself on his lap, her thighs straddling his. The tip of his cock brushed her, hard against her softness, and they both went still.

"Gently brought up ladies wear drawers," he said, his voice low and deep. He couldn't seem to let the subject go.

"Perhaps I'm not a lady after all." And she wound her arms around his neck, and kissed him.

His tongue was in her mouth, and she met it, her body clinging to his. His hands were caressing her beneath her gown, and she gasped as his finger slid inside her. "Please," she whispered, moving against him. "Sebastian, please."

He was inside her, sliding easily into the core of her, filling her. She made a little sound of frustration as she tried to move against him and failed. She wriggled about so that she was able to rest her feet on the bench either side of him, gaining purchase, and then she smiled.

"That's better," she whispered, pushing herself upward on his shaft, and then sinking back again. Her body tingled, urging her on. She shifted slightly, so that he rubbed against the swollen nub that was demanding she be so selfish. She bit her lip to stop herself from crying out.

"That's it," he groaned. "Use me, Francesca. I am here for you. I am yours."

He held her thighs, steadying her, but otherwise he let her do as she willed, giving her the permission she needed to chase after her own pleasure.

It came soon enough, wave after wave, her body clenching around him as she gasped wordlessly. And while she was half conscious and dizzy with joy, he drove himself into her again and again, until she thought her bones had turned to water and her heart could never belong to anyone else but him.

Chapter 28

Francesca's heartbeat was gradually slowing beneath the palm of his hand. Sebastian smiled. He felt he had a right to smile. She'd screamed. He'd had to kiss her to muffle the sound. He didn't think he'd ever made a woman scream before during lovemaking.

It was Aphrodite who had told him to dare her, to make it a matter of pride, so that she could pretend she was not simply giving in to her desire. Not that he was about to share that information with Francesca. But the courtesan had known exactly how he needed to act in order to persuade her to let go of her inhibitions and begin to inhabit her deepest needs and fan-

318

tasies. No polite speeches and gentle courting for his Francesca.

She was a child of the storm.

He could imagine her at ramshackle Worthorne Manor, bathing naked in the lake. Or lying naked in his bed. His grandmother, he decided, would smile with approval upon the new lady of the manor. A woman after her own heart.

He felt himself grow hard again, and bent to kiss her cheek, her neck, murmuring words that had no meaning. "Francesca. So beautiful. Let me . . ."

She seemed more than content to let him.

Sebastian slipped the narrow sleeves farther down her arms, exposing her shoulders and, with exquisite slowness, the pink tips of her breasts. They were hard little peaks, and he couldn't resist putting his tongue to them.

She arched her neck and groaned softly, clasping his head to her, her fingers mussing his dark hair. He could feel her body still enclosing him, as he began to move within her once more. There was no urgency this time, and he made it last, watching her face as she slipped from passion to ecstasy to boneless joy.

When it was over, she seemed almost too sated to open her eyes.

"Francesca," he whispered, brushing her cheek with the backs of his fingers. "We must return. There will be talk."

"Hmm."

He rearranged her dress, covering her breasts,

adjusting her sleeves. The acres of red rose satin surrounding them rippled and rustled as he lifted her gently from him, and placed her on the bench beside him. She watched him with sleepy eyes as he dampened his handkerchief in the water from the fountain.

The cloth was cold against her skin as he cleaned her, and she gasped. He took his time, wiping away the evidence of their lovemaking.

When he was done, he tugged her gently to her feet, rearranging her skirts, smoothing them down, until she stood before him once more in a respectable state.

"There," he said, looking up at her with a smile as he bent to twitch out a kink at her hem. "As beautiful and proper as you were before."

She was watching him, and there were tears in her eyes. "I didn't know," she whispered.

Sebastian's brow creased as he tried to understand. "Didn't know what?"

"That it could be so wonderful between a man and a woman."

But there was no time to answer her. Someone was approaching, his steps quick and very close. Startled, she put her hand up to her hair, smoothing her ringlets, straightening her encircling wreath.

"Damn and blast it!" Sebastian muttered, and stood up, hastily brushing at his knees, and tugging his own clothing back into order.

"It could have been worse," she said levelly. "They could have come by five minutes earlier."

Sebastian grimaced, hurriedly smoothing back his hair. "I don't know how you can joke about it."

"It's probably just someone out for a breath of—"

"Francesca?" William Tremaine stood silhouetted outside the gate.

She jumped as if hell had opened before her.

Sebastian thought that if her uncle hadn't suspected she was up to something before, her guilty demeanor would soon convince him of it. Clearly it was up to him to take control.

"Mr. Tremaine," he said, as if there were nothing at all the matter. "Miss Greentree and I were just taking a stroll. She finds the crowd inside oppressive."

"Is that so?" There was a chill in his voice.

"Actually, we were just about to return," Francesca said, reaching to unclip the gate and swinging it open.

He caught her arm. It must have hurt, because she gasped, but he didn't release her. "You're a liar," he growled, glaring down at her. "I can read it in your voice. I can see it in your face. If you're going to lie, at least learn to do it properly."

"I'm not—"

"You are your mother's daughter."

"Uncle William!"

He had her outside the gate now, and he shook her so hard that some of her ringlets came loose and tumbled over her shoulder.

Sebastian had been momentarily too shocked to act, but now he saw red. Memories of Barbara rushed back, and with them regrets and anger and a sincere longing to make amends. He couldn't let Francesca be bullied like his sister. *He wouldn't.*

He launched himself at William and, roughly grasping the front of his neatly pressed shirt, hauled him away from her.

"Don't touch her," he said, and shoved the older man, hard, so that he stumbled backward and only just saved himself from falling.

Slowly Tremaine straightened, his frigid gaze fastened on Sebastian. "You've overstepped the mark, Thorne or Worthorne or whatever your name is," he said, his voice full of fury. "Stay away from my niece. I don't want you near her, or my house, again."

"Uncle William," Francesca began, her voice trembling, "you cannot—"

He turned on her. "I can do whatever I please," he snarled. "I am the head of this family, and you will obey me or I will make your life a misery. Do you understand me?" And when she stared back at him, silent and stubborn: "Do you understand me!"

She flinched, and Sebastian couldn't stand it anymore. He wanted to grab the man and shake him. He wanted to knock him down. But he couldn't. Even as angry as he was, he realized that to create such a scene would only make things worse for Francesca. Her reputation hung in the balance as it was, and her uncle had the power to destroy her entry into society before it had even begun.

Don't rock the boat. Be patient. Your time will come.

"Go with your uncle. Let him return you to the

ballroom," he said quietly. "Go on, Francesca. It's all right."

She looked as if she might disagree, but when she met his eyes, he tried to persuade her without words that it was the right thing to do. At last, with her chin held high, she turned and began to make her way back toward the house.

Tremaine started after her, but then he hesitated and turned back to face Sebastian. "Stay away," he said, in that savage, icy voice. "Or I'll destroy you. I might just destroy you anyway."

When they were gone, Sebastian stood alone by the fountain, beset with turbulent emotions. Once he had thought it amusing that Francesca was so in awe of her uncle's temper, but no longer. Tremaine was a bully, just like Leon. Was he like Leon in other ways? Did he use physical punishment? But Sebastian dismissed the idea. William Tremaine was more subtle than that.

But it didn't make him any less dangerous.

The next few hours were the most difficult Francesca had faced since she was in the schoolroom, and was forced to conform to her first governess's ideas of what a young lady should be. Punishment had become a way of life—until Amy realized what was going on and sent the woman packing.

Uncle William danced with her, stiff and furious and—most terrifying of all—perfectly correct. He was a good dancer, and it should have been enjoyable, but in her current state of mind she didn't appreciate his talents.

"Uncle, please . . ."

"I will speak to you when we get home," he said, between his teeth. "There will be no hint of scandal, Francesca. Not the merest whiff. I will not have it."

When the music finished, he bowed, and she was left to her next partner. Attempting to make polite conversation was agony, and smiling was worse, when all she wanted was to burst into tears. And find Sebastian.

I will see him again, she told herself angrily. *I don't care what Uncle William says. He does not own me. I am five and twenty, and I am in charge of my own life.*

"You blush delightfully," her companion murmured, thinking she was reacting to whatever he had said. Little did he know, thought Francesca with a rueful smile, that it was rage that was putting the color into her cheeks.

Amy, completely ignorant of what had happened in the garden, gushed with pleasure when it was finally time to say their farewells to Lady Annear.

"What a marvelous evening!" she declared in the carriage. "Francesca, you were such a hit. Lady Annear complimented me on you several times." She smiled. "And naturally I took full credit."

"Mama . . ."

"By the way, where did Mr. Th— that is, Lord Worthorne go? Lady Annear was looking for him, but he seemed to have disappeared. Did he say he was leaving early?"

Francesca glanced sideways at Uncle William, but he was staring out of the window in silence. "I think he had another engagement," she said in an emotionless voice.

"It's a pity Helen wasn't invited," Amy went on, stifling a yawn as the carriage turned into Wensted Square. "She would have loved every moment of it."

"Helen is an embarrassment we were better off without," William said sharply, without turning his head.

Amy ignored him. "I still can't quite understand why we were invited. I don't know Lady Annear, and she says she barely knows you, William. I can only think our names were put forward by some other party."

Francesca sat, staring straight ahead, but she felt her uncle turn his gaze on her. "That must be it," he said levelly. She was grateful when they stopped outside the door, and she was able to accompany Amy up the stairs and into the house. Soon, she thought, she'd be able to stop pretending and weep and rage as she'd wanted to ever since her uncle found them by the fountain.

One of the maids had sat up by the front door to await their return, and now she came, sleepy-eyed, to help Amy and Francesca with their outer garments. They were starting toward the staircase when William's voice stopped them dead.

"I wish to speak to you, Francesca. In the library, if you please."

Her heart grew heavy with dread. Not another scene! She was tired and emotional and the last thing she wanted was further accusations from her uncle. "Uncle William, I am sure anything you have to say can wait until morning. I am tired and—"

"It won't wait. In the library, now." He sounded icy. Uncle William at his very worst.

"What do you want with Francesca?" Amy asked. Even without knowing what had happened in the garden, she had finally sensed the tension between her brother and her daughter. "It can't be urgent. I'm sure the morning will do. We are all very tired, and things may be said that are later regretted."

"Amy, you are interfering in something you know nothing about. Go to bed and leave this matter to me."

But his impatience had the opposite effect. Francesca could see Amy's back stiffen, and knew she wasn't about to be sent off like a naughty child.

"No. If you speak to Francesca, then you will have to do so with me present."

Francesca took her mother's hand, squeezing it in gratitude. "Thank you," she whispered.

Uncle William looked from one to the other, his mouth twisted with distaste. "If that's what you want," he said, leading the way into the library. "We do not wish to be disturbed," he called out to the servant, who was watching them, goggle-eyed. "Go to bed."

The girl bobbed a quick curtsy and hastily retreated into the shadows.

William closed the door and then walked to the table with the brandy decanter upon it. He poured himself a hefty glass, while the silence grew. Francesca had the awful sensation that she had slipped into her own past, while the hateful governess had taken on the form of Uncle William.

"I suppose I shouldn't have expected anything more, with your mother," he said at last. "You can't help what's in your blood. But I hoped my sister would have taught you better manners than to let yourself be tupped by a shady creature like Thorne. In the garden of a house in Belgravia, no less!"

"William." Amy's voice was trembling with outrage. "I can only think you do not know what you are saying, or else you are drunk. Francesca danced one dance with Lord Worthorne . . ."

"You don't even know what's under your very nose," he snarled, turning to face them. "She was out in the garden with him. I was watching."

Francesca felt the color drain from her face. He had seen them, her and Sebastian? The moment had been wonderful beyond anything she'd imagined, exciting and pleasurable, but at the same time she had never for a moment felt threatened or sleazy. Not until now. She knew she would hate her uncle forever for doing this.

He was nodding, his nose twitching as if he smelled something rotten. "The daughter of a whore. What could we expect?"

"How dare you pass judgment on me," Francesca whispered. She was trembling inside, but her anger had replaced her fear.

"I dare because I am head of the family."

"Not head of *my* family," Francesca retorted.

"While you are under my roof you will obey my rules," he shouted.

Amy gasped, but Francesca refused to be brow-beaten. "Then I'll leave your house tomorrow. Now! I don't need your roof, I don't need you. You may frighten poor Helen, but you don't frighten me."

He glared at her a moment more, the sinews of his neck standing out with his anger, and then suddenly he relaxed, folding his arms. For a moment Francesca thought he was going to be reasonable, but a moment later she understood that he was still upset with her. He was simply shifting his angle of attack.

"It must be lonely, being an unwanted child. I suppose you think by throwing yourself at men like Thorne you can find love."

"William, what are you saying?" Amy wailed.

"He's saying that my parents were glad to be rid of me," Francesca answered for him, her face pale.

"Yes, something like that," William agreed. "Your father certainly was. He vanished and has never been seen again, and then your mother was so care-less of you—too busy with her own tupping, no doubt—that she mislaid you for over twenty years."

Amy began to protest, but Francesca spoke over her. "You're wrong! My mother loves me and my father . . . he loved me, too."

"You don't even know his name!" William re-torted, his pale eyes challenging her.

"I do. It was Tommy!"

He stilled, something stirring in his face, but she couldn't read him. She'd never been able to read what he was thinking. Perhaps she'd never cared enough to try.

"I suppose it was your mother who told you that?"

he said dismissively. "How do you know it's true? She could have plucked the name out of the air. The woman is a liar and always has been."

"She had a letter from him before he died," Francesca replied triumphantly. "In it, he spoke about me and his plans for my future."

"Where is the letter now?"

"Lost. You're wrong, admit it. I *was* loved. Just because my birth wasn't as you'd have liked it doesn't mean I wasn't wanted."

Amy slid an arm about her shoulders. "Of course you were, dear. William, that is enough." Her face was wan and angry, and even her brother could see that she'd been pushed beyond her tolerance. "I am taking Francesca to bed, and in the morning we will be packing and returning to Yorkshire. I'm sorry it had to end like this between us. I had hoped for some sort of reconciliation, at least for Helen's sake, if not for our own."

"What about the ball?" William reminded her. "Is that to be canceled at this late date?"

Amy put a hand to her eyes. "I had forgotten about the ball. Helen will be devastated. Well"—with a deep breath—"she will just have to come and stay with us and we will hold a rustic ball of our own."

"You are too hasty," William said mildly.

His sister gave him a suspicious look, and he raised his eyebrows at her.

"I haven't asked you to leave, nor did I intend to. The ball can go ahead as planned. I won't interfere, spend what you will, as long as there is no breath of scandal. Is that understood?"

Amy turned and looked at Francesca, and she realized her mother was waiting for her to speak, to make the decision. She was very tempted to say no. She had seen a side to her uncle tonight that made her very wary of him, and he had said things that were beyond forgiveness. But there were other considerations, such as Helen and Amy, and the many guests they'd invited.

And the fact that London suddenly held an appeal for her that it had never held before. Sebastian was here. She reminded herself that while she remained, there was a chance she might see him again.

"Very well," she said. "We will stay."

William smiled as if they had never been anything other than friends. "Good," he said, and poured himself another glass, raising it like a toast in their honor. "To family," he said, "and the lengths we must go to to protect our good name."

Chapter 29

The door to Amy's bedchamber was hardly closed when Francesca burst into apologies. But Amy held up her hand. "Stop. I don't want to hear what happened, or what you did. I make it a practice not to interfere in my daughters' private lives. It was something I learned after Vivianna came to London, and then Marietta ran off with that dreadful man. I cannot stop any of you following your hearts, so I simply don't try. It is a question of retaining my sanity."

Francesca began to laugh. She sank down on the bed and found that after a moment there were tears running down her cheeks, and she wasn't sure whether she was still laughing, or crying, but whatever the case, she felt better for the release of emotion.

She loved him. She loved Sebastian Thorne, or the Earl of Worthorne, or whoever he was. She had done the most foolish thing the daughter of a courtesan could do—fall in love.

"Mama, you are a very wise woman," she said at last, when she had mopped her cheeks and blown her nose.

Amy looked melancholy. "Do you know, sometimes I think I am a very stupid woman. Or at least a very blind woman when it comes to those I love best." She seemed to be debating whether to disclose a secret. "Helen spoke to me not long ago about something that I never for a moment suspected, and it has been troubling me ever since."

"Tell me what she said," Francesca said quietly, kicking off her slippers and making herself comfortable against the pillows.

Amy lifted her arms and began to unpin the wisp of lace decorating her fair hair. "I probably shouldn't, but I know you will be discreet, Francesca. You are good at keeping secrets, my dear."

"I try." *I have plenty of my own.*

"Helen told me that, years ago, after she had married Toby, she had an affair. I was living in Yorkshire at the time, and I knew nothing of it. The man loved her, or so she believes, but they decided there was no future for them and they had to part. Probably the fact that William found out had something to do with that," she added wryly. "But that's not the worst of it. After the man had left the scene, never to return, Helen discovered that she was with child. 'Forbidden fruit of an adulterous union,' was what William called it. Toby was more forgiving, but he refused to take on the child as his own. Helen went away to have the baby, and they said she was staying with friends. Later on she returned to London as if nothing had happened. The child was adopted by some acquaintance of William's, and he refused to speak of the matter again, so she never knew what became of it. But it was a girl. She held her baby for a few moments after it was born, and she knows it was a little girl."

Francesca lay in her comfortable nest of pillows and grieved for her aunt. "Poor Helen. So when we were shopping, and she was saying that she wished she had a daughter of her own . . . ?"

"She does have one, but one she's never met. When it was all over, William and Toby swore her to silence, and she's been too frightened to break her promise until now. The girl would be twenty-one, and I think Helen would love to find her, but she's afraid to make the attempt."

"Afraid of William? Mama, that man has much to answer for."

"There is that, but I think she is more afraid that if she did find her, her daughter would hate her for abandoning her. She has seen enough of abandoned daughters to know it is not all plain sailing when they are reunited with their mother," she said with a smile at Francesca.

"And perhaps her daughter won't have been as lucky in her adopted home as we were," Francesca added, smiling back. "Yes, I see."

They were quiet, contemplating the mystery of Helen and her child, separated at birth, and whether they would ever find each other again. At last Francesca heaved a sigh and climbed off the bed. She found her slippers and, carrying them in her hand, made her way to the door. She paused and looked back.

"Thank you, Mama," she said softly.

Amy, brushing her hair with long, slow strokes, met her eyes in the mirror. "What for, my dear?"

"Just thank you."

Aphrodite lay in Jemmy's arms, completely happy and content. He stroked her back, fingers light and pleasing, and smiled into her eyes. "Do you remember when we met after all those years apart?" he asked.

She laughed softly. "Of course I remember. I will remember it always. You gave me myself back again."

"I wish sometimes I'd done something sooner. It feels as if I wasted years . . ."

"No, my love, do not have regrets. They are useless. We found each other, that is all that matters. We are together now."

He kissed the end of her nose.

"There's still one person needs sending to hell."

"Yes." She sighed. "But I believe that now Mrs. Slater and her spies are in jail, he will think twice before he hurts anyone ever again."

"What if he's driven to it?"

"How so? I have not spoken out, and Francesca cannot. He is safe. Perhaps he will be content with that."

"I thought you wanted him named?" Jemmy said.

"Maybe it is better to let sleeping monsters sleep on undisturbed."

"Do you really believe that?" he demanded, sitting up.

"I don't know." She shrugged. "I nearly died. It has made me cautious for what I wish for."

Later, when he was sleeping, Aphrodite rose, wrapped a silk robe about herself, and took her diary from a drawer. Earlier on, she had been writing in it, and now she wanted to read over her thoughts. Sitting down in a comfortable chair, her legs tucked up under her, she opened the red leather-bound book and found her place.

> I have not been to Dudley Street for many years. My father died and my mother does not want to see me, but one day I decide I will go again.
>
> I wear my oldest clothing and I walk the streets I used to know so well, but still I feel their stares of resentment and distrust. I do not belong here anymore, and the people know it.
>
> I think of Jemmy. I cannot help it. I wonder if he is happy with his wife and whether he has children. He has made the life for himself that he wanted for us, at a time when I was too foolish to realize what a treasure he was offering.

My mother sits in her chair, her flesh loose upon her bones. She has dark hair and eyes like me, and she used to say we were of Gypsy stock. She does not say much, while I am making awkward conversation with my brother's wife, who takes care of her now.

It is strange. To sit in the parlor, to look upon people who were once so familiar but now are strangers. My mother is so small.

"Do you remember Jemmy?" my brother's wife says. "He was here asking after you not more than a month past."

I don't know what to say. I cannot imagine what he wants.

"Someone told him you were dead," she laughs. "He only just heard you were alive."

I look at my mother then, and see her eyes. And I remember she and my da telling me that Jemmy was wed. Was that a lie, too?

"Why?" I ask her, my voice breaking with the pain. "I loved him."

But she smiles. "You didn't deserve him after what you did. You stepped outside the place you were born into. You turned up your nose at the life you were given."

Such bitterness, and for what? Because I dared to be different and follow my heart. I tell myself I would do it again no differently. But would I?

Jemmy is looking for me!

That gives me the sort of hope I have not

*felt for years and years, and as I leave my
past—I swear I will never visit there again—I
begin to think that perhaps I will find happiness in my future. But I do not want to get my
hopes up, in case it is not so. I have had my
hopes raised before, and it has ended once
more in misery.*

*The club is still closed, and I am thinking of
the night to come and all the tasks I have before me. I do not see the man sitting on the
steps beneath the front portico, waiting. I do
not see him until he calls out my name.*

*Not Aphrodite. My real name. My old
name.*

*He is standing now, watching me, his hands
hanging at his sides as if he doesn't know what
to do with them. His face is lined, and his nose
has been broken, and his hair is graying. But
it is Jemmy, my Jemmy.*

*We look at each other for a long time, and
then I say, "Will you come inside for a
while?"*

*"Aye, I will," he says, "for a while." And he
follows me through the door.*

*He does not go home that night, or the next.
From that moment until this, we live together.
And we are happy, at last.*

Aphrodite smiled, and closed the book. It was a
good ending, a happy ending. There was still the
other matter, of course. The other man. But despite

what she had told Jemmy, she was hopeful that it too would be resolved. She had engaged Lord Worthorne, and she had great trust in him.

It was simply a matter of waiting, and she knew she was good at that.

Someone else was waiting. He was good at it, too, but he knew he couldn't afford to wait much longer. Francesca Greentree would have to be gagged before the truth came out. If the letter came to light . . .

Mrs. Slater and her cohorts had led him to believe that there was only one way to do that, but now they were gone, he had time to consider the matter more rationally. Murder was all very well, but there was always the fear of being caught. Look what had happened to Maeve! He knew he would have to help them all, Mrs. Slater and Maeve and Jed, bribe the authorities to soften their sentences. They would expect it. It was part of the bargain for their silence—apart from the fact that they were frightened of him.

He could cast them off entirely, knowing that his word would always be believed over theirs, but why take the chance that some of their mud might stick? He had a reputation to maintain.

No, he decided, there would be no more murders. He knew there was a different way, a better way. After all, Francesca was no longer a child. She was a well-brought-up and well-mannered young woman, with all the skills that would be required of a London society wife.

She was also beautiful and desirable.

And he was a man.

Chapter 30

Lil, her hand tucked around Martin's arm, all but skipped as they made their way through Covent Garden. He had taken her to see a play about a Scottish king whose wife was mad, and there were witches and a great deal of bloodshed. She'd loved it, even if sometimes it was a little hard to follow.

"Never mind," he'd said, "you can choose next time."

So, she thought, there was to be a next time.

Some of the tarts who were always standing about the place called out, pursing their rouged lips and wriggling their hips. Lil stuck her nose up in the air and pretended not to notice. Martin only laughed, calling out that he was taken and to mind their manners in front of a lady.

That had caused even more hilarity.

Except that his words made Lil want to cry.

They walked a bit farther, but the joy had gone out of the evening for her and she wanted nothing more than to go home and lock herself in her room and hide. She couldn't bear for him to hate her, and yet Lil knew she had been in this exact same place once before, when she'd been too scared to tell Mr. Keith the truth. She'd run away and married Jacob, and, yes, she'd regretted it bitterly.

I don't want to run away this time.

But what if she told him and he looked at her in disgust? Or simply walked away from her? She'd curl up and die, she would!

"Lil, what is it?" He was watching her with his eyes sparkling and a hint of a smile on his mouth. "You look like you've lost a sovereign and found a shilling."

"It's nothing, really."

"Was it those silly girls back there? You shouldn't take any notice of them. They're only doing what they can to make a livin'. We mustn't think any worse of them for it."

He sounded sincere. She almost trusted him. Perhaps tomorrow she'd tell him, or the day after . . .

And then she heard it, her own voice saying, "I used to be one of those silly girls. What do you think of that, Mr. Martin O'Donnelly?"

He looked shocked, and the sight of his face was too much for her.

Lil took to her heels and ran.

She could hear him calling her, but she didn't stop, she was too frightened. Now he'd be sorry for her! Oh why, why had she opened her big mouth? It would have been better to pretend she wasn't interested in him than to be pitied, or worse, despised.

"I can't bear it, I can't bear it," she whispered frantically.

"Lil, what are you trying to do to me, kill me?" It was Martin, gasping for air, doubling over and coughing. His eyes were streaming. "God, I hate the London air! No wonder you moved up north." He gulped, recovering himself somewhat. "Why did you run away from me?"

"I . . . thought you might rather I ran away."

He looked puzzled. "Why would I want that? You were telling me something interesting about you being one of those girls. I have a ton of questions to ask you, Lil." He smiled. "You're an amazing person, do you know that? I can't tell you how much I love you."

Lil blinked. His face seemed to go muzzy, and then popped back into clear, sharp lines again. It was still the same. Warm, smiling mouth, with love in his eyes. He meant it! Of course he did. This was Martin.

Lil laughed.

"I love you, too, Martin," she said, shyly.

He tilted his head. "What was that you said, Lil? I can hardly hear you. Can you say it again?"

He was watching her with that smile, waiting to see what she'd do.

Lil threw her head back and yelled it out as loud as she possibly could. "I love you, Martin!"

"That's better," he said, reaching for her, folding her in his arms. "Lil, my love, that's much better."

"I can't expect her to upset her family over me," Sebastian was saying. "He was furious, and she was frightened. I wanted to kill him . . ." He shook his head, qualified his words. "I wanted to bloody his nose."

"Many of us feel like that about William Tremaine," Aphrodite assured him.

"If I call on her, I know I will only make things worse for her."

"Francesca knows this. She may call on you."

"Unless he's watching her. I wouldn't put it past him."

"Love will discover a way through the obstacles," Aphrodite said blithely. "With a little help."

"Speaking of help, I did as you said." He gave her a glance that was almost shy. "I dared her. And you were right. She reacted just as you said she would."

"Francesca is not a female who likes her men to be tame. She seeks out the dark and the dangerous—in her imagination, anyway. That is why she likes you, Sebastian. You can be the dangerous man of her dreams, and yet she knows she is always safe with you. A woman needs to be safe while she is naked in her man's arms."

He smiled, thinking that he very much enjoyed Francesca's imagination, but in another moment he was serious again. "I worry about her, Madame. She's in a precarious position."

"Ignorance keeps her safe, and as yet she is ignorant as to the truth."

"All the same . . ."

Aphrodite reached out and touched his hand. "Enough. You cannot always be serious. Francesca will be here in a moment, and I wanted to ask you whether you wished to accompany my daughter on another adventure, my lord? You should take every opportunity to bind her to you with addictions of the flesh. She will be returning to her dreary moors soon, and then you will need to prise her away from them. If she is in love with you, or at least in lust with you, the battle is already half won."

"Madame . . ."

"I have been giving it some thought, and I believe the Bacchus Room will do the trick."

"The Bacchus Room?" Sebastian wondered whether he'd ever get used to Francesca's mother instructing him on what was most pleasing to her daughter when it came to the art of love. Probably not.

"One can let one's imagination go wild," she said, a twinkle in her eye. "And my daughter has a very vivid imagination, my lord."

"Yes, she has."

"I will send her to you, *oui*?"

"Please do."

"Good! Now, let us set the scene. A forest glade. A maiden all unaware, and hiding in the bushes, watching her, lusting after her . . . the satyr." She tapped her finger on her cheek, deep in thought. "I believe you would make a very good satyr, Sebastian."

He tried not to choke. "A satyr it is then."

"And remember, you must bind her to you. I do not want Francesca to return to those dreadful moors. She belongs here in London, where she can shine like the diamond she is."

"She belongs in Worthorne Manor."

Aphrodite smiled broadly. "I see we are thinking along the same lines, Sebastian. That is good, that is very good . . ."

Francesca was glad to see Aphrodite looking more like her old self again. She even had ink stains on her fingers. Her mother was "resting" in her boudoir, but had smuggled some of her ledgers up and was now busy tallying figures. Or at least she had been until Francesca arrived.

"I'm surprised you were allowed out to visit me," Aphrodite said with a watchful glance.

"You mean 'allowed' by Uncle William?" Her voice was dry.

"Lord Worthorne tells me your uncle was not very happy with you at Lady Annear's ball, *petit chaton*."

"No, he wasn't. But he seems to be trying to mend bridges. I'm surprised, I admit, by the change in him, but it's very welcome."

"Perhaps he wishes for a reconciliation with Amy, after all."

"Yes, perhaps."

But Francesca didn't want to talk about Uncle William. Strangely, she felt almost disloyal remembering the night of the ball. He'd been so different ever since, so affable and friendly. If he was really trying so hard to make amends, then she owed him some loyalty. But the question remained, why the sudden change?

"Perhaps it was the letter," she said, speaking to herself as well as her mother.

"The letter?" Aphrodite went still. "What letter is this, Francesca?"

"The letter from my father. Tommy. You told me about it when you were unwell, Mother. When we returned from Lady Annear's ball, Uncle William was very angry. He said my—my father didn't want me, that I was searching for love because I was an unwanted child. I had to show him that wasn't true, and so I told him about the letter."

Aphrodite sighed. "My poor darling. I see it all now. What did he say, when you told him about Tommy's letter?"

"He changed. Perhaps he realized then that he was wrong. He's been making a real effort ever since. For example, when I came down to breakfast this morning, he held out my chair for me to sit down, and complimented me on my complexion. Even Mama remarked upon how much things have improved. I think she is hoping she will be able to write to Mr. Jardine very soon and ask him to travel to London to be with us."

"Yes, I can see she would be relieved at the change in her brother." But Aphrodite didn't sound impressed. Perhaps, Francesca thought, she was tired. It wasn't long since she had been in bed, close to death. She still had nightmares about Maeve's confession and the journey she had made with Sebastian to see . . . But suddenly Francesca registered what Aphrodite had said earlier, and she forgot all about Uncle William.

"You mentioned Lord Worthorne, Mother. Has he been here?"

"He's here now, *petit chaton*."

"Oh." She felt herself light up with all the brilliance of a gas lamp. She couldn't help it.

Seeing her reaction, Aphrodite smiled. "He's waiting for you in the Bacchus Room."

"The Bacchus Room?" Francesca repeated curiously.

The courtesan pushed her ledgers to one side and swung her legs down from the sofa. "The Bacchus Room can be shocking for some people. Take care."

Now her curiosity really was piqued. "What should I take care of?"

Aphrodite leaned closer and looked deep into her eyes. "Satyrs," she murmured.

Francesca started to smile, but there was no answering gleam in her mother's eyes. She felt a shiver run through her, excitement mixed with trepidation. "And Sebastian is in that room?"

Aphrodite nodded. "It is the door at the end of the corridor, if you dare."

Francesca rose instantly to her feet. "I dare," she said, and began to make her way down the plush corridor toward the door. The outside was painted white with gold trimmings, just like the other doors, but written on the main panel was "The Bacchus Room."

Her flesh was tingling; her blood was pumping. She felt alive, and excited. Sebastian was waiting for her. They were about to take another adventure together. Francesca opened the door and stepped inside.

Her mouth fell open.

The Bacchus Room was decorated like a wild woodland, with trees and vines painted directly onto the walls, and draperies of various colors strung from the ceiling, making it difficult to see more than a step or two in front of her. Cushions and bolsters were scattered across the floor. The colors were so vivid that for a moment, Francesca really did feel as if she was lost in a forest. Picking her way to the side, she looked up and saw that she was facing a mural.

It was a depiction of a man, or half a man. He had hooves instead of feet, and horns sprouted from the long hair at his temples. And because he was standing side on, with his hands on his hips, she could see that his manhood was hugely erect. Was this the satyr?

She stepped back, shocked despite herself, and bumped into someone standing behind her. She gave a faint scream.

His arms closed about her, his lips pressed to the side of her neck, and he said in a deep voice, "Hmm, female flesh."

Francesca knew who he was. She'd known instantly. But he was behind her and therefore invisible, and so she could let her imagination soar.

"Mr. Satyr," she said breathlessly, "please don't hurt me."

"Francesca . . ."

"Shhh." She giggled. "Let's play the game."

He reached up and cupped her breasts. "How do you know I'm not a satyr come to ravish you?" he said gruffly.

She leaned back into his arms. "I always imagine satyrs smell rather like goats," she said thoughtfully, "and you smell of clean laundry and shaving soap." She turned into his arms and smiled up at him. "But I'd rather be ravished by you than a satyr, anyway."

"There is a resemblance, however," he said, with that wicked glint in his eyes.

"Oh?"

He nodded toward the mural.

Francesca dissolved into laughter.

"You mock me, female?" he said in his satyr's voice. "We shall see!" And he lowered her onto a nearby pile of cushions.

Sebastian began to undress her, planting kisses as he went, and soon her giggles turned to gasps and moans. She was dizzy with desire by the time he stood up and began to strip off his own clothing. Francesca watched him through half-closed eyes, enjoying the view.

"You were right," she said dreamily, "you are very like a satyr."

He growled and reached for her. To her surprise, he turned her over, his mouth hot against her nape, and then moving down her spine toward the small of her back. His hands closed over the ripe cheeks of her bottom, and he lifted her slightly and slid one of the smaller cushions beneath her hips.

She turned her head to look at him, puzzled, but not at all anxious. "Sebastian? Are you being a satyr again?"

"Why do you think satyrs creep up behind mortal women?"

"To frighten them?"

"To caress them into compliance."

"But a woman would know it was no ordinary man!"

"Perhaps, or perhaps by the time she realized, she would no longer care, and then . . ."

He lowered himself to his knees, and she felt his shaft brush against her, sliding down to the core of her. He gripped her thighs, holding her firmly, and as she peered back over her shoulder with widening eyes, he slid deep inside her. She had a sensation of fullness, but actually watching him do it made her gasp with excitement.

Was that why the club had mirrors on the ceiling? So that people could watch themselves making love?

His chest was hot against her back, the hairs on his body abrading her softer skin. "Once the satyr has the mortal woman in his power, he can have his pleasure with her," he whispered, his breath deep and breathy against her ear. "She is helpless against his powers. She is being made love to by the king of lust."

The movement of his body in hers was pleasant, but she did not feel the same level of excitement as she had in previous encounters, the same swell of passion. And then, as if aware of her plight, he slid his hand beneath her and began to stroke the swollen nub between her legs.

"Oh!"

His other hand found her breasts, tugging gently at her nipples, enjoying the way they moved with his thrusts. She lifted her head, gasping now with pleasure, and found the mural directly before her gaze.

Was the satyr grinning at her? He was ugly, but he was certainly all male, and suddenly her imagination took flight, imagining Sebastian in such a guise. She, of course, would be the maiden all unaware, strolling in the forest glade, and then he would pounce upon her and before she knew it he would be . . .

His stroking fingers pushed her over the edge.

It seemed to her that the fantasy and the reality mingled in her mind, making the moment even more intense and pleasurable. Sebastian growled as he reached his peak, moving powerfully. He remained inside her, breathing heavily, and in that second Francesca almost thought it was true.

He was her own satyr.

And then he bent forward to kiss her ear and, clasping her in his arms, rolled over so that they were lying together on their sides, her back to his front. It was as if the world outside had ceased to exist.

"I've missed you . . . so much." Francesca sighed, when they had caught their breath and her head had stopped spinning. "I hated leaving you at Lady Annear's ball. It was awful."

His leaned up on his elbow, and his gaze slid over her flushed face and tumbled hair, and fixed on her mouth. "I was tempted to pick William Tremaine up and tip him headfirst into the fountain."

"I'm glad you didn't, but I thank you for the thought." She touched his face, her own eyes warm and amused. "I know you think I need looking after, like your sister, Barbara, but I don't. I'm strong-willed, like my sisters. I would never allow a man like Leon to hurt me."

He searched her eyes. "Is that what you think I want to do? Look after you?"

"I think you're the sort of man who will always take care of those he thinks are weaker than himself."

"Ah, and what sort of man is that?"

"A hero," she said simply, and kissed him, wrapping languid arms about his neck.

"Francesca . . ." He smoothed her hair back behind her ear. "I'm no hero. I've made mistakes, and I've done and seen things I would not share with you, but I have found one redeeming feature in myself. You. I love you. I think I've loved you since the day you dragged me from the mire, and we trudged through that god-awful storm together. You have brought me back from whatever hell I've been gradually slipping into. You have made me strong enough to face up to who I am and what I must do."

Her fingers trembled against his lips. "Hush," she whispered, "don't say it if you don't mean it."

"Damn and blast it! Of course I mean it. I love you."

She laughed shakily. "You love me? I thought this was my grand passion, and as far as I'm aware from my readings of the poets, such things always end in despair. Or madness."

"Well, we can be different. Our grand passion will end in a long and happy marriage. That is," he added, almost shyly, "if you will marry me."

"Oh Sebastian," she whispered. "I love you, too. I realized it the night of Lady Annear's ball."

He stroked her face, his eyes gentle. "The life of an earl isn't as dangerous as that of Mr. Thorne, but if it wasn't for you, I would never have had the courage to face my past. You've changed me, Francesca. You've healed me. And I can promise you that I will cherish you forever."

"You didn't need healing," she said. "You are already perfect."

Sebastian grinned. "Wonderful! Now, I want you to repeat to me those exact words every morning over breakfast."

"I haven't said I'll marry you yet," she reminded him, smiling.

"Hmm. What else can I tempt you with? I have very large grounds," he went on, and his grin turned wicked. "Perfect for running through. Naked. Perfect for satyrs and maidens."

"Yes," said Francesca promptly.

"Darling Francesca, I want to marry you more than anything in the world, and live my life with you. We can announce it at the ball." He hesitated, frowned. "Am I invited?"

"You are. But if you're thinking Uncle William will not approve, then you're wrong. He's a changed man."

"I hope for your sake it is so."

"And you're an earl, Sebastian," she teased him. "Uncle William will be beside himself. Can we marry at Greentree Manor? On the moors, in the middle of a rainstorm?"

He eyed her suspiciously, and she burst into laughter. "You wretch," he said, holding her close. "No, we will not. We'll marry here in London, and spend half the year at Worthorne Manor, and half the year in Yorkshire."

"On the moors?"

"Very well."

"In the thunder and lightning?"

"If we must."

Francesca sat up, her hair a dark cloud about her, her eyes full of love and passion. "You would do that for me?" she breathed. "Sebastian, now I know you really do love me."

Chapter 31

~~~~~~○○~~~~~~

I t was a very long time since the Tremaine house had hosted something as grand as a ball. Candles glowed, and greenery and flowers banked the staircases and filled the rooms. The sight brought Helen close to tears. Toby was in a jolly mood and seemed inclined to humor her, perhaps because he was looking forward to imbibing enormous quantities of free food and drink. Amy was also moved by memories of the past, although she was missing her husband.

"I will be returning home after the ball," she told Francesca. "I have had enough of London."

"Home?" Francesca repeated uncertainly.

Amy raised her eyebrows in surprise. "You do not

sound pleased, my dear! I had thought you were homesick. Do you wish to stay longer? Vivianna or Marietta would be pleased to have you, I am sure."

"I am homesick. I'm sorry. It is just that . . ." But she couldn't explain, not yet.

"No, you must not apologize. I am so glad you are enjoying yourself at last," Amy went on, patting her hand.

Francesca almost told her then, but managed to bite back the words. She had been hugging her news to herself ever since the Bacchus Room, and every day it grew more difficult not to share it with her family. She had found the perfect man, the love of her life; why shouldn't she be happy?

Her sisters were also here. Vivianna had arrived from Candlewood, the house she ran for orphans, after settling Rosie in. The little girl, she assured Francesca, was fitting in well and seemed very happy with her new home.

"She confided in me that Aphrodite's Club was full of old people," Vivianna said with a laugh. "She was relieved to find Candlewood full of children."

"She made Dobson promise to visit her," Marietta said. "Although I think that had more to do with him bringing along Jem, the puppy."

The ballroom sparkled, and supper was laid out in the drawing room. William had insisted on a room being set aside for card playing, for those who did not dance, but other than that he had been true to his word, allowing them free rein when it came to the preparations and the expenditure.

Francesca decided she really had misjudged him.

He had made her promise him the first waltz, and she planned to thank him then for his kindness. He would never take the place of her father, Tommy, but Francesca admitted to herself that she was beginning to see her uncle William in an almost fatherly light.

"Francesca?" It was Amy, ethereal in pale blue silk with a net overskirt attached by white bows. "Do you think Cook remembered to cut the roast beef thinly enough? I caught her making sandwiches like doorstops earlier. And the ices . . . it would be dreadful if they melted before they were served."

"Dreadful indeed. I will go and make certain that the beef is thin enough and the ices have not turned to water," Francesca soothed.

Amy watched her go. Her youngest daughter was looking beautiful tonight in a yellow so pale it was more like cream. With her hair a cascade of ringlets and her eyes shining, she might have been Aphrodite made young. Not that Amy would dare say such a thing to William! He had been amazingly good-natured of late, and she didn't want to spoil it.

As if her thoughts had conjured him up, her brother came to stand by her side, and for a moment they both watched Francesca.

"Amy, I wonder if I might have a word with you before the guests arrive? In private."

She gave him a harassed glance, but he kept his gaze firmly on hers, and in the end she nodded and followed him to the library. "It will have to be quick, William," she reminded him. "There is still a great deal to do."

"Of course. I understand. You have done a marvelous job already. Quite like old times, eh?"

"Francesca deserves it," Amy said, smiling brilliantly and keen to share her pride in her daughter. "She looks absolutely gorgeous. I'm certain she will be a great hit."

"Yes, she is certainly a beautiful young woman." He moved to the fireplace and rested his arm on the mantelpiece, watching her. "Actually, Amy, it was Francesca I wanted to talk to you about."

"Oh?" she said warily, and couldn't help but remember the last discussion they'd had about Francesca in this very room.

It was as if he'd read her thoughts.

"Now, don't look like that, Amy! You know I've come to see the error of my ways where Francesca is concerned."

"I'm glad, William. I know you have been getting on together so well, and I appreciate the effort you are making."

"Yes." He tapped his fingers on the marble, and she waited, curious as to what was occupying his thoughts. "I wonder if you remember the conversation we had after you arrived in London?"

"There have been so many—"

You spoke to me about my marrying and producing an heir. I was annoyed at the time—I apologize for that. It is something that has been playing on my mind and you touched a raw spot. Mrs. March had been, eh, suggesting that she was the woman for me."

"Good heavens! I didn't realize. No wonder you

were cross, brother." Amy shuddered at the thought of Mrs. March becoming Mrs. Tremaine. "Mrs. Slater's daughter!"

"Exactly, although I didn't know that at the time. Still, that's in the past. I am looking to the future."

"Are you?" Amy said, surprised. "Don't tell me you've found a prospect, William! I was beginning to think you were far too fussy to be pleased."

She was sorry as soon as she said it, because he looked hurt.

"As a matter of fact I have found someone," he said in the haughty voice he used when she annoyed him. "Someone you know."

"Don't tell me, William, let me guess. This is fun. Who could it be . . . ?" She tried several names, but she could see he was growing impatient with her, and brought her game to a abrupt halt. "Tell me then, brother. I can see you're dying to do so."

He smiled. "Francesca."

Amy found she couldn't speak, and when she finally managed it, her voice came out as a squeak. "Francesca? She's your niece!"

He wasn't in the least concerned. "No, she isn't," he said, coolly rational. "She is no blood relation. There is no impediment at all, Amy."

"But, William . . ." She was floundering, too shocked to be able to argue in a way that might sway him. Even now he was looking at her as if she were nothing more than a hysterical woman.

He began to list the benefits. "I am older than she, and can supply a steadying influence. I am settled, and I have a large house and plenty of money. I can care for her in a proper manner. And when we have a child, it will want for nothing. Marrying me is the sensible option. What on earth would Francesca do if she returned to Yorkshire? Stride about the moors in the rain and weather? No, no, it won't do. Marriage will be the perfect solution to both our problems."

Amy took a breath. "William, I don't think Francesca sees her current situation as a *problem*. And besides, she is talking of staying in London."

"Well, perhaps she is already aware of my feelings for her."

"Your feelings for her . . ."

"My admiration and . . . and esteem."

"I see."

"She is young, and needs someone older and more mature to guide her through life."

"Does she?" She swallowed, searching desperately for some way to shake his certainty. "William, I really don't think—"

"I thought it best for me to approach you first, before I propose to her."

"Why did you think that?"

"I'm relying on you to let her know how greatly a match between us would benefit the family. She'll listen to you. She trusts your judgment, Amy, although God knows why. You have made some very silly decisions in your own life."

"William," she murmured, irritated by his comment but still not wanting to hurt him. "I know Francesca. She is my daughter. And I am certain that she will never agree to—"

"Ah." He cocked his head, listening to the sound of horses outside. "There's the first arrival!"

Amy felt as if she'd just awoken from a nightmare. William wanted to marry Francesca, and he expected her to smooth the way for him! It was sheer madness. Impossible. And yet . . . he had made it sound so plausible that for a moment, a very brief moment, she almost found herself agreeing with him.

In his eyes it *was* the perfect solution.

She had to find her daughter and warn her. But it was too late. Guests were arriving, and she could see Cook gesturing to her from the doorway, a look on her face that told Amy something had gone wrong in the kitchen.

Surely, Amy asked herself, William would not propose until the ball was over? Let Francesca enjoy the ball, and then Amy would put a stop to this appalling situation once and for all.

Francesca found herself dancing every dance. There seemed to be more partners than she knew what to do with, and her sisters were here, smiling and encouraging her. She looked about for Sebastian whenever she was able. She had sent him an invitation—without Uncle William's knowledge—and he had sent a note this morning promising to come, saying he may be delayed. As yet he hadn't appeared.

Had he changed his mind?

But that was nonsense. He loved her; he wanted to marry her. She trusted him with her life, and had

done so more than once. He would come, she told
herself. She mustn't believe otherwise.

Despite Amy's concerns, and a slight problem
with the cook's cat taking a fancy to the ham, the
supper was both lavish and delicious—even Toby
would have difficulty making inroads on such a
spread. Francesca sipped the lemonade her partner
had fetched her and listened to the conversation.
Vivianna's husband, Oliver, was smiling at her, looking as devastatingly handsome as always, and there
was Max, slipping his arm around Marietta when he
thought no one was watching.

The sight of her sisters' happiness only made her
more aware that Sebastian still wasn't here. The secret that had sustained her so far began to weigh
heavily upon her. All her life she had been afraid of
being hurt, of her emotions leading her into heart-
break, of being the sort of woman who could not
control her passions.

Surely her fears had not come to pass?

What if Sebastian abandoned her? She would be
left alone, wandering the moors like a wraith. She
pictured herself wearing one of Mrs. Hall's dreadful
dresses, wet and bedraggled, Wolf limping at her
side. It really was a depressing image.

She was so deep in her own concerns that she did
not hear it at first. The stirring among the guests, the
shifting and murmuring of the crowd. And when at
last she looked up, just as a hush fell, her eyes widened in amazement.

Aphrodite stood in the entrance to the supper

room. As usual she was wearing black, and those closest to her had moved away, so that there was a large circle of open floor between her and them. She did not seem to notice. Diamonds flashed at her throat and on her fingers, and she lifted her chin proudly, and turned her head from side to side, searching for someone among those watching her.

Francesca was about to step forward when someone grabbed her arm to stop her. "How dare you come here without an invitation!" Uncle William said loudly by her side.

Aphrodite turned to the sound of his voice, and it was as if she'd found who she was looking for. "William," she said in ringing tones. "So we meet again."

Francesca could see such fury in his eyes that she was stunned. He had shown this hatred of her mother before, and she had never really understood it. Was it really explained by her profession and the scandal he felt she brought to his family?

"You are not wanted here," he said. "You are not invited."

But Aphrodite was unfazed. She began to walk toward him, her black silk skirts rustling, and people moved aside to allow her to pass. "I apologize to my daughter for interrupting her evening," she said. "But it cannot be helped. I must put an end to this now, for all our sakes. Before someone else is hurt. Or murdered."

The word riveted everyone. Not even a murmur passed the hundreds of lips.

"You *stupid* woman—"

"I have something to show you, William."

Francesca had never seen him so angry. His lean cheeks were flushed, his hands were shaking, and his words tumbled over themselves in his fury. "Get out! Get out now!"

Aphrodite was holding up a piece of paper. She stretched her hand high above her, so that everyone could see it. William began to push his way toward her through the guests, knocking them aside, not caring who he offended. He was like a different man.

"It is a letter," she announced, anxiously watching his struggle. "It was written to me by Francesca's father. He talks about his love for his daughter and his plans for her future. He talks about—"

"Play!" William roared, gesturing at the orchestra. "Play, will you! What do you think you're being paid for?"

"He talks about leaving her all his money and his property, of making her his true and legal heir. He says that he wants Francesca to have it all."

"You don't know what you're talking about," William shouted angrily. "Get out of my way!"

Someone fell. There was a scream.

"Mrs. Slater had this letter. Maeve stole it for her. This morning she recovered enough to give it to Mr. Thorne. You were meant to marry her daughter, William. She isn't very happy with you." She turned wildly, catching sight of Amy. "Amy, look, look! You must recognize the handwriting. It was penned by your brother Thomas. Thomas Tremaine was Francesca's father."

Amy's mouth dropped open. Helen gave a squeal

and fell back into Toby's arms. But William was staring in blind hatred at the woman who had just destroyed him. "You bitch," he howled. "I always loathed you."

Aphrodite, pale and shaken, was unimpressed by his venom. "And I thought that you had loved me, once. You told me so often enough. Or was that just because you knew I had belonged to your brother, and it gave you some sort of twisted pleasure to have me, too?"

"William," Amy gasped, turning on him, "how could you? Francesca *is* your niece!"

"But she wouldn't have known it," he said, with careless bitterness. "And I couldn't let her take everything that belonged to me. Thomas told me, you know. He wrote to me at the same time and told me what he planned to do. I have been trying to find and destroy that letter for twenty-five years. And now it has destroyed me."

"You took my children!" Aphrodite cried. "You stole them from me so that you could keep what was not yours."

"If Mrs. Slater had her way they would have been smothered," he said. "I let them live. I let my sister take them in. And now look to what straits my generosity has brought me. I should have given her her way. I was squeamish, and it's been my downfall."

Francesca felt herself swaying. It was all too much. She couldn't listen to any more . . .

"Darling girl," a voice murmured, and Sebastian wrapped his arm about her, pressing her tightly to his side. "I am so sorry. Madame insisted on a dramatic scene. It appears such things run in your family."

"Sebastian . . ." Relief. She clung to him, not caring who saw her. What did anything matter, after the scene they had just witnessed?

William, ranting and raving, was taken in charge by several police. Then Sebastian was leading her through the crush, and it wasn't until the door closed behind them that she realized he had brought her to the library. The smell of leather and cigar smoke made her feel nauseated, reminding her of Uncle William shouting, and her mention of the letter—*the letter!*—and the way he had seemed to change. It all made dreadful sense now.

"Uncle William . . ." She tried to get the words out, but it was as if her throat had closed up.

"He was always your enemy. He wanted you dead," Sebastian said.

"He kidnapped all three of us!"

"I suppose he thought if he only took you someone might discover the truth."

"He left my mother all alone. He must have hated her to do that. He almost killed her . . . twice. Once through grief, and once through poison."

"Madame Aphrodite is a strong woman, my love. She has triumphed in the end. I don't think William will be able to escape his fate this time. I might even be able to persuade Mrs. Slater to give evidence against him. She isn't happy he didn't marry her daughter as he promised, and instead took the opportunity to get rid of her."

"Yes. He deserves to be punished. He almost destroyed so many lives." Francesca leaned against him, soaking up his strength. "I thought you weren't coming," she whispered, burying her face in his shoulder. "I thought you'd abandoned me, and I would have to wear black, like my mother, and go wailing on the moors."

"My love, I swear I will never leave you. You are all my happiness. Aphrodite was terrified that something would happen to you before she could confront your uncle. She said it had to be at the ball, before everyone. There had to be no way he could wriggle out of it, or allow someone else to take the blame." He stroked her hair, then tilted her face up. "It is over. Mr. Thorne has completed his final case. I can set him aside with a clear conscience."

She returned his kisses.

After a moment the portrait over the fireplace caught her eye. Two brothers, one smiling, the other cold-eyed. Thomas Tremaine, her father, gazed down on her, the man who loved adventure, who loved her. He had died in India with Sir Henry Greentree, his best friend, and Francesca had been brought up by his sister Amy. Was that a quirk of fate, or had William truly meant it to happen? Could she allow herself to believe there was some spark of goodness inside him?

"I am a Tremaine," she said quietly. A tear ran down her cheek, and then another. "How strange. I was taken in by my own family, and I never knew it."

"Here you are!"

The door had been thrown open, and there was Vivianna, with Marietta close behind her. They looked pale, shaken by the events that had taken place, but relieved to find Francesca safe and sound. Two pairs of eyes went immediately to Sebastian, who was still holding her in his arms.

Behind her sisters, Francesca could see Amy, and Aphrodite, and Helen and Toby. It seemed that everyone had come to find her. Her family. She heard Sebastian clear his throat.

"I have an announcement to make," he said. "Francesca and I are to be married."

And after all that had happened, or perhaps because of it, the cheers were deafening.

Epilogue

Francesca sighed and picked out a book that looked as if it might hold her interest. She tucked it safely under her arm and opened the door into the hall. Wolf was waiting for her, lying sprawled on the rug on the floor of Worthorne's great hall. He lifted his head with a yawn, and she set the lamp down on a table and bent to scratch him behind the ears.

"We miss him, boy, don't we?" she murmured. "The manor seems empty without him. When do you think he'll be home, hmm? It's already been four days."

Wolf didn't have an answer, and with another sigh

Francesca straightened and . . . there was someone behind her.

Big, warm hands grasped her upper arms in a firm grip. For a moment she froze, enveloped in a familiar male scent, and then she pulled free and backed away. Her heart was thundering in her ears, but fear had already given way to excitement and anticipation.

"Who are you and what do you want?" she whispered dramatically.

"I am the ravisher of Worthorne Manor and I want you," he declared.

There was a moment when neither of them spoke or moved, and then Francesca threw her book at his chest, crying, "Then you'll have to catch me," and took off across the hall to the side door.

Sebastian glanced at Wolf, winked, and ran after her. Wolf put his head back down on his paws and closed his eyes as if he'd seen it all before.

Sebastian knew where she was going. She always went there. It was her favorite adventure, and he had to admit it was one of his favorites, too. He'd been thinking about her all the way home from London, where business had taken him, and to find her in her nightgown, with the light of the lamp shining through the thin cloth and outlining her curves . . .

Sheer heaven.

Outside, the night was clear and warm. He could see her ahead of him, her pale nightgown fluttering in the dusk like moth wings. She tossed aside her shawl, as if it might slow her down, and then she lost her slippers. He cut through the orchard, ducking beneath boughs heavy with fruit, disturbing a family of owls.

She had almost reached the calm waters of the lake when he caught up with her. Hearing his steps and turning to see him almost upon her, she shrieked and tried to outpace him. He caught her, and after a brief struggle, they sank down onto the grass. She was breathing hard, but laughing, too.

"I have missed you," she gasped, clinging to him.

"Of course you have. I'm your grand passion, remember?"

"How could I forget?" she whispered, dark eyes hazy with love.

He kissed her then, and by the time he'd finished she was no longer interested in running. That was good. He'd ridden hard to get home tonight, and he was eager to love his wife as she was meant to be loved.

"Francesca," he said, and set little butterfly kisses on her hair, her cheeks, her eyelids. He felt the wild beat of her heart as he cupped his hand around her soft, full breast.

She squirmed, drawing him closer. To be lying in the grounds of Worthorne Manor with his wife was his perfect fantasy.

Well, almost.

Sebastian reached to divest her of her nightgown, tossing it aside and looking down on her creamy nakedness.

Now, it was perfect.

Next month, don't miss these exciting new love stories only from Avon Books

The Duke's Indiscretion by Adele Ashworth

An Avon Romantic Treasure

Famous soprano Lottie English has a secret . . . and when Colin Ramsey, Duke of Newark, asks her to be his mistress, Charlotte must think quickly or she will lose everything. But when she is threatened, will they be able to find true love in the face of grave danger?

One Night With a Goddess by Judi McCoy

An Avon Contemporary Romance

Chloe is the Muse of Happiness—it's going to take more than a year on Earth to bring her mood down. Thriving as a wedding planner, Chloe never expected love to come her way. But handsome doctor Matthew Castleberry is everything she ever wanted—if only she could find a way to overcome that pesky issue of immortality . . .

Wild Sweet Love by Beverly Jenkins

An Avon Romance

Teresa July is ready to make amends for her past, and a job with one of Philadelphia's elite is the perfect start. When she meets her boss's far too handsome son, Teresa is faced with the one thing she always desired and never thought she could have—a future with the man she loves.

The Devil's Temptation by Kimberly Logan

An Avon Romance

To unmask her mother's murderer, Lady Maura Daventry must turn to the one man who could prove to be a threat to her vulnerable heart: Gabriel Sutcliffe, Earl of Hawksley, the handsome and seductive son of the very man once accused of her mother's death.

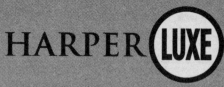

Avon Romantic Treasures

Unforgettable, enthralling love stories, sparkling with passion and adventure from Romance's bestselling authors

Avon Romances
the best in
exceptional authors and unforgettable novels!

AVON TRADE *Paperbacks*

978-0-06-083120-2
$13.95

978-0-06-057168-9
$13.95

978-0-06-082536-2
$13.95

978-0-06-117304-2
$13.95 ($17.50 Can.)

978-0-06-114055-6
$13.95 ($17.50 Can.)

978-0-06-085995-4
$13.95 ($17.50 Can.)